DROWNED

The Second Cyd Re

"The passenger list in Wendall Thomas's *Drowned Under* is a cavalcade of randy former nuns, gigolos, stowaways, near-extinct marsupials...and one brilliantly sexy disaster of a globetrotting travel agent named Cyd Redondo. Thanks to her wildly creative mind, the fruits of which produce frequent affronts to her dignity, Cyd is easily one of my favorite amateur sleuths in fiction today. Thomas's writing flows effortlessly, and her plotting is complex but perfectly tied together. This is a remarkable novel in what is shaping up to be an exciting and hilarious series. Don't miss *Drowned Under* or its predecessor, *Lost Luggage*. You'll love Cyd, perhaps the funniest heroine out there. Highest recommendation."

—James W. Ziskin, Anthony and Macavity Award-winning
author of the Ellie Stone Mysteries

"Bravo. Cyd Redondo, Redondo Travel, is at it again. What a wonderful sequel to *Lost Luggage*. With her clever mind, tart comebacks, and Balenciaga tote bag, Cyd is a fearsome force. I love her pluck, the way she digs her way out of trouble, and her willingness to do everything she can—even die—for her clientele. What a heroine for the modern age. Do not miss this!"

—Daryl Wood Gerber, Agatha Award-winning,
national bestselling author of the Cookbook Nook and
French Bistro Mysteries

"*Drowned Under* is laugh out loud funny. With its finely tuned timing and zany, emotional protagonist, this novel puts Thomas in a class with Carl Hiassen and Janet Evanovitch."

—Nancy Tingley, Lefty-nominated author of
the Jenna Murphy mysteries

LOST LUGGAGE
The First Cyd Redondo Mystery

2018 Macavity Award nominee for Best First Novel

2018 Lefty Award nominee for Best Debut Mystery

"Thomas makes a rollicking debut with this comic mystery featuring an unconventional protagonist who proves to have the skills of MacGyver. With its sexy overtones, this fun, character-driven novel will appeal to Janet Evanovich fans."

— *Library Journal* (starred review)

"Thomas packs a whole franchise's worth of adventures into her heroine's debut..."

— *Kirkus Reviews*

"Laugh-out-loud funny and enchantingly ridiculous...highly entertaining..."

— Jessica Howard, *Shelf Awareness*

"A breath of fresh air in a world gone mad...my vote for one of the best new characters in mystery/crime."

— *The Reading Room*

"I've been waiting for years to find a successor to Janet Evanovich, and I've finally found one."

— *Kittling Books*

Drowned Under

Books by Wendall Thomas

The Cyd Redondo Mysteries

Lost Luggage
Drowned Under

Drowned Under

A Cyd Redondo Mystery

Wendall Thomas

Published by Poisoned Pen Press, an imprint of Sourcebooks, Inc.
P.O. Box 4410, Naperville, Illinois 60563-4410
(630) 961-3900
Fax: (630) 961-2168
sourcebooks.com

Library of Congress Cataloging 2018959448

Printed and bound in the United States of America.
SB 10 9 8 7 6 5 4 3 2 1

For James Bartlett, my irreplaceable, ever-patient husband,
who first told me about the thylacine, laughed at my jokes,
and helped me with every aspect of the book.
It would not exist without him.
And for all the tigers—past, present, and future.

Acknowledgments

Everyone says the second book is tough. This one was, but it would have been much tougher without the profound generosity, support, and kindness of the following people.

First, thanks to my sister, Kim Thomas Stout, for the cruise stories, the "instant" reads, and her lifelong support of my writing. Thanks also to my Sisters in Crime—Rochelle Staab and Tammy Kaehler—for early reads and invaluable notes, to Ray Stout for the info on Narcan, and to my CHHS compatriot and travel agent extraordinaire, Debbie Clark Kaiser, for keeping me honest.

I am grateful to all of my friends and family, but particularly to Keith Sears, Carol Bartlett, Smith Richardson, Michele Mulroney, Nancy Tingley, Daryl Wood Gerber, Jim Ziskin, Hallie Ephron, Kate Carlisle, Rick and Carter McGarry, Mary Lou and Jack Cass, and my dad, Grady Thomas. Special thanks to James Utt and Daryl Cameron for their friendship and for the title. Jeff Koeze—you asked for it.

I cannot say enough about Tasmania and the wonderful people there. Mark Hosking, of the Maritime Museum of Tasmania, took time out of his busy schedule to help me with my research, and the Thylacine Gallery in the Tasmanian Museum and Art Gallery provided both location and inspiration. The Tasmanian Marine and Rescue Services and the Hobart Police were enormously helpful and nothing like their fictional counterparts. Everyone I met, from the hotel staff to local limo drivers, contributed to the atmosphere of the novel. I hope they will all forgive me for taking considerable artistic license with their gorgeous city and its historic buildings and institutions. Continued thanks to Gerry Morris and the wonderful Chadwick's in Bay Ridge. They may not have a real Tiki Night, but they do have the best crab cakes in the Northern Hemisphere.

This year I had the privilege of meeting a host of booksellers, librarians, and reviewers. Their support for *Lost Luggage* kept me going during book two. They are all fighting the good fight and often don't get the recognition they deserve. I owe them a huge debt, as we all do. And of course, I am so grateful for all my kind and generous readers.

Finally, thanks to the staffs at Twist Eatery, Maggianos at the Grove, El Coyote, and the dearly departed Xiomara, for all they've done to keep me fed, sane, and writing.

Chapter One

December 2006

It was Tiki Night at Chadwick's. A dusty neon palm tree—sporting a Santa hat—pulsed behind the bar. Fire hazard, I thought, as I flashed a holiday-watt smile at the Wednesday regulars, most of whom had moved down the bar to get away from me.

I was currently both the most loved and most hated woman in Bay Ridge, Brooklyn. Mostly most hated. The drinker sitting three stools down, swaddled in a crusty L.L. Bean field jacket, considered it my fault he'd lost his job. Maybe, but it was not my fault he had overdone the whole Catholic thing and fathered seven kids. In my opinion, moderate birth control displayed good citizenship, akin to recycling. I told the bartender to put his next three drinks on my tab anyway. Call me Cyd Redondo, Secret Santa.

I'd just jabbed myself in the eye with the pink mermaid in my Winter Windjammer Special, when a polar draft slammed through the padded swinging door.

"Cydhartha!" There was nothing like an eighth-grade nickname to ruin a girl's night, especially when it was bellowed across the bar by her ex-husband.

Barry Manzoni and I, like most Catholic school survivors of our generation, had endured Sister Ellery Magdalene Malcomb's obsession with Herman Hesse's *Siddhartha*. During one of her dramatic readings of the German classic, Barry had christened me with a spitball and I'd been "Cydhartha" ever since, except, thank God, during sex.

He shook off his overcoat to reveal he'd lost about forty pounds since he'd married Angela Hepler. I'd always considered her a succubus, so it made sense. He had the same oversized, slightly bugged eyes and the same dimpled chin I remembered, but hitherto hidden pecs had emerged and there were new worry lines around his mouth. I'd won exclusive Chadwick's "visitation rights" in the annulment, so what the heck was he doing here?

He sidled beside me onto one of the four empty bar stools, gestured for two of what I was having, then stared at the drunken reindeer napkin the bartender set down.

"Make yourself at home." I said, and waited. "What? What is it?"

"You know my parents went on a cruise to Australia?"

I took a long pause. "I heard." It was a sore subject. After we split up, his parents, their extended family, and half of the Masonic Lodge had taken their travel business to my arch rival, Peggy Newsome—a pit viper disguised as an advertisement for plastic surgery. So I'd not only lost a husband and lifelong friend, I'd lost fifty Redondo Travel clients. "Did she get them the free excursions? Because you know, I could've."

"I don't know what that means." Barry rapped his fingers on the bar, then shot his drink—no small feat since it was blended.

"Spit it out, Manzoni."

"They're missing."

I really hoped the Captain Morgan's rum was affecting my hearing. "They're what?"

"Missing, Cyd. My parents are missing."

I texted my Aunt Helen to say I'd be late for dinner, mostly to avoid Barry's panicked expression. I recognized that look. It was the same one he'd worn walking out of that Wedding Chapel in Atlantic City three years ago.

"How long?"

He gestured for another drink. "Two days."

"Two days?" How did I not know this? News in Bay Ridge usually set land speed records.

I instantly forgot all the times Barry's mom, Sandra, had mentioned my weight or my inability to conceive in the three seconds Barry and I'd been married. However they might have treated me, the Manzonis were senior citizens, they were missing, and they were at best a twenty-two-hour flight away and, at worst, shark bait in the Bass Strait.

I couldn't help myself. I grabbed Barry's hand, then dropped it. "Peggy Newsome is their travel agent. What has she done about this?"

"Nothing. I can't reach her. I guess she's gone for the holidays." Typical Peggy fricking Newsome, I thought. Barry looked down into his empty mug. "I know it's a big ask, but will you help me?"

It was a big ask, considering. "Of course." I looked him in the eye. "We go back."

I wrote down the name of the cruise ship and we caught up on our mutually disastrous lives for a minute, then I ordered a round of drinks for my detractors at the bar and told Barry I would call him with an update.

It was a shock to see him. I'm not going to lie. I still had some residual affection for the man. After all, I'd known him since I was four and had named my Madagascan chameleon after him. Mostly, though, he inspired sadness and regret. And fury re: Angela Hepler.

My Charles David kitten heel boots slid through the grainy, gray-black "snice" that had been mushing up our sidewalks for weeks. I pulled my Dooney & Bourke silver quilted jacket (eighty percent off with coupon at Century 21) closer. The red and white icicle lights around the Redondo Travel sign gave it a rosy glow. I breathed in the frigid air. The smell of soon-to-be-uneaten fruitcake baking in every house almost masked the ever-present tang of truck exhaust and garlic.

I locked the door behind me, sat down at my desk, and switched on the computer. Someone was already lurking in the machine, going through my files.

Chapter Two

My Uncle Ray was at it again.

He had a history of intervention, starting with taking me and my mom in after my dad died in a crash on the JFK Expressway. I was four, the youngest of the ten cousins, and the only girl. Ever since then, he'd been my surrogate father, my travel agent mentor, my landlord, my employer, and a million other things until a month ago, when he entered a Martha Stewart-esque minimum security prison for a two-year stretch.

The whole thing was a touchy subject, as half of Bay Ridge thought I'd as good as put him there. I'd uncovered an endangered animal smuggling ring in Tanzania, not knowing he'd been a part of it on the Brooklyn end. He'd used the proceeds of his crime to save our floundering travel business. In the end, to protect his equally guilty son—my "brousin" Jimmy—he'd turned himself in.

Before he did, he'd signed Redondo Travel over to me, impending bankruptcy and all, saying it would be safe in my hands. Still, the benevolent, old school sexist part of him couldn't quite trust me to handle things on my own. He saw his bi-weekly spying as "protective." I saw it as likely to provoke ten minutes pulverizing the punching bag I had hanging in the supply room.

I changed the password for the forty-eighth time (thank God Linda Ronstadt had a huge catalog), settled on

PoorPoorPitifulMe!2, closed the computer down, and did a few roundhouse kicks, pretty much evenly divided between fury and guilt. I loved my uncle. He was still the reason I tried to go above and beyond in my job, but he had broken my heart. And right now, I wanted to punch him in his substantial gut. Everyone has repressed anger toward the ones they love, right?

The first time Uncle Ray brought me to the office to help, I'd been ten. And nervous. After I'd alphabetized all the files, swept the front steps, and cleaned the coffee machine, I stood near the door, staring at the Orient Express poster and bouncing from one leg to the other.

"Cyd! Don't just stand there, you'll drive me crazy."

"What should I do?" I was terrified of being sent home.

"Find out what time it is in Cairo."

I spent the rest of that afternoon memorizing all the international time differences, with and without Daylight Savings. Just about everything in the world had changed in the last twenty years, except Greenwich Mean Time. It was eleven in the morning, tomorrow, at the Darling Cruises corporate offices in Sydney, Australia. The Manzonis had been on one of their ships, the *Tasmanian Dream*. I kept seeing Barry's crisis face. I hoped, for his sake, they were okay. I gave the bag one more punch, then headed back to my desk.

There was no point in calling Peggy Newsome. Not only would she refuse to help, she would find a way to blame the whole thing on me. Better to keep her out of the loop and catch her red-handed, slathered in incompetence. Or kickbacks. It was easier to break into her files.

I guess hacking ran in the family. To be honest, it wasn't the first time I'd breached Peggy's Patriot Travel security. I rationalized this particular misdemeanor as "researching your competition." It helped that I had arranged a free trip for the IT guy at our travel server, so he could pick up his Ukrainian bride. Comping IT guys was always worth it, but to be honest, I could have figured out her password myself—DameDiana#1—as she fancied herself a cross between Princess Diana and Diane Sawyer.

I found Peggy's Manzoni file, clicked on it, and swore. The woman's irresponsible travel agent behavior never failed to astound me. She hadn't even arranged travel insurance for them. I, of course, included it in everyone's original quote. There was no way I was letting my clients die of sepsis or be buried in an unmarked grave in Belize because the family couldn't afford to get the body home. I'd had enough clients encounter emergency situations to know how much they could cost.

I swore again. She'd charged them the full fare, then given them the discount package. This meant that they would spend the cruise thinking everything was included, then owe thousand of dollars for drinks and extras, which had to be paid before they were allowed off the ship. Peggy must have a kickback with Darling Cruises or with someone on board.

Maybe the Manzonis figured this out and jumped ship to avoid the extra charges. I knew for a fact Fredo Manzoni was a cheapskate of the highest order. Barry's cannoli hadn't fallen far from that tree.

Before I called the cruise line, I checked HighseasSleaze.com for the latest scoop on any dubious cruise events. This week there had been a mob-sized fistfight off Zanzibar, a suicide off St. Bart's, a slip-and-fall near Ensenada, an onshore robbery on Turks and Caicos, a customer overboard (while taking a selfie, of course) off the Greek coast, and two couples missing off the Australian coast. But it wasn't the Manzonis. I couldn't find them anywhere, even cross-referencing for location and crime. This might seem like a good thing, but the cruise lines were notorious for avoiding bad publicity at all costs. The worse the event, the more likely they were to cover it up, so it could also be bad.

Darling Cruises was one of the better choices for travelers with hip replacements and bad knees—in other words, my clientele. The line had slightly smaller, classier boats, fewer drunk freshmen, proper art auctions, and, as much as I hated to say it, a standard three-coffin morgue. They sailed to bucket list locations and hadn't had a norovirus/fire in the engine room/sinking disaster in the past few years, so I felt better putting my clients there. Apparently, so did Peggy Newsome. It was probably the only responsible thing she had done in her too-long life.

Harriet Archer, the Travel Agent Liaison for Darling Cruises, was my main contact and my favorite. She'd worked her way up in what was a tough, male-centric organization, and we had been phone buddies for years. A few months ago, she'd flown to Manhattan for a conference and we'd had champagne cocktails in the Oak Room at the Plaza. We both had a history of hapless, unsatisfying boyfriends, and loved coupons.

"Harriet? Cyd Redondo, Redondo Travel."

"Cyd! How great to hear from you. Happy Holidays! A classic oxymoron, if you ask me, but no one's asking. What can I do for you, love?"

"I'm calling about some passengers booked through another party."

"Would that party have a stick up her ass the size of Uluru?" Uluru was a sacred mountain in the Australian Northern Territory. Dollars to donuts Peggy Newsome did not know this.

"That would be the one."

"That derro. She's lucky I haven't kicked her dazzling crowns in. What's going on?"

"There's a couple named Sandra and Fredo Manzoni. They were on the *Tasmanian Dream*. Their son says they're missing." There was a long silence. Too long. "Harriet?"

"I don't know anything about this. And I should. They booked through Peggy?"

"Yes. And I wish I could say I'm surprised she hasn't done crap."

"She's a middle-aged wasteland. Last time she took a Darling Cruise and the Wi-Fi and cell reception were crap, she commandeered the ship-to-shore radio when the steward didn't leave a chocolate on her pillow. I'll get into it and call you back as soon as I can."

I did a quick check with my contacts at Tiger Air and Jetstar to see if the Manzonis were booked on any flights from Tasmania back to Sydney. No Manzonis anywhere.

The phone rang as soon as I hung up.

"Cyd Redondo, Redondo Travel."

"What are you doing there at this hour? Are all the doors locked?"

Honestly, from prison? "Yes, the doors are locked, Uncle Ray."

"The Manzonis are missing." Light speed, like I said.

"I'm on it. I'm waiting for a call back from Darling Cruises."

"I'm happy to handle it if it's, you know, awkward for you. I wouldn't help that son of a bitch Barry, but Fredo and I go back."

"It might be tough for you to orchestrate on a payphone. I'm fine. Really."

"If you're sure. Love you, bye." It was only a couple of minutes before he was hacking into my files again. What could I do? Have him arrested? The phone jangled, making me jump in my ergonomic chair. It was Aunt Helen.

I sighed. "Coming."

Chapter Three

I ducked into a deli for Aunt Helen's ricotta *salata*. It looked dry—even for dry ricotta. I was going to hear about that. She was out of her mind, but she still had standards. She and Uncle Leon had moved into our house when he retired from the Natural History Museum and was on a fixed income. I use that term loosely, as the "fixed" part seemed to fluctuate, depending on how he did at the races.

Being a former taxidermist, he had a weakness for horses who appeared half dead, so the fluctuation was mainly down. I had already slipped him most of my Christmas fund, which meant I'd have to resort to the humiliation of the "homemade gift." As if I needed another reason to dread the holidays.

I took a left onto 77th Street, where the season's blaring Santas, reindeer, elves, and spruce trees—lit up to be visible from space—closed in on me. I passed a Nativity scene with Wise Men resembling forwards for the Knicks. Mrs. Hunt, never one to take chances, had covered each figure in shrink-wrapped vinyl like an unused couch in her best parlor. The cracking plastic winked under the foggy streetlights. One house up from us I glared at our neighbors' glowing, twenty-five-foot high snowman, so tall its puffed face peered into my bedroom window. It had been giving me recurring *Ghostbusters* nightmares, minus the comedy.

Finally, I reached our house. Except for a brief respite during my ill-fated time as Mrs. Manzoni, the brick three-story with the A-line roof (currently hosting a rusting, blinking Santa's sled and our remaining three blow-up reindeer) had been something of a "love prison," full of various incarnations of the Redondo family. The changing of the guard never affected the surveillance they maintained on me.

I stopped on the steps, wondering, as usual, whether I should turn and run. Too late. The door opened, throwing me into a spotlight from the fifty light fixtures in our hallway. My mother, Bridget Colleen Colleary Redondo, stood backlit in the doorway, her waist-long, red-gray hair down for once. I gestured rudely at the leering snowman and went in.

I squished my Dooney & Burke into the coat explosion already hanging on the rack. Aunt Helen, an inflated human comma, hobbled toward us, shoved her way past my mom, and jerked the ricotta out of my hand. She looked down at it and sniffed. "Everything's cold."

My Uncle Leon, his whippet-like physique in a fitted, early Beatles suit and tie, emerged from the den. He winked at me and took my mother's arm. I followed them down the scarlet wallpapered hallway, past the obstacle course of extra chairs, and through the swinging door into the kitchen.

No one said anything as Aunt Helen sprinkled the ricotta on top of her bowl of *pasta norma* and placed it directly in front of my mother, like a poisoned chalice. Mom pushed the bowl my way.

"Okay, what's going on?" I took a sloppy spoonful of the eggplant-drenched penne. The two women looked at each other, while Uncle Leon threw up his hands, then used the downward momentum to snag the Parmesan. I looked at my mother. "Well?"

She stared at the tablecloth. I imagined her leaning, and falling, over a low railing into the Caribbean and felt weak for a minute. "Don't tell me you want to go on a cruise? Because it is not happening." I grabbed the cheese.

Aunt Helen stopped chomping her salad. "Why not? She's not as good as your clients, your own mother? She deserves it. Especially since no one in the neighborhood has invited her, or us, for a single holiday extravaganza. Since you put your uncle in prison, that is."

"Mom?"

"It's nothing."

"Nothing is right." Aunt Helen forced a piece of romaine down her throat, for suspense. "No rummage sale for The Lady of the Angels, no caroling for the unfortunate, no tree-trimming parties, no Punch Drunk Love Potluck, nothing. We're all boycotted. Because of you. It's just one big Redondo blackout." Uncle Leon shrugged and Aunt Helen slapped his negligible bicep. "What do Bridget and I have without holiday gatherings and the Holy Trinity? You, Mr. Big Stuff?"

Oh, God. Then I saw a tiny wobble in my mother's chin. Was she crying? Or laughing?

"I just think cruises are dangerous," I offered.

"The Manzonis are missing. Old news. They deserve it. That's no reason to punish your mother."

At that point, Mom burst into full scale laughter. "She's right about that. Sandra Manzoni can rot in hell, the shameful way she treated you. But really, the potluck? The last two times we all got food poisoning."

"It's the principle."

"Of what?" my mother said. "Equal opportunity dread?"

"That's called society, missy." She turned to me. "And you. You need to fix this."

She was right. It wasn't fair that the whole Redondo family was paying for my mistake. Even if it wasn't technically a mistake. I felt bad enough already for inadvertently putting my uncle in jail. This just made everything twenty times worse. I was officially the Grinch of Bay Ridge. And chartreuse was not my color.

"I'm so sorry, Mom, I didn't know. I thought they were just boycotting me."

"Don't worry about it, honey. It gives me more time to pursue something new."

Oh, no. Last time, that meant a blacksmithing class. We used to have a garage. "What do you mean?"

"Here it comes." Aunt Helen slugged more wine into her glass.

"What? What's new?"

Mom blushed. My cell phone blared. It was Harriet. I pushed my chair back.

"Mom, I've got to take this." I'd just made it to the swinging door when she shouted, "I've signed up for Catholic Blend."

I asked Harriet if I could call her back.

"Seriously, Mom? Online dating? It sounds like a bad bag of coffee."

"Why not? We don't have any holiday plans and it will get me out of the house."

I couldn't handle my mother's Internet dating preferences and seeing my ex-husband in the same night. "We can talk about this later. I have to go back to the office. I love you." I kissed her on the head, then moved toward the swinging door.

"That's fine. I'm used to doing the dishes by myself," Aunt Helen announced to the room.

Uncle Leon followed me out and gave me "the look."

I'd been waiting for it, as I'd heard at Chadwick's that Old Rugged Cross had come in ninth in the fifth. I pulled out the emergency hundred I keep in the secret compartment in my wallet for just these increasingly frequent occasions.

"You're a doll." He kissed me, then headed into the den to watch *Nova*. What can I say? When I was little, he used to let me run around the dioramas in the museum at night. I loved him. And I hated that he and Aunt Helen were suffering because of me. Maybe I should just disappear until New Year's so all the remaining Redondos could have the jolly old time they deserved.

Chapter Four

Thanks to my kitten heel boots and the Bay Ridge Municipal salt trucks, I made it back to the office in six minutes. I thought about my mother the whole way, about how I would feel if she were missing, and the risks I would take to get her back. And I thought about Barry in kindergarten, giving me half his ham salad sandwich.

I opened the door, pulled my frigid feet under me, and stared at the picture of Barry the chameleon and her five babies, which had pride of place on my desk. At least the reptile side of my family wasn't suffering from potluck withdrawal.

I picked up the landline and dialed. "Hey, it's Cyd."

"Well, there's vaguely good news. The Cruise Director said couples rarely go overboard together. Usually one of them pushes the other, then denies all knowledge. Or one slips over during a photo and the other raises a pointless cry for help. It's not often that one falls in and the other one dies saving them—that usually only happens on honeymoons. If they're both missing, odds are they're onshore."

"But they could be onshore and dead." I started scribbling a timeline on my Bay Ridge Leather shoe-shaped notepad. They had restored my red vintage Balenciaga shoulder bag after my last trip, matching the red leather to fill in the bullet hole and bleaching out the cobra venom stain, so I felt compelled to do cross-promotion. I could still see the damage, but from four feet away, it was invisible. Like with most people, I guess. I had bought the bag in a vintage shop in Williamstown ten years earlier. In Africa, it had actually saved my life.

"When was the last time anyone saw them?"

"They won a dance competition the night before the ship docked in Tasmania. They were booked on our Historic Penal Colony Breweries Tour excursion, but apparently they cancelled at the last minute. After they came down the ramp in Hobart, no one's seen them. They're not on any footage the Staff Captain could find." She paused. "He said."

"What does that mean?"

"It means he isn't known for his veracity." That meant he and Harriet had dated. I'd ask her about that later.

"Did they book a private excursion?" Private excursions during a cruise were more expensive than ship tours and offered a more private experience focused on a passenger's particular interest. But they had a downside. Cruise line-sanctioned trips provided insurance and refunds, and they would wait for you if you were late. If you booked privately, the ship wasn't responsible financially or otherwise, and if you weren't back in time for Embarkation, they'd just leave you. It was your responsibility to find your own way to the next port. I'd been forced to arrange a few speedboats for tardy clients.

"If so, no one admits knowing about it. Including Peggy."

"You talked to Peggy?"

"I made sure to time the call in the middle of her massage. She said they were grown-ups, and she was on vacation."

I wanted to walk over and throw a firebomb through the Patriot Travel window, but everyone would know it was me. Making my brousin Frank arrest me during the holidays, after I'd lost him his promotion, was too much.

"So there's a chance they're still in Hobart? Maybe they decided to stay and see Port Arthur." I'd booked a few private tours there with a limo driver named Gary. "Harriet?"

"Why aren't they answering their phones?" she said. "You checked the outbound flights, right?"

"Yeah. But what else?" I could hear it in her voice.

"Everyone's being cagier than usual about this one. The crew is hiding something. I want to know what it is." Harriet had moved up so fast in the company because she knew where all the lifeboats were buried. I trusted her instincts. "And, one of the cabin stewards told me the Manzonis aren't the first passengers to go missing on this route over the past few months."

"Seriously? How many?"

"Six. That we know of."

"Six! Are you fricking kidding me? How is that not on *HighseasSleaze.com*?"

"Because we have a great PR person?"

"Harriet!"

"Because I want to keep my job? I'm kidding. I'm on it, I promise."

"How about the Hobart police? Coast Guard? Can I do anything from here?"

"Not from there. I do have an idea, though," she said. "I'm sure you want to be with your family, but I've got free vouchers that run out on the third of January. Any chance you want to share a free double balcony cabin on the *Tasmanian Dream* with me? Same route. Same crew. It leaves from Sydney tomorrow morning, but you could catch us up in Melbourne on the twenty-second. I can talk in person to my informants and you can keep your eyes and ears open, all while drinking free mojitos. Plus, it stops in Tasmania."

It was a tough call. I had always, always wanted to go to Australia. On the other hand, a cruise was my idea of hell. Why anyone would want to be stuck with thousands of people desperately trying to have fun, often with people they despised, was beyond me. If I wanted to be pressed up against a lot of partying morons with no escape, all I had to do was take the

R train to Manhattan on a Friday night. Besides, I had grown up in an overflowing house with no privacy and thirty people at dinner every night, in a neighborhood where everyone was always trying to do the same five things in the same five places. I basically lived on a stationary cruise ship, minus the waterslide.

My ideal vacation involved quiet, privacy, and no more than two people. There was a time one of those people was Barry. He was my ex-husband, my oldest friend, and his parents were missing. It was only a few days. I could stand it, for his sake. And my exit would open up access to a host of holiday festivities for all the Redondos and potentially postpone my mother's entrance into the middle-aged white slave trade via Catholic Blend.

"You'd have to leave right away, even to make the Melbourne docking, though."

There was no one to cover for me at the office anymore. But the reality was, everyone who was traveling for the holidays was already ticketed. Clients staying in Bay Ridge for Christmas week only came in to avoid their families, not to book a wine tour of Provence.

I had my BlackBerry for emergencies, and Eddie still had Uncle Ray's old satellite phone somewhere.

"Yes. I'd love to."

"Fantastic," Harriet said. "The Manzonis notwithstanding, this is going to be fun."

Chapter Five

Easy for Harriet to say. She was an orphan. I hung up and did some quick calculations. Could I book a ticket, pack, get to the airport, fly twenty-four hours including layovers, and get to Port Melbourne, all while losing a day at the International Date Line? This was the sort of trip I helped my clients plan for months. I had seven hours.

I called my contact at Qantas. I could go through Dubai or Los Angeles. As a single woman who favored mini skirts and *LA Law* reruns, it was a no-brainer. It was great to think no matter where you lived, you were really only one day away from anywhere. It's just that most of the time, it didn't feel that way. If you lived in Bay Ridge, Chelsea could feel like Antarctica.

I was able to combine my credit card frequent flier points, travel agent discounts, and three coupons to upgrade Harriet's coach seat into Premium Economy for both legs, round trip, with the potential for an upgrade to Business if someone rich didn't show up. This was great, as I could now tell my clients for sure whether that extra two grand for Premium Economy was worth it. It gave me a rush to be using all my travel agent skills for myself, for a change.

I tried to not freak out about the cost. The cruise was comped, but I would need to buy maximum travel insurance. I knew what could go wrong—missed connections, slip-and-falls, noroviruses, emergencies that required airlifts, "disappearances," etc. The cruise lines used freelancers and subcontractors to weasel out of most lawsuits, so insurance was mandatory. So was cash for tips on the ship and enough room on my Citibank card to cover on- and off-board expenses. I put an IOU in the Redondo Travel "foreign currency" drawer for the Australian dollars I lifted.

Of course my passport was current, with a well-lit photo. I kept an emergency travel kit, cosmetics ziplock, and pre-packed carry-ons for hot and cold weather in the upstairs apartment next door. Technically, the late great Mrs. Barsky of Pet World had willed the apartment to me, but there was still an international manhunt on for her executor son. For now, I just kept it clean and hid a few things there I would prefer my family didn't know about. Like birth control pills. It was a cruise, after all.

I had six hours and too much to do. I printed all my clients' itineraries, put them in my BlackBerry, and emailed them to myself and Harriet. I would wait to send out a mass email about the office closure until I was safely in Pacific Standard Time. Otherwise, the whole neighborhood would be calling my mom in the middle of the night.

I peeked out the front door. The street was empty save for a snowplow shoving gray blobs of snice onto the sidewalk, where it could do the most damage. One door down, I slipped into the former Pet World. No amount of Glade could remove twenty-five years of bird droppings and fish food. Until it became a crime scene, it was where every kid in the neighborhood got their hamsters and parakeets. I missed Mrs. Barsky every day. I crossed myself in her honor and headed up the back stairs.

I unlocked the door and went straight into the bedroom, a designer's bowl of sherbet, with its hot pink chenille bedspread, electric orange pillows, and lime green curtains—vintage Barsky all the way. I opened the closet door and yanked my "hot weather" carry-on bag onto the bed. I removed the navy polka-dot bikini (Donna Karan at Loehmann's), as the bullet scar in my waist was still puffy and I didn't have the heart or time to try it on. Who in their right mind would do that to themselves in December, especially if they'd been ingesting stress Oreos?

I checked for my emergency black sequin, boatneck, backless mini dress, for anything formal, then pulled out my luggage scale. Qantas had a serious weight limit—only two carry-ons in Premium Economy, neither weighing more than fifteen pounds. I'd gone heavy on the chiffon. Chiffon had to be dry-cleaned, but it weighed nothing and masked a host of ills, especially around the upper arms, where I was suffering from worry wings at the moment.

My tiny cosmetic bottles were always filled. I squished them, my makeup kit, my BlackBerry, and my Balenciaga into the smaller carry-on, then weighed the bags. One was still eight ounces over, but I could carry the extra half pound on my person at vital weighing points.

Beep. There was a text from Harriet:

> I found one person who saw them in Hobart. Maybe they just missed the boat and decided to stay—it is a great town. Can't wait to show it to you, decimate my drinks allowance, and maybe meet a Christmas fling. I'll meet you at the terminal in Melbourne. Safe travels. Xxxxx.

I couldn't wait to see her.

I lugged my bags downstairs, locked up Pet World, and caught sight of the crocheted Christmas tree in the bookstore across the street.

My stomach hurt. It would be the first Christmas, ever, I wouldn't be home. My best friend, Debbie, and I always had lunch on Christmas Eve, but she was off to warmer climes herself, care of free coupons I'd gotten her, so she wouldn't miss me. And I wouldn't miss going to the annual potluck, because Mr. Malmon always touched my ass, then, after I decked him, said, "I like 'em sassy."

I tried not to think about Christmas morning and all the years I crept down three flights of stairs to look at the Christmas tree and pre-open all my presents, then got caught by Uncle Ray. He never told anyone, he just helped me rewrap them. Well, I wouldn't be missing that, at any rate, as he would be keeping secrets for white-collar inmates instead. I flicked a stupid tear off my check as I rolled the bags back into the office.

I was about to close up when I heard a key in the lock and Eddie walked in. He was the oldest of my brousins, tall and still skinny with the exception of a beer belly the size of a dodgeball. Lately, he looked like someone had winged his jet-black hair with Silly String and there were smudgy purple bags under his eyes. Since the FBI had closed down my uncle's import business, Eddie had been picking up daywork at the docks, but he had an ex-wife, two kids who were about to graduate from high school, a new wife, and another baby, so money, always tight, was positively constrictive. I knew he slept in the office sometimes, but we'd never talked about it.

"What's with the luggage, Squid?"

I'd taken a gunshot. It was time he understood I was thirty-two, not twelve. "None of your beeswax. Want a drink?" I got out mini vodkas for us.

He took a swig. "You know the Manzonis are missing."

"Yep. Barry came by Chadwick's." I took another drink. "I thought I might go look for them. You know, make myself scarce so the parish doesn't have to punish the Redondos."

"You didn't need my permission last time." I had withheld information the last time I'd asked him to cover for me, like that I was running away to Africa with a man I'd only known for two days.

"I'm just telling you, so, you know, you can keep an eye on everyone."

"Are you telling them?"

"Are you insane? They'll feel like they have to guilt me into not going, even if they really want me to, and I'll lose all the frequent flier miles I just spent on the ticket. Check into the office once in awhile, could you do that? Oh, and maybe check up on the other Barry? Use my name." I had gotten a lifetime membership to the Brooklyn Zoo when I'd donated a pregnant, endangered chameleon.

"You sure about the cruise thing given, you know, your situation?"

I was not sure about it. At all. "Absolutely."

He raised his eyebrows, then kissed me on the head. "Okay. Watch yourself."

Chapter Six

Back when we were fifteen, Barry Manzoni and I used to sneak out to go ice skating on Wednesday nights. We had a "pebble" code we used on each other's windows. Throw one handful, count to three, then two handfuls. I have no idea why.

As it was now three in the morning, I was hesitant to call the house, or even Barry's cell. Angela Hepler wouldn't appreciate it. Not that I cared what his wife thought, but I didn't want Barry to have to pay for it, given he was already stressed out about his parents. And Christmas. I wondered whether he still suffered from the "worry-triggered" insomnia he'd had during our brief marriage. If he did, he'd be up, watching QVC. His starter home was only a block away. I had ordered a town car from a new, non-Borough company, to avoid broadcasting my escape, and I just had time to swing by Barry's and back before my ride arrived.

A slit of Christmas tree light flashed between the curtains at the front of the house. Perfect. But where were the pebbles? Of course Angela had to have the perfect lawn, with pine straw rather than gravel around the boxwoods. I could have just knocked on the window, I guess, but I was sentimental.

I reached into my bag and found one of my boxes of Tic Tacs. I portioned a few out in my hand, got right up against the window, and threw. I couldn't even hear it and I was two inches away. I tried one more time. In the end, I threw the roll of emergency quarters in my bag. I saw a shadow and Barry came to the window. I waved. He held up his finger. A few seconds later, the outside lights went out, the door opened, and I heard a whisper.

"Cyd! What the hell are you doing here?"

"Did you or did you not ask for help with your parents?"

"Yes, of course I did. Sorry, I just don't want Angela to think anything."

"What could she possibly think?"

"Well, she has kind of a thing about you, you know, as my first wife."

"Why? You've been married six times as long as we were. I mean, according to the Vatican, we weren't even married at all."

"I don't think it actually went all the way to the Vatican. Come on, it felt like we were, didn't it? For a little while?" If Barry had still been single, this might have warranted an answer. As it was, it didn't. "It's just, right now she's more paranoid than usual."

"And why is that?"

"You know, now that she's pregnant."

I froze. Angela Hepler, chronic high school organizer, was having my baby. First, how did I not know this? In this neighborhood? People couldn't even keep their hemorrhoids to themselves.

"We were waiting to tell everybody until, you know, we got through the first semester."

"Bar, this isn't Junior Year Abroad, it's a baby. How come you didn't tell me this?" He threw his hands in the air. Okay, I guess I understood why.

"Well, congratulations. That's great news." It was, for them. For me, not so much. This Christmas positively sucked so far. "I'm here because I wanted to leave you info on your parents before I go."

"Go where?"

"To Australia. To find them."

"Seriously?" He took a deep breath. "God. Thanks, Cydhartha."

"*Keine ursache.*" That was high school German for no problem. "I'll be in touch."

"Oh, just try it, you slut. What, you think because I've gained a little weight it's open season?" There was Angela Hepler in what could only be called a granny gown. Yikes.

"You haven't gained any weight, honey."

Angela had seven inches on me to start with. At the top of the stairs her height advantage was super unfair. She also had a seven iron. It missed me, but took out a plastic Santa on their porch railing, which ricocheted off the Pinskys' elf cutouts and rolled down their driveway, activating a host of motion detector lights. I moved into the shadow of a mammoth oak tree. Motion detector lights are not flattering to anyone. I looked for a hefty fallen branch, just in case. Then I remembered she was pregnant, and pulled a flat, lime-green Tupperware container out of my Balenciaga instead.

"Go find your own husband, you worthless slut," Angela yelled. A few neighborhood lights came on.

"Not if it means I'm going to wind up wearing flannel nightgowns."

"This is Ralph Lauren!"

"Really? Let's see the tag." I could tell at fifty paces it was a Lanz from ten years ago.

She moved back. "I cut my tags off. They irritate me." We both looked at the seven iron, which was midway between us. Angela looked at Barry. "Right, honey?"

I saw her spot the Pinskys, leaning out of their upstairs window. Angela Hepler loved an audience. "At least I don't live with my parents. It's easy to parade around in lingerie when your mother does the dishes."

"My mother does the dishes because I'm supporting my entire family."

"And whose fault is that?"

That hurt. "At least I work. I don't just parasite off my unemployed husband."

"My what?"

Crap. When we were at Chadwick's, Barry had confided that he'd lost his job. Apparently, he hadn't told his current wife.

She glared at him, then ran down the steps in her bunny slippers. I sprinted for the seven iron in my kitten heels. We met in the middle. Just as she went to slap me and I raised my defensive Tupperware, we heard the brief, paralyzing bleep at the beginning of a siren, and a cop car pulled up.

"That's enough, ladies," came the loudspeaker. "And this isn't a show, Babs Pinsky." The Pinskys' window slammed shut. A few more opened up. "Really, Cyd?" the cop loudspeaker boomed.

Shit. When you had relatives in the law enforcement, towing, taxidermy, and plumbing services, chances are one of them was going to show up when you weren't at your best.

This time, it was my brousin Frank, recently demoted from detective to patrol cop since his father—my Uncle Ray—was indicted right under his nose. He got out of the car and walked toward us, armed utility belt clunking. I kicked the seven iron out of Angela's reach.

"Hi, Frank," Barry said.

"Great, one of your relatives to the rescue again." Angela hid behind Barry.

"Look," Frank said, "someone reported a disturbance. I came out. I'm not thrilled that Cyd started it either."

"I didn't start it! I'm here because Barry asked me to help find his missing parents. If Angela doesn't trust her husband, that's between them. But for her information," I said, moving so she could see me, "I barely had sex with him when we were married. I have no intention of doing it now. Right, Barry?" I saw his face fall. Could I possibly do anything right today? I could. Leave. Which is what I was doing.

"Yeah, well, why didn't you just call?" Angela yelled.

"Because nobody needs their beauty sleep more than you!" She headed toward me again.

"All right, all right, ladies. Barry, you really going to let this happen?"

"What am I gonna do? You can't stop it and you're a cop. I'm just a guy."

"You're not just a guy, honey, you're fifty times the man any Redondo is. They're all a bunch of lowlifes," Angela yelled.

I felt Frank stiffen. "That's enough, Angela. Just because your dad greases everybody's palms at the docks doesn't mean you're above a 'drunk and disorderly' charge."

"What?"

"I can smell the rum from here."

"That's eggnog! We had eggnog in our own house. Holidays don't count."

"Tell that to the breathalyzer. Now, are you going to go inside? Barry?"

Barry put his arm around Angela Hepler and started to guide her up the steps. She turned.

"What about her?"

"Is that her seven iron?" Frank asked. All of us looked at it.

"No. It's mine," Barry said.

"Then I'll consider Cyd was operating in self-defense," he said, "and take her home."

"Wait," I said. "I need to give him this." I handed the Tupperware to Barry.

"Look, my contact thinks it's likely they just stayed in Tasmania. Here's all the info you need and all the contact numbers for the cruise line and local police. By the way, Angela, I have my name taped on the bottom, so you can return my Tupperware when he's done."

She had once kept one of my prime pieces after a wake, saying she had no idea it was mine and how could I prove it? The hag. Fine. I would walk away, take the high road, be the generous ex. I reached into the boxwoods to retrieve my roll of quarters.

Barry started to push Angela inside. She yelled past him. "Low rent pygmy!"

"Rebound wife!"

Frank couldn't quite hide his grin as he propelled me toward the police car. I looked at my watch and panicked. I had missed the town car.

"Sorry," I said to Frank.

"Don't be. That's the most fun I've had all night. If I didn't hate Barry Manzoni's guts so much, I might feel sorry for the guy. Now what's going on?"

I considered lying, but the Tupperware was pretty much out of the bag and I figured I owed him that much, so I spilled. "Now I'm late and I might miss the plane."

"Not if Officer Frank Redondo can help it," he said. "If they're going to stick me in a fricking patrol car, I'm damn well gonna use it."

Five minutes later, sirens blazing, I was on the way to departures at JFK. We made it in twenty minutes, mostly passing on the right. Frank had honed his driving skills at Eldorado Bumper Cars on Coney Island.

"Christmas won't be the same without you, Squid," Frank said as he lifted my carry-ons out of the cruiser.

"Yeah, well this year it wouldn't be the same with me, either," I said, thinking of Uncle Ray and Jimmy. I hugged him, hard. "Stay away from the sausage balls and don't let Mom date a serial killer, okay?"

"On it," he said.

He did a short burst of the siren for me as he drove off, like he used to do when I was ten.

Chapter Seven

Fewer than ten hours after I'd agreed on impulsive international travel, I was in my window seat on the first leg of the flight. It was the only one that left on time.

While we were stuck on the ground in L.A., I texted Harriet. She replied:

> No worries. You have a five hour window once you land.
> Some interesting developments here. Xxx.

I needed to be out of the continental U.S. before I talked to my mother, but Uncle Leon should know I wouldn't be covering his bets until the New Year.

He perked up at the mention of Tasmania. "I know a girl there name of Amanda Heep," he said. "She knows the truth."

"The truth about what?"

"About the tigers." He gave me the number and hung up.

We landed in Melbourne four hours late.

I tried Harriet the instant I was through the forty-five-minute Customs Line. No response.

I'd read Australian taxi drivers resented the class distinction of fares sitting in the back, so I climbed into the passenger seat. It felt completely weird, especially being on the side where I was usually in control of the vehicle. At least my tourist status allowed me to press my face against the window so I wouldn't constantly scream, "We're on the wrong side of the road!" or "I'm too young to die!"

I kept my brake foot pressed into the floorboard and my eyes glued for exotic scenery. No such luck. I was starting to realize, the ten miles around any international airport looked the same. Hideous. Just low, cheap, industrial buildings, chain-link fences, and sadness.

I perked up at the sight of the Melbourne skyline, though, and, fifty minutes later, the driver told me we were approaching Port Melbourne. I was already over-tipping him and gathering my things when he stopped in a tiny roundabout, ringed with palm trees and surrounded by polished, generic condos, and insistent, well-manicured bike paths. The glistening floor-to-ceiling condo windows looked out on the choppy water all the way to Tasmania and then, Antarctica. Neither was visible, sadly.

There were other things which weren't visible. First, people. Second, the cruise ship.

For a minute, I couldn't even locate the terminal until I glimpsed the "Station Pier" sign on the quaint, inflated, World War II-green Quonset hut in front of me. It was barely big enough to hide an SUV, much less a two-thousand-passenger ship.

I looked at my adjusted watch. 3:30. It should still be here. A security guard in a too-tight uniform and patchy red beard approached, grinning.

I smiled back. "Could you please give me the time?"

"I can give you a lot more than that." Seriously?

When he saw my face, he looked at his watch. "Half four."

I had mis-changed my watch over the Marshall Islands. Dammit.

"It went right on time. Need somewhere to stay?" He raised one ginger eyebrow

"For thirty seconds?"

He glared at me and stomped off. What were the rules on sexual harassment these days? If you rebuffed them and it hurt their feelings, were you supposed to back off the rejection to make them feel better? Or kick them in the balls?

I grabbed my BlackBerry and tried Harriet. No response. My chiffon was damp and itchy and I could feel my false eyelashes going limp. I realized that, minus one or two hours of interrupted sleep on the plane, I'd been up for two days.

There was a tiny nautical-themed bar beside the terminal. I was headed there when I heard a whistle. I whipped around to see a slight but gorgeous man in a dark blue golf shirt running toward me. As he got closer I read the white word Police on his chest.

"You Redondo?"

I hitched up my Balenciaga and held out my hand. "Cyd Redondo, Redondo Travel."

"Scott. Harbor Police. Friend of Harriet's."

"Thank God. What did she say?"

"For me to drop you on the boat."

"Fantastic. Thanks so much." It was just like Harriet to be kind enough to arrange a speed boat. Bless her.

Scott the cop grabbed my twenty-two-inch rolling bag and gestured me down the pier toward the police boat. I reached into my purse. I would need a scarf for my hair and my heaviest duty sunglasses to keep my lashes anchored. What else?

I usually went for tight skirts, to give my hips a longer line, but they did restrict movement, so for ventilation and room for going up and down cruise ship stairs, I had opted for a Bisou Bisou permanent pleat swing skirt in a pale push-up ice cream orange. It swung like a beaded curtain just above my knees. With my nude-colored Steward Weitzman strappy sandals, I figured I looked continental enough for a boat ride.

"Will we get wet?"

"Not if we're lucky." Scott winked. I had always heard that men outside of America appreciated more mature women, but I'd thought it was just wishful thinking or PR.

We arrived at the speed boat, then passed it.

"Oh, no," I said as he stopped in front of a police helicopter instead.

This wasn't the first time I had been rescued by a helicopter. I hadn't been dressed for it that time, either. My scarf might be good for an open boat, but was possibly Isadora Duncan territory with rotor blades. I folded it back into my purse. Scott reached for my carry-ons.

"Is this covered by my trip insurance?" Helicopter-to-ship transport started at thirty-five thousand.

"It's covered by the fact I dated Harriet's sister and it's a slow day."

"What about your paperwork?"

"No worries. Standard casino check."

Australia didn't allow gambling on cruise ships until they were more than twelve nautical miles out.

"Clever. I didn't realize the ship was big enough for a landing pad."

"It's not."

Chapter Eight

"I thought you said you were dropping me on the boat."

"I am. Glad you dressed for it," he grinned, checking out my whirly skirt. It was only eight inches below my Chantelle "Africa" thong. I had bought the whole set at La Petite Coquette's End of Everything sale. Why, why hadn't I put on the matching boy shorts instead?

Scott stored my luggage, while I gripped my purse. Once we were inside, he explained we'd be traveling with the doors open, so I needed to be strapped in. That was reassuring. I insisted on attaching the handles of the Balenciaga to an S-clip on my harness. I tried to keep visual contact with my other two bags, for whatever good that might do.

My stomach dropped as we lurched straight up off the dock. A couple of other cops on the blue and white police boat waved as we headed away from the skyscrapers and cranes of Melbourne, south and out to sea. I looked through the door at the water below and reminded myself that in eight seasons, Thomas Magnum, P.I. had never fallen out.

"How long will we be flying?" I needed to calculate my drop prep time.

"Not long. They're only about five miles ahead. Probably still doing a muster for the add-ons. Still inside our jurisdiction."

"How far does your jurisdiction go?"

"How far do you want it to go?" He moved his hand from the gear shift to my thigh.

"Not that far."

He put his hand back on the gear shift. "Understood. Six miles."

"Just six miles? That's not very far."

"Six for the Melbourne and Harbor Police. Twenty-four for the Victoria State Police."

"And if something happens further out?"

"Up for grabs. Interpol, sometimes. Coast Guard, sometimes. Some of the cruise lines have their own investigators. Depends. It's pretty much the Wild West in international waters."

"Do you have a lot of cruise crime near the port? Robberies? Rowdy tourists?"

He laughed. "Nah. Almost none, as it goes. Occasionally some drunken crew members. All the really good stuff happens two hundred miles out."

"I can hardly wait," I said.

"That's what they all say." Scott took the helicopter higher.

"So when you say 'drop me,' how exactly does that work?"

"We prefer to call it lowering."

"It's pretty damn low, all right. In the United States we would call this a bait and switch."

"Harriet said it would be better to surprise you."

"She absolutely did not."

"Okay. She didn't. I wanted to enjoy at least part of the flight."

"Bastard. I'm serious, what am I going to have to do?"

"See that rope ladder right there?" I looked over and saw a coil of string.

"That thing that looks like a shoelace?"

"It's super cord, it can hold up to five hundred pounds." Thanks to the psychotic Qantas weight limit, even with my carry-ons, I could stay under that. I just hoped I'd have enough weight to keep the ladder from flying up into the rotors. This was crazy. Why was I doing this?

Then I thought about the Manzonis, wherever they were. I thought about Harriet and how many favors she'd called in to get me this trip, not to mention the private port-to-stern transportation. I thought about my family, and how I needed to redeem myself to them and all of Bay Ridge or it wasn't really worth making it home alive.

"So, talk me through it," I said.

"Okay. I'll get as low as I can and throw out the ladder, then you climb down, and jump from there onto the deck."

"Just sort of free form? Can't you attach me or something, in case I get wobbly or lose my grip?"

"Do you really want to be attached to a moving helicopter?"

"Yes or no?"

"I can, but it will make it harder once you get close to the ground. You'll have to take it off or unhook it."

"I'll take my chances. How about a life jacket?" He rolled his eyes. "I saw that."

"Do you really think I'm going to miss the boat and drop you in the Bass Strait? Besides, I'll keep hold of you until you stabilize yourself on the ladder."

"Don't you need to keep flying?"

"I'm dexterous." He winked.

This was the second time in two months I'd had a chance to flirt with a helicopter pilot. I wondered whether, as a group, they were good in bed? They were capable of concentration, and speedy action if necessary, but they could also be, well, flighty, and quick to exit.

The last time I'd been in a helicopter, I'd been rushing to save my plus one, Roger Claymore, from death by poison dart frogs. Looking back, I'm not sure he fully appreciated my efforts, and the layers of lies he'd told me, even if they were necessary, still stung. So I tried to appreciate Scott's muscled forearm as it pointed to his target, the *Tasmanian Dream*, coming up on the horizon. I sat up straight and opened my Balenciaga. Purse, don't fail me now, I thought.

I pulled out headbands and hair ribbons, bobby pins, hot pink duct tape, and one of my Tupperware nesting boxes. Tupperware had not only saved my life, but the life of my Madagascan chameleon on my last adventure. This time it might save a few other crucial items, including my passport and false eyelashes. Extensions were never quite the same after they got soaked.

"Don't look. Drive," I said to Scott, who was staring at me.

"It's called flying."

"Then fly."

It was no easy task to peel off and hold onto my eyelashes beside an open helicopter window. Thank goodness I always used extra glue. I managed to peel them off and stick them to the front of my passport in the Tupperware. I encased it in pink duct tape, and put it back in my purse. Then I put the purse in my rolling backpack. I could handle the wheels digging into my back for the short time I had left to live. It wasn't easy getting it on while strapped in, but updrafts were the mother of invention.

Now, I just had to anchor my other rolling carry-on to my body. Which was stronger? The shoelace rope or my La Perla? This was a tough one. I didn't want my decision to be affected by the fact that Scott was watching my every move with disbelief, so I went for both. I took two hair ribbons and tied them tight through the rolling pack handles and the backpack handles, then hooked them through my bra straps. That way, even if the harness broke, my stuff would land, or sink, with me.

"You can't take all of that on the ladder," Scott said. "If there's too much weight when you jump out it can unbalance the copter." Great. "Just let me throw it down."

"How's your aim?" I asked.

"I'm the best bowler on my cricket team."

I had accidentally seen a cricket game on ESPN. "I'll hold it."

"It's your party. There it is." The *Tasmanian Dream* was coming up too soon.

I had done my research on the ship before I left. It had twelve decks and could carry nineteen hundred passengers and seven hundred crew—a "good ratio," as we say in the travel business. The ship had been built in 1986 and was commissioned to Darling Cruises in 2001.

None of these facts prepared me for the sight of the wedge of blue and white cutting through the heliotrope water—I got heliotrope wrong on the SATs, so now I used it as much as possible.

Scott was right, it didn't look like there was anywhere for the helicopter to land. Actually, it didn't look like there was a lot of room for anything to land, including me. The largest portion of the top deck had a swimming pool in its middle. Dozens of passengers in orange life jackets were rammed in around it. I guessed they might scatter if I screamed loudly enough on what looked like a long way down.

I could handle the drop. I knew I could. Given my family's John le Carré level of spying, the only way I had managed any kind of social life had been climbing/jumping down from my fourth-floor attic room on a regular basis, usually in stilettos. I could probably stay on them at twenty knots. And I was good at holding tight to my bags, at least in a gunfight with an amputee. Those things weren't really the problem.

The problem was, I couldn't swim.

Chapter Nine

I reminded myself that in *Butch Cassidy and the Sundance Kid*, Sundance couldn't swim either, and he made it down that river. Long term, though, not so much. And as Butch said in the first scene I ever saw with swearing, "Hell, the fall'll kill ya."

Not if I could help it. I looked down at the purple-green waves and the orange deck below. My stomach did a preemptive jump. This was nuts. What was I doing? And for Sandra Manzoni, who had pricked a hole in my diaphragm? Twice? No, I was doing it for Barry, who punched Ralph Pinkowsky's nose when he stole my lunch. I tried to sit up to my full height.

"Ready, Robocop?"

"Almost."

I took two flat, elastic Jackie O headbands and tied them together. I stuck my feet through my improvised headband-belt, and wiggled it up and over my pleated skirt to anchor it around my thighs. It would make landing harder, but at least it reduced my chances of flashing the passengers and crew, who would surround and judge me for the next five days and six nights.

I nodded at Scott. He hooked a rope through the S-clamp. "Want to practice unhooking this before you're airborne?" I opened and closed it a few times. He looked down at my shoes. "Sure you want to wear those?"

"Least of my problems." The idea of climbing down in bare, flat feet was much more terrifying.

I had prepared for (1) wind, (2) swinging, (3) moisture, and (4) death. Hair disaster was the only probability left. I swirled mine up, tied it, then secured it with the bobby pins. This was going to be fine. It probably wasn't much farther down than a roller coaster on Coney Island. I felt the copter slowing down.

"Time to unhook. I'll hold onto you and throw out the ladder."

"And you've done this a bunch, right?"

"Once. With a U.S. Army Seal. You're going to have to stand up. Good thing you're short," Scott said.

"Screw you. And stop laughing. How do I get on the ladder?"

"Just pretend you're climbing backwards into a swimming pool. And don't look down until you hit the final rung." The last time I'd climbed backwards into a pool my brousin Jimmy had tried to drown me.

Great. I wasn't going to let him know that his advice might as well have been in Chinese. Okay, here went nothing. I checked that I was still attached to the safety rope and that my carry-ons were secure. I took a deep breath, unhooked my seat belt, then grabbed onto it as I turned to face Scott.

"We'll always have Melbourne." He tucked his card into the front pocket of my carry-on.

I reached back with my heel into—thin air. Thin, whirling air. I jabbed my leg around until my stiletto finally caught a rung of the rope ladder. Scott gave me an encouraging smile.

"Keep the damn thing still, will you?" I yelped.

My other foot found the rung. I felt pretty "back heavy" and had to lean forward to stay stable. I took Scott's advice about not looking down as I repeated the process—air, rope, air, rope, rope burn. It would be okay. At that moment, a huge gust of wind caught the ladder and I almost lost my grip as I floated too close to the landing skids. I heard squeals below. I must have clinched my glutes then, as my headband-belt broke and released my swirly skirt. Upward.

"How many more rungs?" I yelled.

"Do you really want me to look?"

Then I could tell that I was close, because people were scream-ing "Jump!" So much for my stealth vacation, secretly investi-gating the crew.

Were they just cheering me on, cheering my Chantelle thong, or something worse? I finally looked down and saw the deck, no farther than the bottom of our fire escape. Of course, I was used to landing on grass, not concrete. I decided a broken leg was really going to hamper my vacation. Water gave me the willies, but there were dozens of people in life jackets to retrieve me before I drowned, so it might be a good idea to swing out over the pool before I let go. But I didn't want my luggage wet, especially my purse. Even Bay Ridge Leathers would have a hard time with red leather and chlorine. I noticed a tall, buff man with a lifeguard tank top and matching Speedo staring up at me. From this angle, he had nice dirty blond hair, at least on top.

I pointed to my bag. "Can you catch this?"

He nodded. I was having to trust a whole lot of strangers today. I unhooked and tossed the larger bag first, to test his reflexes. He caught it and placed it on a lounge chair. People clapped. Good. He had an audience, which meant incentive.

There was still my backpack, with my Balenciaga inside. Bad things had happened the last time I'd let go of it, so I hesitated. I heard Scott yell for me to hurry up. As I moved to unhook the rolling backpack, my fingers slipped and I lost hold of the ladder.

Chapter Ten

The weight of my rolling bag forced me back and, for a second, I was free-falling.

Finally, after about a quarter of my life flashed before me, the S-clamp jerked me up. My rolling backpack was half on, half off and I was swinging in a large circle, too close to the copter's landing gear. I could hear Scott yelling, but he was drowned out by the *Poseidon Adventure* level of screaming below me.

The lifeguard held out his arms and I decided, at worst, his significant torso would break my fall. I apologized to my mother in my head, waited until my swinging slowed, then unhooked the clip.

My stomach flipped and I blacked out for a second. Then I felt strong arms around me before we both smashed a padded lounge chair onto the damp, concrete deck. The force of our fall swung the wheels of my backpack into my rescuer's face. The entire deck full of passengers burst into applause. I looked up at Scott who shook his head, saluted me, and swooped off.

A pack of life-jacketed tourists surrounded us, like aggressive Cheetos. I tried to get my backpack off the lifeguard's face. One of the straps was around his arm too. When I pulled on the strap it put our faces about an inch apart. He had blue eyes, or at least one blue eye, the other was rapidly swelling closed.

"You first," he said, using his free arm to help me out of my strap and then wiggling out of his.

"Oh, God, you need ice on that." I stared at his eye.

He felt it and winced. "Just a flesh wound. Are you okay?"

I stood up. I thought I was. "Yes, thanks so much. That was pretty valiant."

"Darling Cruises, for all your travel needs." He bowed his head, looked at his watch and said "Gotta go. Thanks for dropping by."

He pushed his way through the spectators, as a disembodied, echo-y voice said, "Will all new passengers please return to their muster stations to complete the safety briefing."

The puffy passengers eased away and gathered back under large, hanging lifeboats. I wanted to hear the safety briefing too. I was just heading for the nearest lifeboat, or what the loudspeaker was calling a "survival craft," when someone grabbed my arm and swung me around. He was short, with dyed white-blond hair, beady black eyes, and a mustard stain just above the three stripes on his otherwise pristine uniform.

"You! Don't move." His tag read Staff Captain Bentley. Given the stripes and his hostility, I took him to be the ex-boyfriend Harriet had complained about.

I held out my hand. "Hello. Cyd Redondo, Redondo Travel."

"You've totally disrupted the supplemental muster."

"The what?"

"The safety briefing for passengers who joined us in Melbourne."

Harriet had implied Bentley might know something about the Manzonis. I decided to be diplomatic. "I apologize for the excitement—Harriet arranged for the helicopter when my plane was late. I assumed she would have told you."

He raised his eyebrows. "Harriet?"

"Harriet Archer. Darling Cruises' Travel Agent Liaison? In corporate? I'm her guest on the cruise." I reached into my bag for my blue Tupperware, ripped off the duct tape, and handed him my travel documents. I had forgotten my eyelashes were stuck to the front, like tiny awnings. I gasped as he brushed them off and they took flight toward Tasmania.

"She said I would be with her in cabin 710?" He ignored me as he went through my paperwork.

The loudspeaker crackled again. "This now concludes the Darling Cruises muster drill and I wish you a wonderful journey with us."

A few guests hovered around, watching me, but most had decided they'd rather drink, shop, or swim, and had dumped their safety gear and run to the nearest bar or buffet. I spotted a fair number of seniors hobbling away. Great. I might be able to generate some much-needed business while I was here.

Finally, Staff Captain Bentley looked up. "Miss...Gepetto, you bypassed the security check. That is absolutely against the rules. We will have to keep you and your luggage in the brig until this has all been cleared."

I was about to remind him of my real name when a brisk woman in a uniform with two stripes and an old-fashioned, honest-to-God Gidget flip hairdo, came running toward us.

"Don't be ridiculous, Sir. Ms. Redondo sends us business all the time. We have one of her clients on the boat now." They did? Who? I must be slipping.

"She's here as the cruise line's guest." The woman turned to shake my hand. "Margy Constantinople, Cruise Director. Harriet told me all about you. Mr. Koeze? Will you get Ms. Redondo's bags?" A boy who looked about twelve, with a pronounced cowlick and jet black eyes, started toward me. The Staff Captain stopped him.

"Miss Constantinople. It is standard policy to check the travel documents and do a security check. I'm surprised you would flaunt cruise standards in this way. Things like that do not look good on an end-of-year review."

Margy sighed. "Welcome to the nation state. All right, go ahead."

The Staff Captain took out a metal detector from his pocket (which seemed weird) and ran it over me. My bobby pins set it off, so I took them out. Finally, I was beep-free.

"Is Harriet here?" I asked Margy.

"Yes. I haven't seen her much. Embarkation is a hectic time for us."

"I can see that. I'm so sorry to have inconvenienced you both."

"Absolutely not a problem. I'll have your trip packet sent up."

"Thanks so much," I said.

"Seven-ten," she said to the steward.

"Right away, ma'am," he said, then gestured for me to follow. I could feel the white-haired Staff Captain's eyes boring a hole in my back, and passengers whispering as I passed by. I couldn't wait to tell Harriet about this little encounter.

Maybe it was because of *Titanic*, but I always thought of cruise travel as class all the way. I guess it depended on what you saw as class. The *Tasmanian Dream*'s classic white exterior, black funnel, and gleaming railings hid garish fluorescent rooms, swirling carpets, and chairs in every Crayola color. Finally, we arrived at a gold-plated (or more likely *faux* gold-plated) elevator.

I turned to the steward. "How do you spell your name?" I hated to get names wrong. I rummaged through my change purse for my vital, opening "over-tip."

"It's K-O-E-Z-E," he said. "Jeff. But everyone calls me the Koozer."

"Thanks so much for helping me, Koozer. I'm sure you have a million requests on the first day."

"A million and thirteen," he said. "So far."

"I'm pretty self-sufficient."

"I kind of got that," he said. "It makes for a change." The elevator came and went. Another cruise guest in ill-fitting active wear arrived. That time, we got on.

"May I ask why we waited?"

"We're not allowed to be in an elevator alone with a single woman."

"How do you know I'm single?"

"No need to feel bad. A lot of women go on a cruise after a breakup."

"A lot," the Lycra-clad guest said, nodding.

Damn them.

We reached my deck and its *Shining*-esque corridor. I felt claustrophobic and slightly nauseated already. The hallway was splattered with ominous sconces, teak-esque doors, and carpet with a half-hearted diamond pattern in gray and brown. I guess it was understandable when you thought about what had been tracked, dragged, spilled, and possibly spewed onto it. No wonder it smelled of air freshener, chlorine, stale rum, and something else I didn't want to know about.

I was grateful, though, that Harriet had put us in the middle of the ship, which was supposed to be the best for seasickness and what I always recommended for my clients. I hoped I wasn't susceptible, as I couldn't ask for advice. Admitting this was my first time at sea would hurt my credibility on all levels. I'd just have to wing it with the nausea and everything else. I vowed to take as many photos and notes as possible while I was here, for my clients' sake. And, if the Manzonis didn't show up, for evidence. I was anxious to know what "developments" Harriet had uncovered.

The Koozer took out his keycard.

"We should knock first." After having teen-aged boys banging on the bathroom door for my whole childhood, I appreciated privacy above all. I knocked once, then harder. No answer. "Harriet?" I shrugged. "I guess it's okay. She must be out."

"I did see her with a blond guy earlier." The Koozer put his keycard in the lock. It went green and clicked. "I'll bring your room cards right up, but you may as well get settled."

"That's great, thanks." I handed him a twenty. Was it enough? For maximum service, you always wanted to give just a touch more than they could reasonably expect. The Koozer's grin said the twenty was adequate, for now. As there were lots of seniors on fixed incomes on this particular ship, I might qualify as a big spender. Fantastic.

I let him go first, as he had the bags. The sliding door was open and the curtains whipped back and forth, hitting the balcony railing in a steady rhythm.

The Koozer jerked still and let go of my bags. They fell backwards. Then, so did he.

He was out cold. I looked down and saw why.

Chapter Eleven

I gasped, frozen, then blinked, sure I must be having some kind of jet lag nightmare.

My friend Harriet lay on the floor between the bed and the open window, in a white linen dress. She was face up, her legs splayed unnaturally, her now sad Miu Miu flats crooked and halfway off her feet. One arm was stretched out, as if reaching for the balcony. There was blood seeping into the diamond-patterned carpet under her head and drops of it on the bedside table above her.

I left the Koozer on the floor and rushed to her. This couldn't be happening. I had just gotten a text from her. I prayed she'd have a pulse, but I couldn't find one anywhere. At least I hadn't let my brousins scare me off from the First Aid course at the Y.

In, out, in, out, and all the pressure I could manage on her chest, for four full minutes, but I got no response. I needed help.

The Koozer was still unconscious. I got up, grabbed one of the complimentary bottled waters, and poured it onto his head.

He sat straight up so fast that he bumped his head smack into my left knee, then looked frightened.

"Oh, God. Did I pass out? They'll send me back to Papua New Guinea and I'll be selling chicken parts again in the street market. You know what that means."

I had no earthly idea how to respond to that, except to point at Harriet. His knees started to go. I grabbed his arm.

"Please don't faint again, they only gave us one bottled water. Can you get the ship's doctor? And the Captain, and anyone else who might help? As fast as you can. Please. Hurry."

"Is she dead or just gravely injured?"

"Get a doctor!"

He pulled a walkie-talkie out of his pocket. "Bright Star Rising! Bright Star Rising!" I just stared at him.

A scratchy voice answered. "Where?"

"Cabin seven-ten."

"Get Doctor Mathis."

The Koozer ran out the door. I heard him thud down the carpeted hallway. I looked down at my friend. All I wanted to do was to lie down beside her and sob. Crying was not going to help her. Breathing might.

I started over with the CPR, even though part of me knew it was useless.

We had only spent one weekend together, but Harriet and I had worked together for seven years and, in lots of ways, she was my role model. Well, until now, as I had hoped to get through my thirties at least. Where was the Koozer? And the doctor? I kept trying, then looked at my watch. It had been almost seven minutes. It hadn't worked. She was completely cold.

I held her frigid hand and, finally, let myself cry. When I couldn't breathe anymore, I reached for my tissues and noticed that the Koozer had dropped his "master" keycard when he fainted. I put it in my purse to give back to him later.

I looked out at the balcony and saw a two- or three-inch piece of khaki fabric caught and flapping on the railing. I looked back at Harriet. Khaki didn't seem like her style. Frank always said the most important thing in a homicide was to secure the scene, without adding your DNA. I reached into the waste basket, slipped the plastic bag over my hand, and opened a drawer. Lots of linen, but no khaki. The laundry basket was empty. Whose was this? Did it have something to do with Harriet's death?

I took pictures of the fabric, wondering where the hell the doctor was. I knew I should leave the evidence, but I took out my plastic nail clippers and cut a tiny piece of the khaki and put it into a spare ziplock. I heard someone at the door. I went to shove the plastic bag under the bed and glimpsed a piece of paper there. There was no time to grab it before the door opened and a figure moved toward me.

He was dressed in a tux with no tie and a ragged pair of brown suede Pumas. He had a black eye. The one I'd given him. It was my lifeguard.

"Hello again. I'm Doctor Mathis," he said. "What happened?"

"I don't know. She was like this when we walked in. I tried CPR, but can you try again?"

I stared at him until he knelt beside me and felt for a pulse. I caught a whiff of sea air, antiseptic, and Gillette aftershave. He gestured for me to do the mouth-to-mouth while he tried to get her heart started. Finally he shook his head and pulled rubber gloves out of his pocket.

"I'm sorry. She's gone. You know her?"

"It's Harriet Archer, she's the Travel Agent Liaison for the cruise line. I was coming to room with her. What do we do? Call the police? Coroner?"

"For all intents and purposes, I am the Coroner." He leaned back on his heels.

"What about the Harbor Police? I mean clearly, it's a homicide."

"Is it? I haven't had a homicide before."

"Well, can we find someone who has?"

He went to lift her head and I squealed. "Wait! Don't touch anything until someone photos the scene."

"Calm yourself, Cagney."

"You just said you have no experience. My brousin is a homicide detective. Trust me, we need photos. Just move back." Grateful I'd splurged on the new BlackBerry Pearl 8100 with camera,

I snapped everything I could as he watched. There was a sharp knock on the door.

Staff Captain Bentley elbowed his way in. He took one look at me, then Harriet, and slammed the door. "You, again! What have you done to her?"

What ever happened to 'the customer is always right'? "Look, this is my friend. And your colleague. She was like this when the steward showed me in. She's clearly been murdered. Why is everyone just standing around? Whoever did this must still be on board. Do something!"

The Staff Captain couldn't quite bring himself to look at the body. "Perhaps she was just clumsy and fell. People often suffer from dizziness on the first day, don't they, Doctor?"

The doctor gave a hesitant nod. "There are a few possible scenarios, Staff Captain."

I couldn't believe this. Were they serious? Dizziness? I had always heard that cruise lines minimized passenger deaths, but this was ridiculous. I mean, she was part of their team. It was hard not to throttle both of them.

Bentley looked toward the balcony. "I'm sure it was an accident, but we should talk to her husband. Has anyone seen him? Perhaps he can shed light on the situation." He picked up his walkie-talkie. "Koeze, report to cabin seven-ten, please."

I wanted to point out the ripped khaki on the balcony, but this guy didn't deserve my help. I could only hope the harbor cops would get here and find it. Bentley looked at the wall, then toward the balcony.

"I suppose it might be a domestic incident," he said. "Do you agree, Doctor?"

I looked at the doctor with raised eyebrows.

"I suppose the husband might have hit her, became overcome with guilt, and jumped off the balcony," the doctor said.

"Let's not scream 'overboard' until we've searched the ship. There's no need to traumatize our guests over something that's purely speculation. And if it is a murder-suicide, we should respect their privacy at this difficult time."

"You're kidding, right? You're just going to brush a murder-suicide under the carpet?"

"Doctor, it seems Miss Geppetto is overtired. Perhaps you can attend to her in the infirmary until we can accommodate her?"

"I don't need to go to the infirmary. I want to know what you're going to do about this. Who you're going to call?"

Bentley turned to Doctor Mathis. "As I said, infirmary. Clearly she's suffering from shock."

Shock? Of course I was in shock. There were so many things wrong with this scenario, I was speechless. To start with, Harriet didn't have a husband.

Chapter Twelve

There was no way I was leaving my unmarried friend in the hands of these idiots without at least halfway securing the crime scene. I wasn't the patron saint of the 68th Precinct for nothing.

"Gentlemen? Before I go, I wonder whether you might give me just a minute to sit with my friend?" I gave them my most ridiculous girly pleading look—the one that never worked with my Uncle Ray, Frank, or Eddie, but did with bouncers and Barry Manzoni.

"It's not within regulations," the Staff Captain said. His forehead crease screamed disapproval. He didn't want me alone in there. That made me more determined to stay.

"There are standard regulations about murdered passengers?" I asked. "What are they?"

"Sir?" The 007 doctor stepped forward and reached for the handle of my rolling bags. "Surely we can just give her a minute? Out of respect. I know you have things to attend to. I'll take her downstairs once she's done." I gave him a grateful look and made sure to hang on to my Balenciaga. He used my luggage to force the Staff Captain out. Walkie-talkies crackled through the door.

I looked down at Harriet. I still couldn't believe she was gone. I couldn't go all weepy or comatose, not now, not when I had five or six minutes, max. I apologized to her and got to work. First, I wanted to know what was under that bed. I had a penlight in my bag and shone it under the bolting that held the bed in place. My arms were too short, so I took off my shoe and used the heel as a hook. I snagged a balled-up piece of paper. And a champagne stopper. I put them in plastic bags and kept looking.

Harriet and I had once had a somewhat drunken discussion about the best place to hide anything valuable in a hotel room. Neither of us thought the safe was safe—every housekeeper had the master code and the batteries were always half-dead.

My favorite, for anything flat, like cash, was under the television. Most people wouldn't bother to lift it. But now every hotel had a flat screen on the wall. It was still possible to tape something on the back of the TV, but there was nothing there, taped or otherwise.

For short-term hiding, Harriet favored cushions. I reached behind the one on the armchair and pulled out her purse. Thank God it was a clutch and fit into the side pocket of my bag. I pushed it in, along with the plastic bags, and kept looking.

Harriet's favorite longer-term hiding place was up inside the lamps. Most lamps had a hollow base that was at least six inches high. It was easy to secret things up there—cash, papers, a flash drive—to avoid detection. It might have worked this time, if everything on a cruise ship—and I mean everything—wasn't bolted down.

I tried the plastic mini-screwdriver I'd managed to get through security with a mascara top, but it was no match for the oversized screws. I could hear rattling at the door. I managed a few loud wails and the rattling stopped. I shot more crime scene photos, then put a tiny bit of Blistex under my eyes, which made me tear up immediately. Taking another look at Harriet, I needn't have bothered.

"I will find out who did this," I promised her with all my heart. I gave her cold, slim hand one more squeeze, kissed her on the forehead, then took out a tissue and opened the door.

Doctor/Lifeguard Mathis stood there with my luggage.

"What do I call you?" I asked.

"Doc."

"Seriously?"

"Well, you could call me Dr. Mathis, but after what we've been through, that seems a bit formal."

"Please don't try to make me laugh. Do you have a first name?"

"Maybe."

I sighed. "How do you go from a Speedo to a tux in five minutes, anyway?"

"Practice. Come down to my office and you can tell me more about Harriet."

I took hold of my bags. I had been nervous without them. He took my free elbow in his remarkably warm hand and gestured me toward the elevators.

"What are they going to do to her body? Just leave it there? Can I cover it up or something?"

"Best to leave it. Once the investigators are finished, we have a morgue on the second lower deck. I know this is tough, but the body shouldn't be your problem."

Shouldn't it? Well, I'd done everything I could right now. I took one look back at cabin 710, then followed him.

The hallway seemed even creepier now. He took me down another elevator and another narrow hallway and unlocked a door labeled "Infirmary." There was a small waiting room with a desk and three closed doors. He opened one and gestured me into a small, well-appointed office with tasteful New England-looking sailing prints and a medical certificate hung just too high to read.

He reached for a silver thermal coffeepot on his desk. "It should still be hot—I was just making it when I got the call." He offered me a Darling Cruises mug, which I took, and a container of powdered creamer, which I declined. He proceeded to dump half the tube into his cup and sat down behind his desk. He picked up a limp ice pack and put it on his eye.

"Sorry about that."

"Occupational hazard."

"Do you usually see patients in a tux?"

He grinned, then got up, grabbed his lab coat, and put it on. "Happy now? Look, are you all right?"

"No. I'm not even close to all right. Would you be?" I just kept thinking of Harriet's body lying there all alone. She had been investigating on my behalf. Was that what had gotten her killed?

"Would you like a sedative or anything?"

"God, no." Actually, it sounded great, but I realized I'd completely forgotten the Manzonis were still missing and, especially now that Harriet had been murdered by an imaginary husband, I needed to keep my wits about me. I had to believe they were still alive, or I would really lose it.

Doc was sucking down his coffee and poured another cup. He held out the pot.

I was about to decline when I remembered that I'd been up for seventy-two hours. I grabbed it and topped myself off.

"You want to explain the whole lifeguard/ship's doctor thing?"

He held out his hands. "Saving lives wherever I go." He grinned. "I'm certified. I fill in sometimes for a pay bump, if there aren't any patients."

"But aren't you on call?"

"I'm never more than a towel and four decks away."

"Do a lot of crew double up on jobs?"

"Only the freelancers. Most crew members don't have time. They only sleep about three hours a night as it is. Speaking of lack of sleep, you look like you could use some."

"Thanks a lot."

"I'm speaking as your temporary physician. And landing pad. Want to explain the whole dropping from the sky thing?"

"The trip was last minute and I had a tight connection coming into Melbourne. I didn't make it, so Harriet arranged to make sure I got to the ship."

"She must have been a pretty powerful woman. I've seen

plenty of people lifted off, but you're the first S.W.A.T. team level arrival so far." He leaned forward. "Seriously, are you all right? Jet lag is bad enough without the sort of shock you've had. Where did you fly from?"

My track record with medical adjacent personnel, like chiropractors, was not great. But I had to trust someone.

"Look, before I tell you my life's story, could you maybe check something for me?"

"If I can."

"There's a couple that started out on the last cruise, the Manzonis. Fredo and Sandra. No one's seen them since the ship docked in Tasmania. Their son asked me to inquire after them while I'm here. Actually, Harriet came out to meet me so we could look for them. Can you find out if they've returned to the boat? Or if the cruise line has any information?"

He handed me the coffeepot and said he'd be right back.

As soon as I heard the elevator ding, I stood on my chair to check out his medical certificate. "Henry M. Jones Medical School of the Bahamas," it said. With the exception of Johns Hopkins, I didn't know how many medical schools were named after a guy.

Then, I tried to check my messages, but I was too low in the ship for reception. I was just about to unball the paper from Harriet's room when Doc came back.

"I'll give you any information I get. Did you say your brother was a detective?"

"Cousin. Yeah, Frank. He's a straight arrow. Great at his job. Under-appreciated," I said as I thought of him on patrol. Maybe he'd have time to give me advice about Harriet's murder. I needed cell reception. I wondered if my phone would work on the main deck. Suddenly, I felt a little bit dizzy and put my head between my knees.

"Any chance of some food?" I asked.

"On a cruise ship? You've got to be kidding. Hey. I don't mean to be pushy, but I think you could use either a chaplain, a B-12 shot, or both. I can at least supply the latter."

"Are you an M.D. or a therapist?"

"Neither." He picked up a syringe. "I'm a veterinarian."

That's the last thing I heard before everything went black.

Chapter Thirteen

I woke up disoriented and rumpled under the covers of a cabin bed. I cracked my eyes. There was a bedside table and a sliding glass door leading to a balcony on my left. To my right was another table and a closet. Just like Harriet's. I guessed most of the cabins looked the same.

Still, how did I get here? Who took my shoes off? What day was it? Or night? The sun was casting long shadows under the balcony railing. These questions became irrelevant when I ripped off the bedclothes and sprinted for the tiny bathroom. The notes of bleach and stale rum in the enclosed space didn't help. Neither did the tiniest hint of vomit in my mouth. I had heard about how miserable seasickness might make you, but apparently cruise lines had colluded to sugarcoat the reality.

I tried to hold my hair up and out of my face. I had gotten a new, shoulder-length bob last week to cheer myself up. Why, why, why had I agreed on long bangs? It seemed like hours by the time I finally sat back against the tub. I was too weak to get up off the tiled floor, which vibrated with the boat engines and seemed unstable. That was probably just me.

I lay down beside the tub. The cool tile felt good against my face. I woke up to banging on the cabin door. I grabbed the toilet for a help up, attempted to scrub my collar and my mouth, then staggered to the peephole.

There were two men standing in the hallway. I got a bad feeling. Their hair was too perfect. I looked down. My crinkled ensemble hardly screamed "travel professional."

"Just a minute, please."

Where were my shoes? And my luggage? I breathed a sigh of relief to find the bags in the closet and my shoes on the floor. I slipped them on and opened the door.

"Miss Redondo?" The taller of the identical, suited men, looked down at a piece of paper. Then assessed me. Apparently I did not pass the assessment.

"Yes?"

"We're from Risk Management. We need to check the room."

"My room? Why?"

"To make sure there's nothing here you can trip over. After the unfortunate event that happened here, we want to be sure you're safe."

"That happened here?" I looked up at the door number in horror: Cabin 710. They had turned around the murder room and put me in it. I emitted a small squeak and stumbled out, bumping into the second, shorter Risk Management man.

"Wait—they put me in Harriet's room? Are you kidding me?"

"According to the Staff Captain, we are at full capacity. Unfortunately, it's the only one we have available. Has it not been cleaned to your satisfaction?"

"Cleaned? I hope to hell not. It's a crime scene." And I had accidentally been throwing up all over it.

"Nonsense. Mrs. Archer had an unfortunate accident and we are here to insure that you don't have one as well. May we come in?"

As they entered, I stole a look at the carpet beside the bed. It was pristine—no sign of blood there or on the bedside table. Had they replaced the entire wall to wall? I glanced out the balcony window. The scrap of khaki was gone too. They began to poke around, taking notes and photos.

"But she was clearly hit on the back of the head. Have the police come and gone? Is that why someone drugged me?"

"Drugged you? Miss Redondo, there's no need for hysterics. We understand you just arrived from the United States. It's been scientifically proven that crossing the International Date Line, combined with a lack of sleep, can wreak havoc on the neurological system. We often have guests who hallucinate on their first few days at sea."

"Do you?" I figured there was about a thirty-second window to stop myself before I kneed one of them in the balls. "Of course. Well, in that case, I should go right back to bed. Thanks for checking on me and for your concern." I gestured toward the door and finally had to partially push the shorter one out. "As a travel agent, it's always nice to experience a cruise line firsthand, so I can give a realistic review to my clients." I slammed the door and smacked the latch closed. Bastards. They knocked again.

I faked vomit noises until the knocking stopped. It would have helped at this moment not to be jet lagged, nauseated, or heartbroken, but I was just going to have to gut up.

I turned on all the remaining lights and started examining the room. How had they managed to replace the entire carpet? How had they had time? How long had I been asleep? I panicked for a minute about my Balenciaga, then found it on the dresser. It appeared undisturbed. I turned on my BlackBerry. No reception, but at least it came on. The time read seven p.m. Thursday. Thursday? Had I been out for a whole day?

No. It was seven p.m., Thursday, December 21, Australia time. I was a day ahead of Bay Ridge. I'd only been asleep for two hours. Well, that was still too long. I'd done nothing to find the Manzonis. Or Harriet's killer.

The first time Harriet and I'd had drinks together, the bartender at the Plaza asked if we'd grown up together. We laughed, but it's funny how sometimes, with certain virtual strangers, it feels that way. We had so much fun, I dragged her to Coney

Island the next day, where we pigged out on Nathan's chili dogs and then got nauseous on the Tilt-A-Whirl. She admitted she envied me my suffocating family—she was an only child with no cousins—and I envied her all the exotic locations she'd managed to explore in her job. She assured me it wasn't as glamorous as I thought. We'd had a memorable few days, giddy on champagne and hot mustard.

I felt a stab of hot grief behind my eyes and would have benefited from a long, wailing, can't-breathe-for-the-snot kind of cry, but I didn't have time.

The immediate sanitizing of the room and the appearance of the Risk Management twins made me even more convinced that the cruise line was hiding something. I had to see if there was anything the "cleaning crew" might have missed and needed professional advice. I dug through my carry-on and found Uncle Ray's satellite phone. I'd charged it in L.A. and, to my delight, it worked.

It was the middle of the night in Bay Ridge, but Frank had a baby, so he was used to getting up.

Unfortunately, his wife, Madge, answered. I was pretty much *persona non grata* with her, since she blamed me for Frank's demotion.

"Miss Fancy, on your cruise. Nice little holiday in the sun while the rest of us have to slave for a living."

"Cut the crap, Madge, I need Frank."

"Running off and leaving your poor mother alone for the holidays."

"My mother is fine. I'm sitting here in the middle of a murder scene and I need Frank, so put him on the fricking phone or I am never, ever babysitting for you again. Or holding a place for you at Century 21." Our only connection was love of a bargain and, as a mother of small children, she wasn't up for the four a.m. MegaSale line. I can't tell you how many times I'd protected her place against violent housewives.

"Get him. Seriously."

I heard yelling, then infant crying, then a long male sigh. "What?" Frank said.

"Hey. Thanks for the ride, by the way. You know my friend who arranged the trip and was helping me look for the Manzonis? Harriet?"

"Yeah. Is there a point?"

"Yeah, there is. I tripped over her body when they let me into her cabin. They gave me a sedative, sanitized the room, and put me back in it. They're calling it an accident, but someone bashed her head in."

"Jeez, Squid, you haven't even been gone a day."

"So? Sorry the timing of my friend's murder is inconvenient for you."

"Are you sure it wasn't a slip-and-fall? Those things happen all the time on ships. Was there blood anywhere else?"

"Whose side are you on?"

"The side of husbands who were trying to sleep."

"Hang up, already!" Madge yelled in the background.

"What do you expect me to do? The Australian Ocean is not exactly my jurisdiction."

"There is no such thing as the Australian Ocean. We're in the Bass Strait."

"I don't care if it's the Ass Strait, I can't do anything."

"You can tell me what kind of evidence to look for. What could the cleaning staff miss? Is there anything I should try to collect? The cruise line is clearly trying to cover this up, and Harriet was my friend. She was only here to help me look for the Manzonis. Do you think that's what got her killed—asking questions about the Manzonis?"

"I always told you the Manzonis were trouble. But did you listen? No."

Frank's disdain for Barry Manzoni was not exactly a news flash. I heard another sigh, but it was shorter than the first one, so I was getting somewhere. Frank was a natural homicide detective and I knew he hated being sidelined from the action. I just had to convince him there was a mystery here. I told him about the ripped piece of khaki on the railing and the things under the bed. "Look, Frank, something horrible happened to her. I have to try, right?"

"No, you don't. I don't understand why you have to turn every vacation into an episode of *The Closer.*"

"The Staff Captain—who keeps calling me Miss Geppetto, by the way—said it might be a 'domestic disturbance' between Harriet and her husband. But I know she wasn't married. The steward said he saw her with a blond man, but I don't know whether he belongs to the khaki, and if so, did he jump overboard or is he still here? Come on, Frank, help me. If Harriet was attacked because of the Manzonis, I could be next. And you were the one who drove me to the airport." I let that sink in for a long moment. "What if it was Chan Lu lying in a pool of blood?" Chan Lu was Frank's partner.

"Do you have any rubber gloves?"

"Of course." I always had a pair or two of extra hair dye gloves in my purse for assorted unpleasant tasks.

"And any plastic bags?"

"Yep. I picked up the other stuff with the plastic bag from the wastebasket. There are a couple more of those and unused laundry bags in here."

"Good. Okay. Here's what you do."

By the time I'd hung up, he'd talked me through a full-on search, as well as how to use my large makeup brush, "Something Shady" eye shadow, and Scotch tape to lift a few fingerprints. I got one clear thumbprint and a few partials on the balcony railing. I photographed the prints, then secured the strips of tape in the place men were least likely to search—my tampon case. I was just finishing up my CSI work by checking all the curtain hems, when there was a knock on the door.

Chapter Fourteen

There was another knock, this one louder.

I hid my evidence and checked the peephole.

It was the Koozer. I opened the door.

"Ms. Redondo, hello. I hope I'm not disturbing you. I just wanted to leave you these and see whether there was anything you needed."

He was holding a tray with a bowl of green apples and a creamy, embossed envelope.

"The apples are for seasickness. Some passengers say they help."

"Thanks, I really appreciate it. What's this?"

"Message from the Captain." Then he stood there, I guess waiting for a tip. I dug out a ten, then held it in my hand.

"Can you tell me what they've done with Harriet's body?"

"I believe it was moved to the morgue."

"How? When?" Then I had a horrible thought. "You weren't the one who brought me here and put me to bed, were you?"

"God no. I mean no, ma'am."

"Do you know how I got here? Or how they got this room cleaned up so fast?"

There was a long pause. "Darling Cruises is an organization of consummate professionals."

"Professional crime scene cleaners?"

His lack of response said it all.

"Christ on a bike. So this happens a lot?"

Again, he said nothing. I realized I should have started with fives, as now the ten in my hand was a demotion. I took another ten out of my wallet.

"We have a lot of elderly people. Some of them die."

"Die as in 'are murdered'? You don't think that was an accident, do you? I mean that was a lot of blood, you saw it." We both looked at the place the blood stain should have been.

The Koozer took the other ten. "Have you ever seen a dead body before? I mean, you seemed to know what to do."

"I have. I wish I hadn't."

"Someone you knew?"

"Yeah." I would have given anything to be sharing a watery decaf with Mrs. Barsky right now. She'd have had some unsolicited advice on this whole situation, for sure.

"I've only seen them in coffins, not in life." What the heck did that mean? He looked out the window, then turned and tried to smile. "Oh, I almost forgot, here are your keycards. Your travel packet should be in the desk." He turned to go.

"Thank you. Seriously, Koozer."

He nodded. "Anything you need, Ms. Redondo. Formal wear, anything."

"Actually, you could do something for me. Was the blond man you mentioned staying with Harriet? In this cabin?"

"It looked like he surprised her—he brought flowers." The Koozer looked around. "I don't know where the flowers went."

"Do you remember anything else about him?"

"Six feet? Blond hair going gray at the temples. Wore a light-colored suit, I think."

Light-colored as in khaki, I thought. "Thanks so much." I was about to let him go when I remembered the Manzonis.

I felt horrible. I'd been here for hours and done nothing to find them. At least they might still be alive. "You weren't by any chance the steward for a couple called the Manzonis on the last cruise, were you?"

He hesitated, thinking. "I think they were on Deck Nine," he said. "They would have been Nylo's, I think."

"Could you maybe arrange for me to speak to him when he has time?" I handed him another ten. I heard his walkie-talkie crackle and shooed him out. I remembered I had his master keycard, but by the time I checked the hall, he was gone.

What had he meant about coffins? Had he lost a family member? Or several? I flashed on being six and seeing my grandmother Redondo in her silk-lined coffin, every gun metal hair in place, like it had never been in life. She looked unconcerned, which bothered me. Wasn't she sorry to leave us? Or past caring? I'd never know.

I sat on the bed and opened the envelope.

"The Captain of the *Tasmanian Dream* requests your company at the Captain's Table this evening. Formal attire. Nine p.m."

Wow. According to my clients, this was a real honor. I imagined in this case, it might just be strategic. I was a travel agent who knew a lot of other travel agents, and my first experience on board had been tripping over my murdered friend.

Maybe the crew just wanted to keep an eye on me. I don't know why I was so convinced Harriet had met with foul play. Maybe it was the speed with which Darling Cruises was trying to cover it up. Maybe it was because Harriet was a lot of things, including a former ballerina, and I just couldn't see her losing her balance in that particular way. It had to be the "husband," but who was he? And where was he? Did the khaki mean he had jumped overboard? Or just over one cabin? And had Staff Captain Bentley actually alerted the Coast Guard? No one had turned the ship around.

Harriet implied she and Bentley had dated. That meant at some point there must have been one thing good about him, at least. Was he as unmoved by her death as he appeared to be?

Or had he murdered her himself? Is that why he was trying to avoid an investigation? My last conversation with Harriet had been just before I took off from JFK. She said she was getting pushback from an upper level staff member on the ship, but she hadn't said which one. Was it the Staff Captain? Or someone else? She'd also said the Manzonis weren't the first seniors not to return from Tasmania, and that she was trying to get the old records, but I hadn't found them in the cabin. Had the killer taken them?

The dinner might be helpful. The crew would be forced to be polite. Even if they were in denial about Harriet, they couldn't ignore me about the Manzonis too. It would just be rude. Plus the wine and drinks at the Captain's Table would be free—an important consideration, since the Koozer was quickly eating up my liquor budget.

Nine p.m. That gave me two hours to get ready, make friends on the ship, and see what I could find out. As I reached for my carry-on, I started to make an amateur cop to-do list, though my jet lagged brain was likely to forget half of it.

I needed to talk to Koozer's friend, Nylo. I needed to talk to the Cruise Director, Margy, to double check the Manzonis hadn't registered for any excursions on Tasmania. If they had, I should book the same ones. I needed to send all the crime scene pictures and evidence to Frank somehow, but the Wi-Fi was too weak in the cabin to send any data. And I needed to charm the Captain, as he was the only crew member who ranked above the annoying Bentley. I had heard ninety-five percent of all cruise ship captains were Italian. And handsome. For that, I needed a shower and formal wear.

As I stood under the low-pressure shower head, I tried not to think about where the water was coming from or where it was going. I had read in cruise ship crew memoirs that the lower you went in the ship, the dirtier the water was when it arrived. There were five decks above me, so I kept my eyes and mouth closed—a practice I had perfected in Tanzania. My formal dress had a boatneck in the front, but was backless to my waist. I exfoliated to make sure my sweaty back wasn't harboring any dead skin, then shaved, moisturized, and diffuse-dried my hair. There wasn't enough room to put everything on the counter and I had to divide my beauty products between the toilet lid and the now-damp floor. I felt I needed another shower by the time I was done, but I hoped people would see me as "glowing" or "moisturized," rather than "post marathon." I reached for my nighttime eyelashes, loaded them up with Create Your Own Awning mascara, and I was ready to squeeze into my dress.

I escaped to the relatively spacious stateroom and pulled out my Felicia low-back bustier (clearance, Loehmann's) and my waist-to-thigh Spanx. To be frank, the whole dress pretty much served as Spanx-wear, since it was made of Lycra, covered in sequins, and squeezed you everywhere. The extra Spanx just made sure it didn't squeeze in the wrong places—as in out. I was glad it was black, as it also served as mourning-wear for Harriet.

For a second, I saw Harriet's body on the floor again and sank onto the bed. I couldn't breathe. I tried to blame it on the Spanx, but it wasn't the eighty-four percent nylon/sixteen percent Lycra blend—it was guilt. I couldn't help thinking that her death had been my fault. Well, partly Barry's fault, and his parents' fault, but most mostly mine. If I hadn't asked for her help, if she hadn't been asking questions, she might be swilling mojitos and scowling at Santas on the main deck right now, instead of lying all by herself in the ship's morgue. I couldn't bear to think of her there.

I felt a knob of despair just under my ribs. Redondos don't do well with despair. We're more comfortable punching someone in their solar plexus or reporting them to the IRS. We always choose flame throwing over therapy. I knew what my Uncle Ray would say—wallowing in self-pity wouldn't do me, or Harriet, any good. I needed to find her killer, which meant I had to get up. And find the right shoes.

I decided on my strappy silver Donna Karan sandals, anchored my secondhand diamond studs, and I was ready. Just as I put a couple of green apples in my purse, I remembered Harriet's clutch and the balled up paper from under the bed. I pulled them out. The paper first. I unwrinkled it. It was smudged. There was a word that looked like *Fort* and then a list of letters and numbers, mostly illegible. The items on the list all started with CI or DT—I wasn't sure—and were followed by numbers and dashes.

I had no idea what the Fort was. Did she mean Port? Port Arthur? Could the rest be a phone number? I would check both of them out as soon as I could get online or get reception on my BlackBerry. I needed to save the satellite phone for emergencies.

I reached for Harriet's clutch. I was relieved it was still there, as the purse had been out of my control while I was unconscious. There wasn't much in it—only Harriet's business cards, a few Australian dollars, her Darling Cruises I.D., and a tube of Chanel Rouge Allure lipstick in Curious Orange. I took off the top and rolled it up. Harriet's lipstick had a flat top, with a tiny dip at the front. It made me want to cry. Where was her passport? Her phone? Had someone taken them out while I was asleep? Or did the murderer have them? And was he/she overboard, or at the buffet?

I put the Do Not Disturb sign on my cabin door and stepped into the hallway. I thought it might be worth checking to see if anyone in the adjoining cabins had seen or heard anything suspicious. I knocked on cabin 708, hoping folks were back in their rooms to rest before dinner. No luck. I would ask the Koozer about them when I saw him next. I put a ten in my bra in preparation.

I moved to the other side, 712, and knocked. This time, I heard a crash and an unintelligible curse, but no one came to the door, even though I knocked twice more. I was too tired for extended obstruction. I leaned my head against the wall.

Buzz. Click. I turned to find a skinny, miserable-looking man in a too-tight suit aiming his camera at me.

Chapter Fifteen

I raised my Balenciaga, ready to whack the stealth photographer with it.

"What the hell are you doing?"

He bowed. "Capturing your fantasy."

"I beg your pardon?"

"I'm the ship photographer. I try to get a few candid shots of each guest. There was something about you standing there, in that dress, leaning against the wall that screamed 'Art shot!'"

"And that's supposed to make me remember my happy vacation?"

"It's not uncommon for a woman who loses her man to seek the solace of the sea. Or perhaps a replacement? What happens on a cruise ship…"

"Gets recorded. Obviously." I was about to stomp off, but he might have recorded the Manzonis, or Harriet and her "husband." I changed my tone to friendly, though I couldn't quite manage flirtatious.

"What's your name?"

"Elliot Ness."

"Come on!"

"I know. But, seriously, it is. My father was an extra on *The Untouchables* and I was born during pre-production. I think he thought Kevin Costner might want to be my godfather, but alas, that was not to be."

I moved closer, but not too close. He reeked of Listerine.

"So you've been taking pictures since Sydney?"

"Yeah, pretty much."

"And how about the last voyage? The one that returned Thursday?"

He hesitated. "Sure. Yes. I was on that route. Why?"

"I'm interested in purchasing photos as gifts. Do you have anything of Harriet Archer, I'm sure you know her? She worked for Darling Cruises? Black hair, pixie haircut, blond husband? And I also had family friends on the last trip. The Manzonis? Older couple from Brooklyn. The man is bald, big chin, usually wears a dress shirt with cuff links, but untucked. Like he's just eaten? She has a bad perm and usually wears a bright, overdone print."

"Not sure about the first woman, but the couple? Yeah. I think they won the Cha Cha contest."

"Really?"

"Against some pretty mean competition. We have this one guy—one of the ship gigolos—who's a monster dancer, but they beat him out. Boy, was he pissed."

"Their son is a friend of mine and I know he'd love to see them. I'll be happy to pay."

"The older cruise shots are all in my computer, in my cabin. You could come with me now." There was something a little bit creepy about his tone.

"I don't want to get you in trouble. I know the crew has rules about being alone with single female guests."

"So you're single, then?"

"How is that relevant?"

"Oh, right. Yes, we aren't supposed to host guests in our room. But I need to pull the old pictures up and make sure they're the right ones, then I can print copies for you. I don't bite. Come on."

I followed him down the stairs. When we stopped, I wondered if he'd noticed I had assumed a basic kickboxing stance, my left leg slightly forward and my back leg about a foot and a half behind. I was a righty, so you always saved your back side as a surprise power punch/kick.

The berth was a mess, with photographs everywhere. I stayed in the doorway while he leaned over his laptop, then brought it to me. There they were, the Manzonis, with plastered grins on their faces and a sort of fake *bonhomie*. There was a man behind who looked familiar, but I couldn't place him.

"Great, that's definitely them. Thanks, Elliot. I'll take any shots you have of them. And of Harriet arriving on this voyage, if you have them. Should I come to the photo shop later?"

"I'd prefer not, since this is off the record. I'll meet you in the Castaways Bar at midnight."

I got directions to the main deck and headed down the hallway, passing a few crew members who all said "Hello, Ms. Redondo." I guess the gossip mill was already grinding.

I looked on a map and stopped by the Cruise Director's office, but it was locked. Was anyone doing anything about Harriet? I knew better than to try the Staff Captain. I figured I would try to meet some of the cruisers, in hopes they'd seen her.

I took the elevator to the main restaurant deck. The door opened. It looked like my options were Calypso, Karaoke, or Carols. I could hear "The Christmas Song." It was tough to remember baby Jesus's birth when the air reeked of SPF 50.

And no matter how many wreaths were splattered on every surface, all I could see was Harriet, eating a Nathan's hotdog, with mustard on her nose.

I felt even more heartsick than I had on Thanksgiving, after I'd found out my Uncle Ray was an animal smuggler. I could still see the horror on Frank's face the first time my mother handed him the electric carving knife.

That reminded me, I needed to send him the photo attachments. I checked my phone. Still no bars.

I walked out to the railing. The setting sun gave a caramel-y glow to the light sparking off the water. Where were we? And what was that bit of land out there? Was it the mainland, or our destination, Tasmania? I had no idea how to navigate out here.

I moved back from the railing and reached deep into my Balenciaga for the silky suede bag that held the one part of my father I always had with me. It was a Wilcox Crittenden compass, made in 1929, the brass needle inside still shiny. It had belonged to my Grandfather Guido and then to my dad, Johnny, who'd given it to me on my fourth birthday, a month before he died. He'd told me as long I held onto it, I would never be lost.

The compass had been, though, confiscated by Interpol when I was in Africa. My plus one, Roger, had stolen it back for me, then had lied straight to my face. I still couldn't trust him. Of course, when did trust have anything to do with attraction?

The needle was facing north, so the dark shape was the tip of mainland Australia. I must be standing backwards. Maybe that was why I felt nauseous. I put the compass back into my purse and turned forward. That didn't help. I grabbed a green apple out of my bag, ate a few bites, then promptly threw up over the railing.

"Sorry!" I yelled to everyone below, as I backed away.

I spun and banged right into Doc, now wearing a black tie with his tux. He smiled. I threw my hand over my mouth, waved him away, and ran for the ladies' room. After brushing my teeth with my emergency travel toothbrush three times, and reapplying both lipstick and Chanel No. 5, I opened the door, hoping I could make a clean getaway.

Doc was still outside. "Just wanted to make sure you're okay." He stepped forward.

I slapped him as hard as I could.

"Ow! What the hell? I caught you when you dropped from a helicopter!"

"Yeah, and then you drugged me and did God-knows-what-else before leaving me in a murder room."

"What?" He looked around, as a few people seemed to have

noticed the altercation. He pulled me down the hall. I jerked back.

"The last thing I remember is you coming toward me with a syringe. The next thing I know it's two hours later and I'm back in the death cabin." Passengers were listening in. After arriving by helicopter and vomiting over the railing, I figured it was too late to be subtle.

He stared at me. "I had nothing to do with that."

"Of course you did."

"No, I didn't. I was going to give you a B-12 shot, but you collapsed before I could. I wasn't sure if you were needle-phobic or just exhausted. I called Margy Constantinople. She's the one who came to get you."

"Well, how did she get me upstairs? On a stretcher?"

"Wheelchair. She didn't want to alarm the other guests, especially in light of…you know. She arranged to have your bags sent up and when I checked with her, she said you were sleeping. I figured that was the best thing for you. I was actually on my way to check on you."

I assessed his story. I wasn't inclined to believe the man who even countenanced the accident theory of Harriet's death, but I did believe that Margy Constantinople, who'd been so lovely, and whom I'm sure was also desolate about Harriet, might have helped me.

"Okay," I said. "I guess." I slumped against the wall.

"Have you eaten?"

"Ever?"

"You're not going to make it easy, are you?"

"Probably, eventually."

"Really?"

"If it involves shrimp," I said, suddenly starving.

"Shrimp," he said, "is my specialty."

"I'm supposed to have dinner with the Captain in an hour."

"The over-the-top service at the Captain's Table really slows those five courses down. I'd suggest an appetizer. You don't want to wind up shoving down bread or having some kind of episode, do you?" How did he know me this well?

He offered his arm. "Madame?"

"That's Ms. Redondo to you, and I don't need your arm."

"It's for me. Fewer slip-and-falls, less work. More time for shrimp, for example."

The way he said shrimp sent a drop of sweat down my bare back.

It got worse when he placed his hand on my hip and moved me toward the Oceana Buffet. I was looking forward to a momentary distraction, since I couldn't do anything about Harriet until dinner. Cruise buffets were legendary and I had always found salad bars soothing. And, just when I had been suffering from a lack of holiday spirit, there it was: an eggnog bar.

I unhooked myself and practically leapt onto the buffet host. Two eggnogs—heavy on the nutmeg and easy on the rum—later, I felt almost human.

I looked longingly at the carousel of crab's legs.

"No," Doc said. He handed me a green apple. "Give yourself at least a day before you binge. Did they really put you back in that room?"

"The Risk Management guys said it was the only room available. Could that be true? Or does the Staff Captain just want to torture me?"

"The Risk Management guys?"

I told him about their visit. He shook his head.

"Hey, you haven't heard anything about the Manzonis yet, have you?"

"No, not yet." He looked at his watch. "We've got time before dinner. Want to look around?" I did, on my own, but I couldn't figure out an easy way to dump him. Clearly nausea didn't work as a repellent.

"Sure."

I stopped to look at the Evening's Events calendar. There would be Carolers in Victorian garb in the "Cock and Bull" pub, which seemed unfortunate on so many levels. I just couldn't quite put the idea of bonnets, thongs, and "The Little Drummer Boy" together. There was also a Seniors "Saturday Night Fever" Dance Competition on in the Disco Lives! Lounge.

"Let's do that." I was homesick. *Saturday Night Fever* had been set and shot in Bay Ridge. My dad had been one of the Barracudas in the rumble scene.

Chapter Sixteen

We could hear "Boogie Shoes" pounding from above. Doc gestured me up the stairs.

"Is this all right? An employee accompanying a guest to a bar?"

"I'm accompanying you as your physician, to make sure you don't have a bad reaction to the pills."

"You gave me pills?"

"No. But nobody else knows that. Besides, everyone on the boat's been asked to be extra nice to you, given the circumstances, so I'm just following orders."

"That's why I'm invited to the Captain's Table tonight?"

"Probably."

We arrived at the Disco Lives! Lounge, complete with a floor of blinking, primary color squares right out of the film. The lounge host nodded at Doc and moved us to a table near the action. I could feel and hear people whispering as I went by.

"Are you sure you should drink?" Doc said. "Speaking as your physician."

I guess he didn't know me that well. Normally, I would have a shot or two of Jack Daniels, given the day I'd had. It was a cruise, though. Maybe I should have a Planter's Punch. Or, given the state of my digestive system, a green apple martini. But before I could answer, a waiter sat a double shot of bourbon in front of me.

"Miss Redondo. Good evening and welcome. My name is Julio. I took the liberty of bringing you your favorite drink."

How did he know my favorite drink? Had the Risk Management guys done a background check?

"Miss Archer was kind enough to inform us of your preferences," Julio said. "But of course, if you'd like something else, I will get it immediately."

I looked at Doc, then Julio.

"Thank you, Julio. This is perfect. It is a lovely tribute to Ms. Archer. I appreciate it."

"My pleasure. And, may I add, many other patrons have offered to buy a drink for our own female Bruce Willis, so I am at your service."

Doc snorted, then ordered a Scotch and a Planter's Punch before Julio bowed and headed back to the bar. I could feel more tip money floating out of my wallet, all because of runway construction at LAX. I turned to Doc.

"Are you trying to get me drunk?"

"I have a feeling that wouldn't be very easy."

"Hey!"

"You just don't strike me as a lightweight."

I shrugged. I wasn't.

"That's what I thought," he said.

"I grew up with ten male cousins who picked on me about everything, including drinking like a girl."

"Don't worry, the Planter's Punch is for me."

I laughed for the first time since I'd left the office. Well, except for during *Little Miss Sunshine* on the plane.

"Does the staff not know Harriet's dead?"

"We try to keep gossip to a minimum."

"On a ship? With three thousand people? Good luck with that. Bay Ridge has eighty thousand and no one can buy an EPT kit without getting a baby shower."

"Cruises are all about appearances. Hey, they're about to start the Early Bird round."

I watched as a man in a powder blue three-piece suit, an

obvious toupee, and a microphone, moved to the center of the dance floor.

"Welcome, Cruisers! We're thrilled to offer a chance for all those on board who remember and love the disco era to show off their moves. Let's give a hand for the lovely couples who are here to win!"

We all clapped. The flashing floor went berserk and a thunderous, and perhaps ironic, "Stayin' Alive" roared through the speakers while ten sets of partners, two with walkers, made it onto the dance floor.

In my experience, when it came to any kind of organized dance, seniors had it all over us. They seriously knew what they were doing. They could jitterbug, swing dance, they'd been through the Rumba and Cha Cha crazes of the sixties. They knew how to move with their partners, lead and be led, in a way that people my age weren't comfortable with and usually sucked at.

So, despite a certain arthritic stiffness, there was some serious moving going on, and suddenly I understood the whole cruise thing. The Grey Panthers might have a dance once or twice a year. This was every night. This was a place travelers of a certain age could actually show off their serious skills and feel young again, without embarrassment or judgment. I loved it. Doc caught me smiling and grinned back.

"It makes you feel young, doesn't it?"

"And not in a good way." I turned back to watch the dancing line.

The next couple came forward. The man was shorter than Travolta, but had his swagger. He suffered from pronounced bow legs, which made his flared pants swing in. He was smooth, though, and I appreciated that he was careful in the big dips, supporting his older partner's arthritic neck. She had purple streaks in her white bob and an orange halter dress that looked like a vintage Diane von Furstenberg.

"Who is that?" I asked Doc, pointing at the gold-laméd mystery man.

"He's one of the 'escorts.' I don't remember his name." He gestured for Julio, who returned with another Jack Daniels and a flourish.

Julio grinned. "That is Monsieur Brazil. He is staff. The cruise line employs certain eligible senior men to make sure all the single women have partners. It is a kindness."

This was something I didn't know, and a great added benefit for my widows.

"How many are there on the ship?"

"Twelve. I only know this because I am responsible for their drinks."

"Was Monsieur Brazil on the last passage to Tasmania?"

"Yes. I believe so. He is often here during the holidays."

When the song ended, "Monsieur Brazil" swirled his partner out and froze, one arm flung up, legs akimbo, creating a horseshoe a three-year-old could get through. She shimmied forward and threw up her arms. I gasped.

It was my former teacher, Sister Ellery Magdalene Malcomb, admirer of Herman Hesse, who was eighty-one and currently wearing orange platform shoes. Just before I graduated from middle school, Sister Ellery met the widowed father of one of her students at a Catholic raffle and decided to bet on men and sex instead of God. The relationship hadn't lasted, but she'd never looked back. As a vested Bride of Christ, she had her retirement, and it turned out she was actually from a wealthy, dead family, had funds galore, and was "Up for anything."

"Cyd," she told me the first time she came in to book a dirty weekend, "you don't know what hell is until you've taught a class of seventh graders. According to the Archdiocese, I'm headed back there when I die, so in between, I'm going to have fun." She'd decided life was not worth continuing without "Sex with someone who knows what they're doing. Stamina's important too, at my age." These are things you really don't want to hear from a nun, much less the one who taught you to write cursive.

Still, there weren't a lot of people she could talk to, and since she'd "retired" and become a regular client, we were friends. Between us, we'd worked our way through every eligible man in Bay Ridge. After my Aunt Noni died, Sister Ellery asked whether my Uncle Ray might be interested in a woman who felt younger than her years and up for lots of sex? She'd held her tongue so long for the Archdiocese, she clearly relished her newfound frankness, which often resulted in TMI. As a former student, there was a certain glee in seeing her that way, so I always looked forward to a visit. By now, she'd had multiple romances, two husbands, and one hip replacement. I'd planned both her honeymoons, one in the Caribbean and one in Hawaii, as well as an "ashes scattering" off the Isle of Wight.

After her second husband died, she'd been wary of living alone. I'd figured out a year-round cruise would actually be cheaper—and more fun for her— than a retirement home, so I'd booked her trip. The only thing was, she was supposed to be in Greece right now.

She took a bow and popped up. I waved and her face lit up. She shuffled toward me, her arms in the air. I braced myself. All of those years with no physical contact had turned her into an awkward and over-enthusiastic hugger. She could never quite pull it off normally, either bruising your ribs, smearing your makeup, or stepping on your feet like a bad prom date.

This time her platform heels rammed into my exposed toes, but I hugged her back just as hard. I was so glad to see her.

"Cydhartha! This is Kismet, certainly. 'Alas, we will meet again, ere long.'"

She turned to her dancing partner, who'd followed her over. Although I was sure I'd never met anyone with a working pompadour or a gold lamé seventies suit, there was something about him, around the eyes, that seemed familiar.

"Cyd Redondo, meet Ron Brazil."

Ron Brazil. Really? I held out my hand. He hesitated, then gave it a limp shake.

"This is so perfect, isn't it, honey? That she's showed up on this cruise? Cyd, would you be my Maid of Honor?"

Chapter Seventeen

If there was one thing Sister Ellery Malcomb insisted on, it was manners. She said, if nothing else, they gave you time to get control of your face. I wasn't sure it was going to work this time, but I loved her, so I tried.

"Congratulations! To the two of you? This is some news!" I hugged her again, then turned to Ron Brazil. "She couldn't be more special. You're a very lucky man."

"I am." He still didn't look me in the eye.

Sister Ellery grabbed his hand. "A very lucky younger man. See? I've learned my lesson. No more old men."

He kissed her hand. "They couldn't keep up with you. My dear, you must be parched, shall I get you a Campari and soda?"

"That would be wonderful, darling."

"I'll help." Doc followed Brazil to the bar.

Sister Ellery grabbed my arm. She might look frail but she still had the grip of a Bride of Christ, circa 1981.

"So, the doctor, is it? And you're the one who landed on him? Nice shot."

"You heard about that?"

"Everyone heard about that, my dear. Think Bay Ridge, times twenty. Any injuries?"

"Just my pride."

"Pride is expendable. At least you're giving yourself a vacation."

"Not exactly." I looked behind me. Our escorts were still waiting at the bar. I told her about Barry and the Manzonis.

"I have to say, after the way they treated you, I'm not sorry."

"Sister!"

"Please."

"Were you on the trip with them?" I prayed she could be my informant.

"No. Ron was, though." She leaned in. "He's a monster in bed."

"Sister!"

"I never pegged you for a prude, Cyd."

I rolled my eyes. "You're supposed to be in Greece. What happened?"

"Ron, of course. We met during a Tango competition on *The Equator* just off Santorini. He had to come back here, at the last minute, and, since we were practically engaged, I decided to surprise him. He'll have met the Manzonis, for sure. They thought they were good dancers." She made a sound that was remarkably like a harrumph.

"You know you could lose your deposit?" I said.

"It's worth it," she said, looking at Ron. His pompadour was starting to deflate in back.

Before I could tell her about Harriet, her disco boyfriend returned with a Campari and soda and what looked like a Jack Daniels, straight up. I stared at him. "Here you go," he said, then looked at his watch. "That took longer than we thought. Doc says you're at the Captain's Table too? Maybe we should take these back to the room, all get dressed and meet there?"

I nodded as Doc walked back with a couple of beers. Ron took one. I took the JD, shot it.

"Thanks, Mr. Brazil."

He gave an acknowledging nod, but still avoided my eyes.

"We'll see you upstairs, then." Sister Ellery leaned forward and gave me a sloppy kiss on the cheek.

"Absolutely." I watched her wobble off with her bow-legged Romeo.

Doc turned to me. "I assume there's a story there?"

"There are about fifteen." I gave him the short version. "She promised me she wouldn't get married again. I have to say, I don't like the looks of this guy."

"Ron? He's a regular on a few Australian routes. European ones, too, I think. He's all right, a little odd sometimes."

"Does he get engaged a lot?"

"Do you?"

"Don't change the subject."

He pushed his ample hair off his forehead. "Can't blame a guy for trying. If he does, it's not common knowledge. Technically, it's against the rules. Although romance has definitely blossomed before between the widows and escorts in the past. What harm can it do? She seems happy."

"She does." I hesitated. "That's the problem. She has a trust fund. Big one."

"Ah," Doc said.

"Any info on him you can give me, I'd appreciate."

"His blood pressure isn't great."

"That might come in handy. I'm going to freshen up. Deck Twelve, right?"

I did a quick trip back to the room for fresh lipstick and mascara, and to figure out if I could bring up murder and kidnapping with the Captain over appetizers, or if I had to wait until the main course. I saw the time and decided to take the stairs. When I got to the restaurant entrance, Sister Ellery was waiting, a shawl tossed over her gaping halter top and dangly earrings hanging from her equally dangly lobes.

"Welcome to *La Courgette*," she said.

"It's amazing how anything French sounds fancy, even zucchini."

She winked at me. "I asked Ron about the Manzonis. He

said I was the second person to ask about them. A woman with short black hair asked, too."

"Harriet Archer, my friend?"

Sister Ellery shook her head. "Maybe. He said she looked familiar, but he didn't know her. She was talking to some of the crew about them. That's the friend who brought you over?" What does she say about it?"

I looked down. "I wish I knew. She's not... Sister, she was lying dead on the floor of our cabin when I got there."

"Holy Mother of Christ." Sister Ellery crossed herself, then shook it off. "Sorry. Old habits. No pun intended."

"And the question is, if word travels at Bay Ridge-speed on a ship, how come you don't know that?"

Before she could answer, Doc arrived, still in his tux, still in his Pumas, still cute. He offered Sister Ellery his arm. He got points for that.

"I saw your date on the way up, Ellery. He said he would be right here and to go ahead."

"Great, it would be rude to be late," I said.

"Yes, it would," Doc offered me his other arm. I caught up and moved with them into the room.

A woman in her late twenties with honey-blond hair stood behind the host stand. She had extraordinary posture, with an undernote of fury. I pegged her as the product of a boarding school she'd hated. She stared down at her clipboard until we approached, then her smile snapped to. I gave her my best Redondo Travel one in response.

"Hello. Cyd Redondo, Redondo Travel. This is Sister Ellery Malcomb. We've been invited to the Captain's Table tonight."

"That's fantastic. And such an honor on your first trip on our line." She smiled at Sister Ellery, then nodded at Doc. She made a few marks on a cruise line clipboard. I wanted one of those. It looked sturdy.

"I'm Ms. Callahan, the Captain's hostess. We're delighted to have you. Please follow me."

As I walked through the restaurant toward a heart-stopping view of the water, I thought maybe it wasn't so bad, being confined with strangers. There was peace in anonymity—or there was until I heard the whispers "helicopter girl," "thong," and "tramp." I might as well have been surrounded by a thousand Aunt Helens, judging my dress, my arrival, and my dinner dates. It was very important right now not to trip. I wished I'd worn my four-inch heels rather than the kitten heel sandals. I was always unstable this close to the ground.

We arrived at the head table. It was beautifully appointed with snowy, kangaroo-shaped napkins, plates bearing the Darling Cruise Line's logo, and glasses and silverware designed for maximum light reflection. Doc placed his hand on my back, giving me an electric shock, as he moved ahead of the hostess to pull out my chair. The hostess glared at him, then smiled at an Icelandic-looking woman standing at the head of the table in full whites, four black-and-gold stripes on her shoulder. She towered over all three of us. I checked her shoes. They looked suspiciously like five-inch Louboutins. I wouldn't know for sure until I saw the red soles. As a feminist, I loved the confidence of wearing spike heels when you were already six feet tall. But as a shrimp, I felt it pressed an unfair advantage.

"May I introduce Miss Cyd Redondo." Miss? Seriously?

I held up my hand. "Redondo Travel. Ms." I added. She reached down. I glimpsed the beginning of an anchor tattoo on the inside of her wrist. She had a strong handshake. But so did I, thanks to Eddie's arm wrestling training when I was five.

"Captain Lindoff, at your service. Thank you for joining us." I detected a slight Scandinavian accent. A woman. How fantastic.

"Such a pleasure to meet you, Captain." I wondered whether I should call her Ma'am or Your Excellency. "Thank you so much for inviting me."

"My pleasure." She leaned down. "It's the least we could do, under the circumstances. I am so sorry for your loss. I would like to discuss the situation, but as you can appreciate, this is not the place."

"I understand." So much for the appetizer questions. "Perhaps tomorrow?"

"Of course. Speak to Lisa and she will make the arrangements." She turned to the handsome couple already seated. They rose.

"Cyd Redondo, this is Mary Lou and Jack Cass. Cyd is a travel agent from America. Mary Lou and Jack are Silver Platinum Members on the Darling line. They're from London." I smiled and shook hands with the couple, who were dressed to the nines and looked fabulous. Mary Lou had a stylish short haircut I could never pull off and which reminded me of Harriet. Jack actually knew how to wear a tux without the cummerbund pooching out. I liked them immediately and wondered whether they booked their own travel.

Mary Lou leaned over, winked, and said "Watch out for that one. She's a killer." My eyes went wide. "Bridge. She never loses."

"You must know her well."

"She's one of our favorites," Jack said, winking. "We've watched her since she was a Chief Engineer, then Staff Captain. We tried to get on her first sailing as Captain, but it was sold out, so here we are."

"It's a very big deal, isn't it, a female Captain?"

"Yes. And lonely," Mary Lou said. "There are certain crew members, who will remain nameless," she looked directly at Storr Bentley, who was hosting one table away, "who are not pleased. I believe the staff are freezing her out a bit."

"Let me guess. The men?"

"Of course the men. I have the only good one left, apparently." She grinned at Jack, who grinned back. They reminded me of the Giannis, my favorite clients from Bay Ridge, who had the same affectionate shorthand that I feared at this point I would never have with anyone.

Mary Lou nodded toward the Staff Captain, who was pouring wine for his guests.

"Storr," Mary Lou said. "He's the worst of the bunch. See, he can barely look at her."

Jack chimed in. "He is not chuffed to be second in command."

"His name is Storr?"

Mary Lou raised her eyebrows. "Storr Bentley. Sexy, yeah?"

I almost spit out my water and Storr looked over. I wondered whether I should apologize to stay on his good side. Then I remembered he didn't have a good side.

"This is my first cruise, so perhaps you two can be my experts?"

"Anything we can do, luv."

By that time, Ron Brazil, now in an ill-fitting and shiny tux, his pompadour deflated by another hour of gravity, had arrived, and was seated between Jack and Sister Ellery. She beamed at him. As before, he avoided looking me in the eye. I felt that familiar nausea again.

I'd heard from clients that the Captain's Table was the one place on the boat where the alcohol was both free and abundant. Although I knew it was stupid to drink when I was this jet lagged, seasick, and had already mixed eggnog, bourbon, rum, and a corpse, I figured I was sick anyway. Why not? I asked for a Jack Daniels, neat. The Captain turned when she heard my order and asked for the same.

Then she asked where everyone had been just prior to the cruise. As the guests chimed in, the waiter appeared with two bottles of wine for the Captain to okay. She put on reading glasses, stylish as her shoes, to read the labels. She sampled the white, then asked me to try the red, unaware that in our family, Chianti Classica was about as deluxe as it got. The red tasted a little bit bad, which in my experience, meant it was expensive and likely to make everyone go "ooh."

"Perfect," I said. "I wanted to apologize for my chaotic arrival."

"No need. Harriet alerted me."

"So, you knew her?"

"We met at a few cruise line functions. She was lovely, it's such a tragic accident." My eyes widened. "But again, perhaps we can discuss this tomorrow?"

"Of course." I added the Captain to the list of everyone Harriet had talked to before she died. I'd finish it when I got back to the room. I realized Mary Lou was talking to me.

"Did you say yacht race?"

"We wondered if that's why you're doing the Christmas cruise? For the Sydney to Hobart yacht race?"

"No," I said. "I just got tired of the snow. Is it a famous one?"

"Very. Starts in Sydney on Boxing Day every year and winds up in Hobart the day after. It usually goes right past us on the way back."

"That sounds exciting."

"It is. For us, it's not Christmas without it. We've even got a friend entered this year. He's not very good. I think he's just doing it to have us cheer him on from the deck."

That made me think about my mom and Aunt Helen, cooking up a storm at home for the E.Coli Potluck. I wondered if Aunt Helen was making Eggplant Parmesan. She mixed Parmesan, ricotta, and fresh oregano in with the breadcrumbs. There was nothing like it.

The appetizers arrived. Oysters. Great. The waiter explained the oysters were from Blackman Bay, Tasmania's best. Oysters had always creeped me out. Enough so that I'd never actually eaten one. They always looked like a viscous version of the snice I'd just left. So this is what I'd been missing in world travel—eating slime. I hesitated, waiting for the Captain to begin.

"Guests first."

Everyone turned to me, including Doc. Could I plead vegetarianism? Fruitarianism? It would be fine. I just needed a lot of horseradish. I would have given my Balenciaga for some ketchup. Most things were a delivery system for ketchup, in my opinion, and with enough of it, I could pretty much get anything down. I went heavy on the condiments, then upended the oyster. It just hung there, swinging by a stubborn tendon, dripping salty slime onto my tongue. Doc snorted. I re-scooped it and lowered it to my plate, daunted.

Mary Lou leaned in "You have to detach it," she said. "And use the other end."

"Bless you." I chopped off the "arm" and tried again. This time, it went right down.

It felt like cream of mushroom soup and tasted like spicy salt. Delicious, spicy salt. There, I could say I'd had a Tasmanian oyster and actually enjoyed it. Sister Ellery was sucking them down like the Cape Cod native she was. Ron Brazil abstained.

The Captain poured me a glass of red. It was still awful. "Gorgeous," I said.

I had to hand it to Captain Lindoff. She was charming, made sure everyone's glass was filled, and in no time had us confessing our family holiday traditions. My stories about sitting on the landing with my Uncle Ray while we waited for everyone to wake up seemed pretty pedestrian, though everyone seemed to appreciate how it felt to be the grown up, sitting there with my brousins' kids. Doc said he and his brother used to leave cookies and milk for the Christmas "lions" in South Africa.

We finished the meal with a traditional Australian dessert called a "Pavlova," named after Anna Pavlova the ballerina. It was so completely covered in whipped cream that I didn't even care what was inside. Whipped cream was second only to ketchup in improving the world, one bite at a time. Just as I finished lapping up the last few swipes of white, Mary Lou said she was heading to freshen up before the photographs.

"Photographs?"

"It's one of the perks of a night at the Captain's Table. You get a complimentary picture with the Captain and with your fellow guests. They post them in the photography studio, so I've learned it's worth a quick check before."

"In case you've eaten off your lipstick."

"Exactly. Coming?"

I nodded and we made our apologies and headed to the ladies' room. I was dying to ask her if she'd talked to Harriet, but I felt I should wait at least twelve hours into our friendship.

When we returned the photographer was chatting with Doc. He turned and smiled. It was not Elliot Ness. Well, surely there was more than one for two thousand guests. Probably on day and night shifts. Which reminded me, I was due to meet him at midnight. I had twenty minutes. I leaned in between the Captain and Mary Lou for the photo, trying not to smile too much, as my eyes always disappeared. He was smart enough to make sure he had at least one good shot of everyone. People always choose the group picture where they look the best, even if it's a nuclear incident for another participant.

I thanked the Captain, told Mary Lou and Jack I hoped we'd see each other again, and hugged Sister Ellery. "Gotta go," I said.

"Shall we have breakfast? Early? Ron and I have a Cha Cha refresher class at eight."

"Absolutely," I said. "I'll meet you at seven."

As I headed for the exit, Doc jogged up beside me. "Do you need an escort upstairs?" He offered his arm.

"I have a date."

"Already?" He shook his head. "American girls."

I kissed him on the cheek and asked Lisa, who was back at her post, how to find the Castaways Bar. She was good with directions, I'll give her that. But when I asked for an appointment with the Captain, she said it wasn't possible, she was fully booked tomorrow.

Chapter Eighteen

Just as I hit the elevator, Brooklyn time finally started to work in my favor. It was five past twelve, which was ten in the morning at home—prime Redondo time.

I hurried down two decks, past a series of passengers who were taking full advantage of not having to drive home. At least I hadn't been the only one retching over the railing in the past few hours. I wondered who cleaned it all up.

I pulled a shawl around my sequined dress, and headed into the Castaways Bar. It was "bar" dark, but I could still make out fake palm trees, coconuts, and fishing nets. There was even a life-sized version of Barrel of Monkeys hanging from the rafters. One of the plastic arms dinged my head as I entered.

The clientele resembled more *Gilligan's Island* than *Cast Away*. I kept forgetting my memorable ship arrival, but no one else had. I braved the whisper/staring gauntlet between the door and the bar, where I spotted someone who might be Ness. He was too close to a wobbling woman, who looked eighteen at best.

"Has anyone ever told you, you could be a model?" He leaned closer.

"Hey, Mr. Ness!" I yelled, striking a blow for female solidarity.

I took his arm, moving him away from his target. Then waved at his under-aged date.

"Hi. Cyd Redondo. Redondo Travel. Would you mind if I

steal him for a minute? And by the way, I took you more for an astrophysicist than a model." That would give her something to chew on. If she remembered it when she was sober.

"Really, Elliot? Jailbait? Aren't you on duty?"

"She said she was twenty-one."

That was too stupid for even an eye roll. "Everyone in the world either says they're twenty-one, twenty-nine, or thirty-nine. How old did you tell her you were?"

"I was building up to that."

"To thirty-nine, you mean?"

"What business is it of yours, anyway?"

"I'm a travel agent. I put people on this cruise line. I'd like to be able to tell my clients that their underage granddaughters aren't going to be hit on by the ship's photographer."

"Fair enough. Can I say something? Purely as a photographer who specializes in portraits? You don't look so good."

One of the fake palm trees was nearby. "Cover me," I said.

He stood in front, as I dry heaved into the palm. He even cleared his throat and coughed to cover the sound, then handed me a cocktail napkin. For a moment, he restored my faith in humanity.

"Thank you. I apologize. I was at the Captain's Table and five courses is too many for my first night at sea."

"Yeah. Usually they only do that to people they want to torture."

"I thought they were just keeping an eye on me."

He shrugged. "I assume you don't want a drink, then?"

"I would kill for a ginger ale." Elliot noticed everyone staring at us and moved me into a darker corner.

"What? Is drinking with me not good for business?"

"In a word, yes. Or I mean no. It's not good. Yet. But I do have a few shots of a new passenger descending that might improve my reputation."

Great. "Can you see my thong?"

"Cosabella?"

"Dammit. I'll buy them, but only if I watch you delete all copies."

"The cruise line won't let me do that."

"Why? It's all digital, right?" We looked at each other for a long moment. "Deleting is not optional. How much? If you throw in the rest of the shots of the last trip?"

"Five grand."

"You've got to be joking."

He shook his head.

"How bad are they? Five grand buys a lot of photos in Brooklyn."

"A man's gotta eat."

"All your meals are comped. I'll give you five hundred. Come on, bulk discount?" He shook his head. I always preferred bartering to threats, but certain vendors just gave you no choice. "Elliot. I just had dinner with the Captain. She likes me. Do you want her to know you were hitting on a sixteen-year-old?"

"U.S. dollars, not Australian."

"Fine, put it on my cabin."

"No can do. This is off the record."

"Do you take credit cards?"

"Would you?"

Seriously? I hadn't even been here for twenty-four hours and I was already almost out of cash. "Only if you throw in one more thing. Any photos of Harriet Archer."

"She worked for the cruise line, right? Audrey Hepburn type."

"Exactly. She got on in Sydney. Anything you might have with her, foreground or background?"

"Why don't I just give you my back-up flash drive and you can look for yourself? It has the last four trips. All the photos are dated. That would make it six hundred, though."

"Great." He walked me back to his cabin, where I paid him and he gave me an envelope with the pictures of the Manzonis and the flash drive. I zipped up my Balenciaga and headed for fresh air, hoping there was a cash machine in Wineglass Bay.

I stood on the deck and looked up. How many people in the world never, ever knew there were this many stars, people who lived their whole lives in the sulfur glow of Texaco stations, stadium lights, and police helicopters? I glimpsed a shooting star and made a wish for Harriet. I hoped she was on a permanent vacation, cruising through the galaxies above me, with no glass ceiling and no Peggy Newsome.

I felt dizzy. Seeing Barry, losing the Manzonis, finding Harriet's body, and Sister Ellery's engagement to a gigolo would have been a tough forty-eight hours, no matter what. When they came with a twenty-eight-hour journey, brain fog, and nausea, they were almost unmanageable, even for a Redondo. That reminded me, it was morning, yesterday, in Brooklyn and safe to call Frank. I hurried back to my cabin and went out on the balcony for better reception.

It took a while to get the satellite phone working, and even longer to get Frank on the phone at the 68th Precinct.

"So, anything?"

He gave an Aunt Helen-sized sigh. "I've got to take it easy—getting unauthorized help isn't so easy, now that I'm on patrol."

"Frank."

"Alright. I just want you to know that this cost me."

"Are you really going to guilt me out? I just lost my friend and possibly the only in-laws I'm ever going to have. And I'm going to miss Aunt Helen's stuffing."

"Bad or good first?"

"Bad." I always asked for the bad first. It seemed logical to cheer yourself up at the end.

"Okay, the prints didn't come up in our database. But you're in Australia. Chances are most of the passengers aren't American, right? They might have them at Interpol. Don't you know an Interpol guy?"

Really? Did every trip I took have to include an Interpol element? Special Agent Graham Gant was the one who had made me betray my uncle and smuggle snakes in my bra. He also hated me because I solved his case for him. Men aren't always great with that. I really didn't want to encounter him ever again, much less ask him a favor.

"Kind of, but I'd prefer that as a last resort."

"Well, I'd try Australian law enforcement then."

I did know someone in Australian law enforcement. But if I called Scott, I would have to give him the news about Harriet.

"Could you give them, like, a courtesy call or something?"

"No. First, it won't be considered a courtesy. Not even close. Especially as there's no concrete evidence this is even a crime. Second, I'm a patrolman in Brooklyn."

"Well, what can you do?"

"Tone, Squid. I can send you digitized versions of the evidence. And I did talk to Dr. Paglia," Frank said.

"You did? God bless you."

"Actually, I picked him up at an illegal poker game in Sunset Park. I said I wouldn't take him in if he looked at the stuff you sent."

"And?"

"And he said head wounds bleed way more than this, so she was possibly dead already when she hit her head. And he said your photos were crap, but if you could send a few close-ups and a blood sample, he'd test it under his "John Doe" budget. He has some funds he has to use before the end of the calendar year."

"That's disgusting."

"That's Dr. Paglia."

"Well, how am I supposed to do that?"

"Just find the body and take them. It's a ship, she's still got to be on it. And she's not going to feel the needle."

"Frank!"

"I'm a pragmatist."

"Are you?"

"And, anyway, how am I going to mail blood?"

"You disappoint me, Cyd. You did ask for help from a medical examiner. What did you think he was going to do, call a psychic? He needs evidence."

".Okay, fine."

"Look, Dr. Paglia is headed for his holiday binge trip to Atlantic City. I'd get it in before the labs close and he starts celebrating. Do they have FedEx on the boat?"

"No. But there's some wine and kayaking stop tomorrow. What day is it there?"

"The twenty-first. Crap. What should I get Janice?"

"Is this a setup?"

"Never mind."

"Diamond studs or a real Cuisinart, so she stops making pesto in the coffee grinder. Garlic and Italian dark roast should never meet."

"Is that what it is?"

"Christ. Yes."

"Don't swear," he said. I sighed. "I heard that."

"I'm thirty-two."

"That's no excuse not to be a lady."

"Who are you, Aunt Helen?"

"Fine. You know if Dr. Paglia starts losing, you're out of luck."

"Got it. Anything else?"

"Janice has an uncle in Palm Beach who's in Resort Torts."

"In what?"

"Resorts Torts—anyway, that's what he calls it. He's an attorney, does slip-and-falls, malpractice, overboards, drownings."

"Great, I'll take anything." I took down Mr. Resort Tort's info. "How's Eddie?"

"Why?"

"He might have slept in the office. You didn't hear it from me."

"Got it. Maybe I can drag him to Bed, Bath & Beyond."

"Or Tiffany's."

That got a laugh. "Love you, Squid. We'll miss you."

"You too."

He hung up before I did. I hung onto the phone for a minute. I didn't miss that damned inflatable snowman, but I missed the smell of pointless fruitcake and I missed Chadwick's, filled with screaming family dinners and the smell of the best crab cakes in the five boroughs.

I'd accidentally gotten Frank demoted, but he'd put himself on the line for me. He'd taught me to make an effort for people, even when it was inconvenient, and that was the least I could do for Barry's folks, and for Harriet.

I didn't know yet how I was going to get evidence to prove it, but if Paglia thought I might be right, it meant Harriet had been killed after a day of asking questions about the Manzonis. As much as I hated to admit it, I figured the two crimes were connected. So, if I found the Manzonis, I'd either find her killer or be bumped off myself. I opened Elliot Ness' envelope. I took one look at my thighs approaching the pool deck and didn't feel so bad about dying before they got worse. It wasn't my best angle. I picked up the photos of the Manzonis.

Ron Brazil, looking none too pleased, was in lots of them. I added checking him out to my already long list of Mata Hari activities. I needed a computer to check the flash drive.

I knew I should go to sleep as soon as I could—tomorrow was going to be a big day. Unfortunately, it was eight-thirty a.m. in Brooklyn. And that meant the Manzonis had been missing for another whole day. Sleeping seemed selfish.

So I went for coffee instead of Tylenol PM, called Dr. Paglia, and formulated a plan.

Chapter Nineteen

The passenger map didn't include the morgue. I hoped it was in the Infirmary. I grabbed my new "Black Mariah" Donna Karan silk wrap (ninety percent off at Loehmann's President's Day sale) and my Balenciaga and decided to take a circuitous route, just to be safe. I only threw up once on the way, swiveling at the last minute to miss a plaid deck chair.

Once I reached Deck Five, I headed for the emergency stairs. I ate a Tums/breath mint combo, went down yet another flight of stairs to Deck Four, and headed down the low, empty hallway. There it was, the Infirmary. No lights. I tried knocking first. Then harder. If Doc was in there, he wasn't conscious. I still hesitated.

I checked for CCTV cameras. Then I remembered the Risk Management guys and my sanitized room. Maybe they didn't want cameras, for plausible deniability. Just when I felt safe, I spotted one at the end of the hall. Thanks to my brousins, I had good aim, but I didn't have anything hard enough to break it. Then, I saw a room service cart. With the scarf over my face, I backed past the camera, then ducked under it and pulled the cart closer.

There was one dinner plate full of toast crumbs and dried egg yolk. It would make a crash when it broke, especially if I missed. Otherwise, there was only silverware, used tablecloths, and napkins. I went through my purse and finally found the perfect thing—something thick, something that stuck to every-thing, something that would take days to wash off.

I rummaged around for a butter knife, then swapped it for a soup spoon.

I pushed the cart as close as I could get it to the wall under the camera, then bent a stack of Redondo Travel "You Can't Take It With You" business cards to ram in between the wheels and lock them on the other side. I made the Sign of the Cross in honor of Sister Ellery, put one foot on the bottom shelf, and clambered on. To say it was unstable would be kind.

I should have unscrewed the calamine lotion before I got on. I wrapped a used tablecloth over my dress and shawl, then filled the spoon with the lotion, which I tried to balance with one hand, while I threw a napkin over my head. I lifted the spoon and flicked its viscous contents toward the lens. I felt the flesh-colored droplets hit my head-napkin and jerked away, loosening the cart. As I tried to right myself, it broke free altogether, sending me surfing down the hallway, headed for imminent crashing sounds. I stretched my leg down and stabbed my heel into the carpet as hard as I could. It finally stopped the cart just shy of the other wall, but broke my heel. Which made it a lot harder getting down than it was getting up. Satisfied that the camera was covered and the rest suggested nothing more than a Thousand Island dressing incident, I limped toward the Infirmary.

I pulled out the Koozer's master keycard, hoping my camera-covering stunt hadn't been in vain, especially as it knocked me down to four pairs of shoes for the last five days of the trip.

I passed the plastic card over the door. Nothing. I tried two more times, then heard a click, and pulled on the handle. It opened. I pulled out my pocket flashlight and hoped (and feared) one of the two closed doors I'd seen earlier was the morgue. The first one was an examination room. The other was locked.

I tried Doc's desk drawer. He had the usual array of bent paper clips, dead Sharpies, and tape. Under a pile of Post-it Notes, I found a picture of him in a suit in front of palm trees with a lovely thin woman, holding a baby. It was not the first time I'd found a photo which threw me. Unlike last time, I tried to ignore it and finally found a wad of keys at the back. I started working the ring until I found the right one. No morgue. No Harriet. Just a supply closet.

Five minutes later, four syringes (in case I didn't know what I was doing, which I didn't), along with rubber gloves, cotton balls, and a bottle of anti-seasickness pills, sat snugly in the smallest piece of my sky blue nesting Tupperware.

I found a detailed map of the lower decks. There was an M beside a room noted as Cold Storage. I took a shot of the map, replaced the keys, and pulled the door closed behind me.

It made no sense to head down more stairs with uneven heels, but going barefoot down here was not an option. Finally, though it killed me, I knocked the other shoe against the stair railing and wound up with flats curved like genie shoes, which kind of defeated the purpose. I headed down two more sets of stairs, into the lower deck, the one with the mysterious "M."

The lower I went in the ship, the more *Das Boot* it got. It wasn't just dark down there, it was crazy loud—engines clanging, generators whirring, washing machines sloshing. None of this helped with the high level dread I felt about what I was about to do.

Just as I'd reached the limits of my claustrophobia, something scurried past me. Scurrying was never good. Neither were morgues. I knew cruise ships had them. They carried thousands of people with untold pre-existing conditions. The latest statistics made the average cruise passenger fifty-five, university educated, married, employed, and with an annual income over seventy-five thousand dollars—your basic recipe for heart failure.

Personally, I'd lost five clients and air-lifted two off cruise ships so far. Given the average age of my clientele, that wasn't bad, but it still broke my heart. And potentially, my pocketbook. Those emergency "assists" started at thirty-five grand, which is why I insisted on client insurance. If a passenger without travel insurance, aside from charging the deceased passenger or their family members for the final medical exam and body storage, all costs were, in the words of Darling Cruises, "up to the travel agent." Thanks a lot. At least if, God forbid, something had happened to the Manzonis, Peggy Newsome would be on the hook for it, not me. I chastised myself for even thinking this and realized I was stalling. I needed to gut up.

Finally, I found the door labeled "Cold Storage." I remembered the Koozer yelling "Bright Star Rising," when we found Harriet's body, and wondered what other euphemisms the ship used to avoid any unpleasantness. Or lawsuits.

I waved the keycard over the door, half hoping it wouldn't work. But the light went green and, holding my breath, I inched the door open.

Although I had a long-term medical examiner client in Bay Ridge's Dr. Paglia, I'd never been in a morgue, except on television. I was a big *Law and Order* fan and still held out hope for *Law and Order: CS (Catholic School)* or *CSI: Bay Ridge*, so I could serve as a consultant. With my viewing background, I felt comfortable with a whole range of fatal, strategically covered-up injuries. Still, I could already smell that this wasn't cable. There were front notes of seawater and bleach, with hints of pet store and putrid.

Someone was on the stairs. I jumped in, eased the door closed, and fell against it. The footsteps passed. I turned on my emergency flashlight. It was inadequate.

I dug into my bag, pulled out some baby wipes, and did a quick sweep of the floor, then rolled up my wrap and pressed it into the crack to block the light.

I hit the switch. When I imagined my clients in the ship's morgue, it was a high-tech, sterilized, well-lighted place. This was a cross between an airline bathroom and a hoarder's closet. I could barely move forward for the life jackets, industrial-sized cans of coffee and peaches, waiter jackets, and body bags. Two plain pine coffins were stacked upright against the wall, like pairs of skies. I had to shove aside a Costco-sized box of cocktail napkins to even locate the body drawers, if that was what you called them.

I cleared a space around them and prepared myself.

I never saw my late father's body. Because he'd been in a crash, he had a closed casket. My Uncle Ray had gone for the identification, to spare my mom. And she'd spared me the truth at first. So, for a long time I believed he was just on Long Island.

When I was old enough to understand what death was, I appreciated what my mother had done, as he would always be the dad sitting on my bed and tucking me in. Aside from losing two grandparents, I'd been able to dodge death until I turned thirty-two, stumbled over my friend and client, Mrs. Barsky, and everything changed.

I'd been watching a lot more PBS the last month, particularly David Attenborough, who, let's face it, looks incredible for ninety-eight, or however old he is. When I watched the violent mating rituals and the gazelle takedowns—what people called the circle of life and I called murder for hire—I realized the thing that really separated human beings from the animal kingdom was our capacity for self-delusion. We pretended every day wasn't a dog-eat-dog day. We pretended if we had a mortgage, we were safe. We pretended that the people around us abided by the same rules we did. But we were kidding ourselves. We were just tiptoeing across thin ice, every day, pretending it was hardwood.

There were three morgue drawers and I had to pick one. I closed my eyes as I tugged on the cold, thick chrome handle of the middle one, jerking back when I felt the weight of something shift toward me, hitting the coffins and knocking one of them over. I moved out of the way, allowing it to slam to the floor. In the midst of the thud, I heard a definite "Ooof."

Chapter Twenty

For a second I thought it might be the Ghost of Cruisers Past. But in my recollection, even Casper the Friendly Ghost had never said "Ooof."

"Hello?"

The coffin gave a slight shake. It had fallen on its lid. I picked up one of the industrial cans of peaches and knelt beside it.

"Hello? Look, you're upside down. If you want me to help you, you're going to have to identify yourself." Nothing. "That was loud, someone might have heard it."

Nothing. I stood up and kicked the coffin.

"Hey!" All right, it was human. I held tight to my peaches as the cheap pine box started to rock back and forth.

"This is ridiculous." I tried to lift it on one side.

"Other side!"

"You're welcome!" I hissed as I lifted in the opposite direction.

A hand with chewed black fingernails and a tiny kangaroo tattoo inched open the lid. At the other end of it was a Goth girl, who didn't look more than thirteen.

We just stared at each other for what seemed like an hour, though it was probably only thirty seconds. We both froze as footsteps ran down the hall. When they kept going, we took a breath and I had a chance to look at her. She had a ripped tank top, spiky hair, excessive earring holes. Despite her tough exterior, she sported a look of absolute fear she couldn't totally remove from her dark-circled eyes. I held out my hand.

"Cyd Redondo. Redondo Travel."

"Esmeralda Kane, stowaway." I hadn't expected her heavy Australian accent.

I grinned. "How long have you been in there?"

She shook her head.

"Look," I said. "I'm not supposed to be in here, either, but someone might have murdered my friend and I'm trying to figure out who. If you can keep a secret, so can I. Okay?"

"Your friend is in there?" She pointed at the morgue drawers with a shudder.

"She's supposed to be. Were you here when they brought her in?"

She nodded. "That was a close one."

"I bet."

"They kept hitting the coffin, trying to jam her in."

"I don't need to know that."

"The truth hurts."

Teenagers. Was there an Australian equivalent of Kahlil Gibran's *The Prophet*? If so, I bet she'd read it.

"Would you mind if I look?"

"Do you have to?"

"Yeah, I do."

She got behind me.

"How old are you?"

She gave the eternal cry of the underaged. "Old enough."

I put one hand over her eyes and eased out the drawer with another, feeling that heavy shift again. I closed my eyes for a minute, then opened them to see three bags of red potatoes.

I reached for the drawer below and pulled again, anticipating Yukon Golds. So I wasn't prepared for Harriet's perfectly manicured toes. I gave a small squeak and slammed it shut again. Esmeralda was even paler than before.

"Get back in the coffin. I mean, I'll help you turn it over, just get back in for a few minutes."

"No. Why?"

"Because I have to really look at her and take pictures and she didn't know you. It's a privacy issue. Out of respect for her. Wouldn't you want your friend to do the same for you?" She stood there rigid, staring at the wall. "What is your problem? You were in there before. Go on. Also, that way I'm the only one who'll get caught if anyone comes in."

Esmeralda shrugged and backed up. I grabbed one of the waiter's jackets and handed it to her. "For padding," I said.

We lifted the coffin back up and once she was in and it seemed stable, I closed the lid most of the way.

"I have air holes," she said. "I'm not an idiot." She pulled it shut.

"Right." I turned once to see if she were peeking, then turned back to the sliding slab.

It made a creaking sound as I tugged on it and released a darkroom smell. God knows what they kept in there before her. Harriet's slim body was covered with a sheet at least. Even dead, she looked better at thirty-two than I did. It took everything I had not to shut the drawer again. I thought about Harriet, and what she would do if our roles were reversed, then folded the sheet off her face.

"What happened to you?" I moved a piece of hair off her forehead.

I replayed my conversation with Dr. Paglia. After I'd talked to Frank, I'd used Uncle Ray's satellite phone to track him down in a coffee shop beside his office. He wasn't happy to be disturbed over his hangover and crullers.

"Who the hell is this?"

"Your favorite travel agent."

"I thought you were in Australia."

"I am. Frank said he explained the situation, right?"

"I vaguely remember something."

"The cruise company says my friend had an accident and hit her head. I think she was murdered."

"What does the M.E. think?"

"There isn't one. Not really. There's a possibly dodgy ship doctor and a staff a little too eager to sweep the whole thing under the rug. Frank said you'd run some samples for me?"

"The doctor's giving you samples?"

"He's got three thousand people to look out for. So I was thinking I could save him the trouble."

"Cyd."

"Look. This is a totally screwed-up situation. She was my friend. And it might have something to do with the Manzonis being missing. Come on, where's your Christmas spirit?"

"1964."

"Yeah, well I hear you. Mine too. Why do you think I'm here and not at Chadwick's? I'm trying to redeem myself and save the company, okay? Besides, who else is going to rotate your criminal activity?" Dr. Paglia was known for counting cards. I made sure he spread his "luck" around enough casinos that he didn't get caught. "Now, what do I need?"

"Nothing you do is going to hold up in court."

"I know."

"You're sure you're up for this? It's not really a girl kind of thing."

I was about to throw three female medical examiners in his face, until I realized they were all fictional. I let it go.

"Yes. Yes, I am."

"Good girl. Okay, this is what you'll need…"

"Hey!" said the coffin. "You done yet?"

"No!" I jerked the sheet back over Harriet. "What, you made it three days and now you can't stay in there for three minutes?"

"Hurry."

That seemed unlikely. I put my purse on top of the cocktail

napkin box and pulled out my camera and the tool kit I'd hobbled together. He'd said to take the photographs first.

I didn't want to, but I made myself. I couldn't stop tearing up every time I looked at her, though, so two or three of them might have been blurry. Someone had cleaned up her head—probably Doc. But that let me get a better picture of the wound. Dr. Paglia told me to open her eyes and check for any broken blood vessels. This was the hardest thing so far—not just because I had to touch and move her dead eyelids, but also because it was really hard to hold them open and take a cell phone picture. They didn't look red to me, but he would know better. Harriet did give off that weird smell, but it wasn't almonds—I knew from Agatha Christie an almond smell indicated cyanide. I found two bruises on her upper arms and then what looked like a tiny mark. Could it be an injection site?

I took pictures of everything I could think of, from various angles, then moved on to step two: blood samples.

I put on the gloves. "Oh, God."

Dr. Paglia had said "It'll be a breeze, it's not pumping. And it won't be bright red, because it isn't getting oxygen, so pretend it's grenadine or something."

"Hey! What's going on out there? Why can't I come out?"

"You can only come out if you know how to draw blood."

I heard the coffin lid creak.

"What are you doing?"

"I'm diabetic."

"You have insulin in your coffin?"

"Of course."

I covered Harriet back up as Esmeralda grinned and climbed out. She looked at my supplies and picked up one of the syringes. "What are we putting it in?"

I handed her the nail polish bottle I'd sterilized with the teapot in my cabin. It was glass, under three ounces, and might fool an idiot, which, given the odds, worked in our favor.

"Okay, don't look. Fainting is loud."

I obeyed her. About a minute and a half later, she handed me the nail polish bottle. "Are you sure this is enough? Sometimes they need a few vials."

"Any ideas?"

We dug through shelves and found a box of mini ketchup and mustard jars. We did our best to sterilize them with the cleaning products at hand. Just as Esmerelda filled the second one, the footsteps went past again. This time they stopped.

"Shit," I said, inching Harriet's drawer closed. I crammed Esmeralda back in the coffin, grabbed my bag, and climbed in with the potatoes. It was the first time I'd ever been happy to be short. There was a knock on the door.

"Es? It's me."

I recognized that voice.

Chapter Twenty-one

"Esmeralda, let me in."

By the time the Koozer had entered and made out for a minute with what I hoped was his girlfriend, I'd manipulated my hands enough to get his keycard into my bra, just in case.

"What's going on?" he said. I waited on tenterhooks. Would she give me up? Where was the blood? In plain sight?

"Nothing," she said. Just about to do my nails." God bless her. "Going a little stir crazy. That's all."

"Sorry I'm late. I know you need to eat. I brought you all the leftovers I could find."

"Perfect, thanks. Can we take a walk, just around the cargo hold? I'm really stiff."

"Absolutely." Would he see my shawl under the door?

"Thanks." I heard him kiss her again. As soon as the door thudded, I slid out, grabbed the condiment-sized samples, retrieved my wrap, and eased the door open. I could hear them at the end of the hallway. When they turned the corner out of sight, I sprinted for the stairway, or sprinted as much as I could in my misshapen flats.

Back in my cabin, I decided to put the samples in my cosmetics case, since a quick glance wouldn't give them away as what they actually were. I was trying to tell my stomach that, especially as we hit a patch of rough water. I walked out onto the deck just in case I had to hurl again, and held onto the doorjamb for balance.

Because it was later in Europe, and my satellite phone was working, I called Oceania Cruises and sorted out Sister Ellery's transfer to the *Tasmanian Dream*. It cost me. I had to agree to send ten people their way in the New Year to pull it off, but they were fond of her, so it worked out. Then I called her travel insurance company and adjusted her itinerary, as I didn't want her going ashore without full coverage. To be honest, I didn't really want her doing the Electric Slide without full coverage, even though, at this point, her replacement hips were younger and more indestructible than mine.

I figured out a plan for the morning, mostly eager to get on land and get the samples off to Bay Ridge. I had an account with FedEx, though I hadn't used it since a faux FedEx driver kidnapped me in Africa. That wasn't really FedEx's fault, but it had left a bad taste in my mouth and I'd been sticking with DHL.

On that thought, I tried to fall asleep. But I kept seeing the morgue and Harriet's face and my nephews sitting on the landing on Christmas morning without me. I had to remind myself I was doing this for my family's reputation (and ability to attend holiday events) and for Barry Manzoni, unemployed almost-father, who, at the very least, would always be my first and maybe only husband.

Although Barry and I had known each other since preschool and shared school lunches and dodgeball blows, he was one of the few boys in Bay Ridge I hadn't actually dated growing up. We'd just been buds, bound by our secret love for adventure novels and peach ice cream. Then, three years ago, I had snuck out of Bay Ridge to attend my first Travel Agents' Convention in Atlantic City.

Out from under Redondo surveillance for once, I wore the little leopard skin dress I'd been hiding in a recycled ink cartridges carton and went bare-legged in a pair of Stuart Weitzman peep-toe pumps. I got enough second looks to know it was a success. But the few men who chatted me up were businessmen.

Businesswomen kick ass, but there's nothing more boring or patronizing than a corporate man. Look around.

The second night, I wound up at the craps table with a few hysterical dental hygienists who didn't get out much either. I noticed a cast of unlikely characters exiting the ballroom at the top of the escalator. There was a lecherous purple Barney groping a shockingly tall Pippi Longstocking and a woman dressed as a bottle of St. John's Wort. Behind them trailed the pirate of my Caribbean: floppy hat at a rakish angle, Captain Hook wig and mustache, buckled shoes, one peg leg and crutch, and a plastic parrot pinned to his shoulder. He jerked out his plastic sword and aimed it at a cardboard cutout of Dr. Phil.

"You, sir, are a simpleton," the pirate said, offering a parry which knocked the oversized, flabby, paper psychologist right over the railing and onto the casino floor, bald head first.

I guess my snorting laughter cut through the casino noise. The culprit looked down at me, grinned, then struck a pirate-like pose, accidentally backing into a passing Cruella de Vil, complete with a real cigarette holder. He turned to apologize to her while I handed my chips to the squealing woman beside me and headed for the escalator.

The pirate started down, but his peg got caught in the moving steps and he lurched forward, his crutch flying. He arrived at the bottom, hard, then struggled to get up, repositioning his peg leg and wig. As soon as he was stable, I grabbed a drink off a passing cocktail waitress' tray and threw it in his face.

"Hey!" he yelled. "What the hell?" He shook his dripping wig and swiveled the soaked eye patch to the middle of his forehead, then saw the melted, still-smoking parrot, hanging by one claw and a safety pin.

"Oh. Thanks, Cydhartha." Barry Manzoni said. "You look fricking gorgeous. Can I buy you bottle of rum?"

"Yo ho ho." I said.

Maybe it was the costume, or maybe it was because casino

cocktails had hosed the heavy film of the neighborhood off both of us, but it wasn't long before the pirate hat was on top of a bottle of champagne and my leopard skin dress was over the lamp. Five hours later we stood in dark glasses, holding hands, in front of the Forever Wedding Chapel. Usually you needed three days for the license, but I knew a guy.

"You sure you don't want to just date or something?" I was still a little wobbly on my peep-toes.

"Cyd, we've known each other since we were five, we're both about to hit thirty, it's too late to date, doncha think? But if it's a bad idea, just say the word. No harm, no foul."

I'd looked at Barry Manzoni, solid good guy, one of the last men in the Borough who wasn't already paying child support. He was right, he knew me as well as anyone. If he thought I was marriage material, who was I to argue? He leaned over and kissed me. He was a good kisser, he had that going for him.

"How do you feel?" he said.

"Lucky. I feel lucky."

Or I did, until I heard banging on my cabin door and remembered I was still on the *Tasmanian Dream*. In death cabin 710.

Chapter Twenty-two

"Just a minute." I put on my wrap and went to the door. It was Doc. He wore a worn Hawaiian shirt and a sleepy grin. He held out a bottle of seasickness medicine and a green apple.

"Just in case," he said. "Sometimes it's worse on the second day. Did you sleep?"

"I tried. What's your plan for the day?"

"Working until we dock, then kayaking in the Bay. Any interest?"

"Can I let you know? I may take it easy, just a walk into town. There is a town, right?"

"I think they believe they are a town," he said.

"Great. I better get dressed. I'm meeting Sister Ellery in ten minutes at the buffet."

"Take those," he said, and left, sparking additional guilt for stealing the pills from his office. I threw myself together, made sure my eyelashes were on straight, and headed toward the Wallaby Buffet.

A cruise ship was like a floating planet. People from everywhere, celebrating every possible end-of-year holiday, were rammed into one place and the cruise line aimed to please every one of them. Everywhere I looked, I found wreaths, holly, and Santa hats beside menorahs for Hanukkah, kinaras for Kwanzaa, and drinks umbrellas and buffets for everyone. My guess was, whatever the culture or the holiday, guilt and overeating were involved. Guilt especially.

Sister Ellery was there when I arrived. She was still favoring a blinding shade of tangerine for her tank top, but this morning it came with a turquoise baseball hat which read "I pitch for Jesus."

I was still provoking whispers everywhere I went, but I decided to take a page from her book and not give a damn.

"So. The doctor?"

"No way. We are not starting with me. We're starting with the Manzonis."

Over hash browns and pancakes, I finally got to fill her in on the whole story and how I was worried Harriet's death was tied up in it all. She'd always been a good listener. Too good.

"So why did you really come in the middle of Christmas vacation? It's not all Barry Manzoni, that's for sure."

"Of course it's all Barry."

"Cyd Elizabeth Sarah Redondo, don't you dare try to lie to a woman of God."

I sighed. "I am doing it for Barry, and for the Manzonis, which I admit is ironic, but they're too clueless to get themselves out of trouble. Bickering is their only skill." I shrugged. "But you're right, it's not just that. It's my family." I told her about the Bay Ridge holiday boycott. "It's already my fault Uncle Ray and Jimmy won't be there, so I thought if I left town, at least a few things could be normal for them."

"It's your Uncle Ray and Jimmy's fault they won't be there, not yours, but okay, that's better. So let's help."

"I have pictures of them in the disco and Ron was in a few. What did he say?"

"He said their finales were always sloppy."

"Is that all?"

"No, he said they were spending time with a couple who was very excited about this place, The Fountain. It's an exclusive spa resort, seniors only. He didn't remember the couple's name, but I can ask around, see if any of Ron's buddies knows anything else. I play poker with them sometimes." Of course she did.

"That would be great. Okay. This Ron guy. Spill."

"I know he's paid to dance with the old gals. But he gets my jokes, we read the same books, and he's a kickass dancer. He's funny looking, but he has a good heart. That's worth its weight in gold at my age. And getting engaged means other people buy you champagne. Plus, he has a great children's charity that he wants me to help with."

Oh, please. Not that old chestnut. I saw her hard-won savings floating toward Antarctica. She patted my hand. "Really, don't worry about me. You find the Manzonis. You know, they were always very sneaky. I'd be surprised if they were dead. Ron and I have a two-hour rehearsal coming up, but we're going to the Cruise-In movies later. Why don't you join us and you can grill him?"

She kissed me and ran off. Charity, my ass. I was going to have to check him out. As soon as I checked in with Margy the Cruise Director and Captain Lindoff.

I circumvented an art auction on Deck Six and ducked into the elevator going up, wondering what to ask Margy about the Manzonis. Then I stopped myself. Harriet had been asking questions and she was dead. If it was murder, whoever killed her was probably still on board. Perhaps I needed to be more subtle. Especially with the Cruise Director. She'd been nice to me, but she also booked all the excursions. The one the Manzonis hadn't come back from.

Chapter Twenty-three

I finally found the Excursions Desk on Deck Eleven, beside the Photo Studio. I was in luck. Margy was at the desk, talking to two couples in matching outfits. All four of them matched. She looked up and smiled at me. I nodded and signaled I would wait next door. I had a few more questions for Elliot Ness.

There was a wall display in the Photo Shop, full of shots from a place called The Fountain. No one was under sixty-five, or less than enthusiastic. It must be the place Sister Ellery mentioned. I didn't see Sandra or Fredo in the pictures, though.

On the opposite wall were last night's photos from the Captain's Table. They'd obviously adopted the Disneyland "Splash Mountain" approach—get them when it's fresh in their minds. It was a reminder to the Captain's guests and created Captain's Table envy in everyone else. It probably made them more likely to join the Premium Gold Club for their next voyage.

It was a smart move and I realized what good advertising a photo of me and Sister Ellery at the Captain's Table might be, sitting on my desk at Redondo Travel, even if it wasn't of my best side. Commerce over vanity, I thought, as I noted the photo number and headed inside.

Inside the studio I found another wall of Captain's Table photos. They were remarkably similar in pose, and to be honest, content. There was always one couple dressed as if for the Met

Gala and one husband in an ill-advised jacket, his face looking like he'd happened into a water treatment plant. Ron Brazil was a frequent attendee, with a steady row of partners—one more reason to check him out before things got any more serious with Sister Ellery. As I followed his hairstyles down the wall, I spotted a particularly ugly and familiar tie.

It belonged to my former father-in-law. I knew that because I'd bought it for him, after he took back the blender he and Sandra bought me and Barry as a wedding gift. His logic was, if it's annulled, it never happened. It seemed particularly low, especially given we got an annulment so Angela Hepler wouldn't have to marry a divorced man.

Barry's dad was a sucker for any kind of flattery and fancied himself a player. I'd found the most hideous, tacky pattern I could find and told him it was rocking Wall Street. Even in the photo, a woman was giving it a look. A dog would give that tie a look.

Sandra was in a yellow, ruffled, off-the-shoulder dress, made for someone who actually had shoulders, rather than just a neck which became her torso. She looked like the top half of a tostada bowl. In the shot, Captain Lindoff was on one side and Ron Brazil, with yet another hair-do, on the other. The Captain had said she didn't remember them. I guess she met a lot of guests, but it had only been five days ago. I would have to refresh her memory. I approached the chirpy college student at the photo counter.

"I'd like two of 103 and one of 734 as well, please?" She smiled and disappeared into the back room. While she was there, I took a quick picture of the Manzoni photo and a few on either side of it myself, just for reference. It was a good thing I did. She came back through the tasteful curtain with an envelope, an apology, and the slick photographer from last night.

"Here are the first two," the woman said, "But I'm afraid one of our computers is down and I can't access the files for the last journey. This is Hal, he'll help you."

He held out his hand. "You're Ms. Redondo. We have several lovely photos of you from last night's dinner. Oh, I see you've found one. Would you like to put a few on your account?"

He laid four more photos on the counter. Sister Ellery looked happy. Doc was scarily photogenic. I looked worried and pale. I was particularly sensitive to looking like death warmed over, since I'd seen it firsthand last night.

"You think this is a lovely photo of me?"

He considered it. "We can Photoshop. Although you look better than most Americans who've just arrived," he said. "Seriously."

"And you don't have the other photo? Could I buy the one on the wall?"

"Oh, we never sell those. You can always check back with me later. Was there any reason you wanted that one in particular?"

"I just liked the photo. Thanks." I put the pictures on my tab, since I was low on cash. "Is Elliot around?"

"Who?"

"Elliot Ness?"

He laughed. "Is this one of those 'do you have Sir Walter Raleigh in cans' kind of joke?

"No. I met him last night. He said he was the ship photographer. I assumed there were two of you."

He and the college student shared a look. "Nope. I'm the only official photographer. Sometimes we get scammers. With this many folks on the boat, it can be hard to keep track. You didn't give him any money, did you?"

"No, of course not," I said, damning jet lag for my weakened scam-o-meter. "Never mind, I'm sure he was just joking around."

What the hell? If Elliot wasn't the ship's photographer, who was he? Just a pervert? Was there even anything on the flash drive I'd paid five hundred dollars for?

"What did he look like?"

"I'm probably just confused," I said as I took my photo and left.

• • ● • •

Margy touched my shoulder. "Ms. Redondo. How are you doing?"

"To be honest, I've been better," I said. "Can I sit down for a minute?"

"Of course." She pulled out a chair behind the counter. "I know it's hard to think about having fun after…you know. But Harriet said you were so excited about seeing Australia, I know she'd want you to. We have a couple of great excursions for Wineglass Bay. Everything from kayaking to hiking, to a private wine tasting." She held out a few pamphlets. "Right now, I still have plenty of spots left for singles."

"I have a few things I'd like to mail. Is there express mail on shore?"

"I'm sure the Bursar can take care of that for you. They take all the ship's mail in on the stop. It would be a shame for you to waste your day dealing with errands."

"That's great to know." I had no intention of entrusting my blood samples to a cruise ship employee, but I let Margy think I might.

"And what about excursions in Hobart?"

"Harriet might have already booked the two of you on something. Let me look." She shook her head. "She probably had a special treat in mind and booked privately."

"Do you know the driver she might have used? It's the holidays. I would feel terrible if someone lost a job or time with their family because we didn't cancel."

"Aren't you a sweetheart? I wish more travel agents were like you. God, I wish more passengers were like you. I keep the private stuff in the back. You understand, we always like to offer our trips first. I'll be right back. Feel free to look through anything that's of interest."

I took her at her word, grabbing her log and excursion book

and taking quick snaps of them, barely shoving them back in place before she came back.

"Here. Once you figure out what you want to do, I'd be delighted to help."

"Margy, you've been a huge help already. I really appreciate it. Did you get to spend any time with Harriet on the way to Melbourne?"

"We had a quick drink in the Crow's Nest. Talked men, of course."

"We used to do that, too. Look, she told me she was traveling alone, but my cabin steward said she was here with her husband."

Margy swung toward me. "He was here? On the boat?"

"Who?"

"Her ex. She didn't say anything to me."

"What ex? She told me she'd never been married."

"Wishful thinking. She didn't like to talk about it. I'm sorry, do you need anything else? I need to make a call."

She disappeared before I could even get up. I took a few more pictures of her desk, then decided to take the elevator up to the Captain's area and bypass Lisa the hostess altogether.

Unbelievably, I caught Captain Lindoff in the elevator. She was still tall, still Nordic, and wearing another pair of stilettos, these gold patent leather, I guess to match her stripes. She was my hero. I asked if I could watch her in action, hoping I could slip in a few questions on the side. She didn't look happy about the request, but was too gracious to refuse. I said I couldn't imagine the pressure of being only one of two female captains in the whole cruise world.

She shrugged. "I have to walk a fine line between delegation and control. I'm probably more hands-on than some captains might be, especially when we're coming into port."

We arrived at the Bridge, which reminded me of a top-flight Manhattan bar, with blinking machines rather than stools. It had a curved bank of tall windows and the best view ever, if you liked an endless expanse of water. Being a non-swimmer, I had mixed feelings about the vast wetness on offer. For a second my seasickness returned in the form of a tiny burp. She noticed and grinned, then introduced me to the seamen at various controls.

Staff Captain Bentley scowled in acknowledgment, then went back to work. The Captain leaned over the Engineer to make some adjustments and we stood at the back for a few minutes, just long enough for her presence to be felt. Then she walked me to her office.

"Do the crew know someone's died? Do the passengers?"

She gestured me into a low chair across from her desk and closed the door. She sat down across from me and I could see how my low chair could give her an advantage with the male crew. I was pretty much below desk, as it were. She leaned forward.

"To be honest, if they're not related to the deceased, and it's an accident, as the crew assure me it was, we try to keep it as private as possible. Everyone is here for a holiday. I hear that you specialize in senior citizens, surely you've had clients pass away on vacation before?"

"I have, of course. It's just. It was Harriet."

"Yes. She was one of the good ones. We didn't have a lot of contact, but she sent me a lovely note when I got my commission."

"Yes, she was like that. Look, Captain, I was the one who found the body. And I have to say, it really didn't look like an accident. One of my cousins is a detective in Brooklyn."

"How many do you have?"

"Ten."

"I only had three older brothers, but I can identify."

"It toughens you up."

"Yes."

"So anyway, I took a few pictures and he said she wouldn't have landed that way if she'd knocked herself out."

"You took pictures? Ms. Redondo. Cyd. You're a woman in a man's world, just like I am. It's only my second voyage. All these accusations—missing passengers, a murder—surely you can see how they will use this against me? And as a travel agent, how it could hurt the whole cruise line?"

Wow. She'd said that out loud. "I do. And the last thing I want, as a fellow woman, is to make things any harder for you than they already are. But you're in charge of the ship and everything that happens here. Don't you want to know what really happened?"

"We will absolutely investigate and I will help you in every way that I can, but if you can just not mention this to other passengers, I would appreciate it."

"Fair enough," I lied. "Have you had any luck finding out who she was traveling with?"

"There is no record of anyone but you booked into the cabin. The steward met a man who introduced himself as her husband, but that could have been subterfuge."

"Doesn't it make sense to have Mr. Koeze try to identify the man before we dock and he has the chance to escape? I could talk to the authorities in Wineglass Bay?"

"No. There's no real law enforcement body in Wineglass Bay. Tomorrow morning I will alert the Hobart and the Tasmanian police and I will discuss this with them. But if there has been a crime, for which there is no evidence at this time, it likely occurred in international waters, so there are jurisdictional issues."

Then she said she needed to return to the bridge.

"Just one more quick question, then," I said. "Have you remembered anything about the Manzonis? It turns out they were at your table on the last cruise."

She rose. "I respect all our passengers, Ms. Redondo, but most of them are not as memorable as you." She opened the door and made it clear I should leave.

I had a lot to process. I looked at my watch. Sister Ellery had said she and Ron Brazil were practicing until eleven—just enough time for me to do a quick scan of his room. If I just knew where it was.

Chapter Twenty-four

I found a house phone and called the operator.

"Ron Brazil's room, please."

"He doesn't appear to be in. Would you like to leave a message?"

"No. He was kind enough to loan me a handkerchief last night, I just thought I'd return it. Can I just leave it outside his room or with his steward? That's Deck Five, correct?"

"Cabin 510."

"Great, thanks." It wouldn't have been hard for the murderer to find Harriet.

I figured on the keycard still working, as the Koozer wouldn't want any extra scrutiny when he had a stowaway girlfriend in the morgue.

The door had a Do Not Disturb card in the lock. I checked the hall. A man in Bermuda shorts and Dockers with no socks walked toward me, so I knocked again. As I waited for him to pass, I wondered why Ron Brazil made me so suspicious. It made sense that I would want to protect Sister Ellery, but this felt like more than that. I broke it down in my mind. There was the gigolo thing, there was the age difference thing, but most importantly, there was the nausea thing. Technically, that could be seasickness, but I didn't think so. Plus, no straight man danced like that, did they? When I heard the elevator go, I checked for cameras, then swiped the keycard, pushed the handle, and yelled out an additional "Hello!" just in case.

The ship escorts needed to maintain the illusion of being guests, which is why Ron Brazil was in an interior guest cabin rather than below deck, where most of the staff got their two hours of sleep a night. So the room was small, but not unlike mine—except there were *Dancing with the Stars*-esque trousers and ruffled shirts on every surface. The congealed room service trays meant the Do Not Disturb sign had been on for awhile. The room had another strange, chemical, and somehow familiar smell. It reinforced my *déjà vu*, mainly consisting of dread.

As I moved toward the bathroom, I glimpsed a head in the mirror and froze.

"Hello! Hello? Sister Ellery thought she might have left her watch."

No answer. I'd sworn the room was empty. Then I heard scrabbling.

"Hello? Mr. Brazil? It's Cyd Redondo. Redondo Travel. Sister Ellery's friend. We met downstairs?" Nothing.

I peeked around the door and saw the heads.

Four of them, floating on white Styrofoam like decapitated Beatles on a bad day. Who, beside RuPaul, had four wigs? Not just wigs. Ugly wigs. One of them was a blond bowl cut. My stomach turned over. A fifth synthetic head was empty. Was Ron Brazil bald? Maybe he was bald. Was it baldist to think that?

Still, no one who wasn't in a one-man show had this many costume changes, not to mention makeup, press-on tattoos, and a straightening iron. Who was this guy?

That's when I heard the baby crying. Actually, it sounded more like a baby coughing. It was coming from the closet.

Chapter Twenty-five

I got closer. The noise stopped, then started again. Scrabbling was up there with scurrying, in my opinion. It belonged in horror movies, not on four star cruises. I didn't need any more horrible surprises. But what if there were someone hurt or tied up in there? I had read about a serial killer doctor who murdered women on cruise ships in the 1920s. And there was always the Lindbergh baby. Or Rosemary's baby. It definitely yowled like a mutant spawn. I looked at the closet. It was a standard cheap "slat" model, which folded in.

I grabbed Brazil's straightening iron and pressed on the middle of the door. It only went halfway—something was blocking it. I edged around on the right side. I eased in and looked down. No damsel in distress. Instead, under the hanging clothes, was what looked like a small pet carrier. The scrabbling and crying was coming from inside.

Was this Ron Brazil's secret? Sneaking a pet onto the ship? It was obnoxious, but hardly a felony. Was this why he didn't let housekeeping into the room? Was this why he wouldn't look me in the eye?

I squished down and sat on the floor, then closed the door again to give myself room. I peered in through the metal squares of the carrier door, but could only make out a dark shape. A tiny claw pushed through one of the holes and poked the air.

"Hi, there," I said. The creature yelped. The claw retracted.

"Well, you're scared, of course you are. I'm Cyd. I'm not going to hurt you. In fact, I'm probably your only chance, given the weirdo who put you in here." Just as I was about to unlatch the carrier, someone knocked on the door. Ron Brazil wouldn't knock on his own door.

Shit. I wasn't supposed to be in here. If I didn't answer, a steward might come in and find me. If I did answer, how was I going to explain myself? I jerked the closet door shut, put the pet carrier on my lap, provoking another yelp, and pulled myself as far behind the hanging clothes as I could, praying this wasn't a dry cleaning delivery. I could see a little through the slats, but not the whole room. Someone opened the door, closed it, and clicked the lock.

Footsteps that sounded heavy, even on carpet, moved to the bed. Then the figure started a whispered, one-sided conversation. "You really think he's stupid enough to keep it in his room?... Hobart...Naw, she's expendable."

Who was expendable? The speaker ended the call. I could see snatches of Bermuda shorts through the slats. The snatches moved to the bed.

Shit, my Balenciaga was there. I watched as he lifted the purse, dug through it with his fat fingers, then dumped everything out—including my nail polish and ketchup blood samples—and tossed the bag on the floor.

So, when he got to the closet and got the door partway open, I didn't regret driving my stiletto through the madras cotton, right into his balls. When he doubled over, I hit him on the head with the hair straightener, waited until he hit the carpet, then slammed the closet shut. I waited the longest ten seconds ever, then put down the pet carrier and eased it to the floor.

I guess I didn't notice that the metal door of the carrier had come open, because something small and brownish shot out, sharp claws swiping my Stuart Weitzman nude patent heels on its way. I spotted black marks on the creature's back before it disappeared.

It seemed dog-shaped, but I'd never seen a dog move that fast. Its speediness was definitely cat-like. I only knew this because of my best friend Debbie's cat, Monster, who held the land speed record for escaping from their back door on 77th Street and shooting down to the river. I couldn't count the times we'd squirmed on our bellies through the aqueduct tunnel calling his name. Cats are discerning, self-contained, and not bound by social convention or unconditional love. Cats just don't care. That's absolutely the greatest thing about them.

The cabin door was shut, so I decided to let the poor thing calm down while I tied up the unconscious bad guy with a couple of particularly hideous ties. Ron Brazil's closet resembled a close-out from Paramount Studios wardrobe department.

I pushed aside the seventies suits, a vintage Armani tuxedo, two sixties Hawaiian shirts, and a FedEx uniform, which provoked another wave of nausea. There was information here my body knew, but I didn't have time to figure it out before the intruder came to, and Ron Brazil came back to change for Wineglass Bay.

It wasn't easy, but I rolled the Bermuda shorts guy on his stomach and turned his head toward the wall, so he couldn't see me if he woke up. I returned the scattered contents to my purse, then got down on my knees. I figured the scared cat/dog had taken refuge under the bed. I mean, I would. I sent up a silent thanks I hadn't worn the La Perla garter belt and stockings I'd considered in the morning.

Of course, the bed was bolted too, so there was no moving it. I wondered if I had anything that would be tempting for it to eat? I usually had an emergency protein bar in my purse, but I'd removed it for the Qantas weight limit. There was a piece of bacon on one of the dirty plates. I didn't want to make the creature sick, but cats ate live bird carcasses. Cooked pork had to be more sanitary, no matter how long it had been out of the fridge. I held the limp bacon bookmark just under the mattress.

A damp, pointy nose on the end of a long, narrow face with goopy brown eyes nudged my hand. It didn't look like a cat, more like if a Dachshund mated with a baby giraffe. It whimpered, nipped me, then grabbed the bacon and disappeared back under the bed. It had serious teeth for something that was half the size of a banana bread. I heard chewing.

It stuck its head back out. It looked sad. And exasperated. Like it was engaged to Madeline Kahn and knew, somewhere deep inside, it should be with Barbra Streisand. Its eyes were the spitting image of Ryan O'Neal's Howard Banister, musicologist.

"Howard?" I said hoping it was a male. One of its little ears perked up. I decided I should make sure it was a boy before I christened it. I'd made that mistake before. But we weren't really at the "check the genitals" stage in our relationship yet. I found more bacon and took it to the pet carrier. It loped after me. I still couldn't figure out what it was. It moved like a cat, was shaped like a hyena, had symmetrical black stripes on its back, and cried like it had too much phlegm.

This was Australia, maybe it was one of those baby-eating dingoes. I hoped not. I felt terrible shutting the carrier again, especially when he did the cough/cry, but Ron Brazil would be back any minute. I wanted to finish searching the room before I snuck out. I headed to the shelves and drawers. I discovered a World Wildlife Fund duffel bag, just like the one Roger used on our ill-fated trip to Tanzania. This one, though, featured an international "No" sign through the logo drawn in what looked like blood. Then I found it. The toy.

It was a small, fluffy, lavender seal, with a massive club bashing its head, and blood red stitching dripping down its adorable little face. It had a tiny tag which read "Planet Reality." I'd seen one of these before—when I was tied up in the back of a hijacked FedEx truck. Suddenly my *déjà vu* nausea made sense.

Oh, God. Sister Ellery Malcomb, my second- and eighth-grade teacher, former nun, serial monogamist, and Herman Hesse and Tantric sex enthusiast, was engaged to international fugitive Grey Hazelnut, aka the Unavet.

Chapter Twenty-six

Grey Hazelnut was an extreme animal rights activist, a crusader for endangered and mistreated animals everywhere, who took no prisoners. When I'd been on the trail of animal smugglers in Tanzania, he'd impersonated a FedEx driver, knocked me out with a chloroformed Handi-Wipe, and trussed me up like a Cornish hen—and we were on the same side. Over the last ten years, he'd kidnapped an animal researcher, trained as a butcher so he could do an exposé on slaughterhouses, and sprayed Lauren Bacall's sable coat with red paint. He'd also started a maimed stuffed animal business because "children should know the truth." Hence, the fluffy clubbed seal. The last time I'd seen him, he'd been carted off by Interpol.

I had to warn Sister Ellery right away. She would be devastated, but better to be devastated before someone stole all your money, than after. It left you with mourning options.

"Ahhh!" Great. Mr. Unfortunate Shorts was awake. He moaned and gripped his nether regions. Good, I thought, heels don't lie. He was still turned away on his stomach. I wanted to keep it that way. I crept up behind and conked him again with the straightening iron. He shut up. This was quite a device. I considered hair appliance larceny, but it would put me over my flight weight limit.

I looked in on Howard and realized he didn't have any water.

Who wasn't thirsty after bacon? I searched in vain for a bowl. Nothing. Finally, I decided to fill the ice bucket up with bottled water. I'd have to let him out of the carrier again, though, as it wouldn't fit through the metal door. I looked at my watch.

I should be long gone, but I couldn't leave Howard parched. Actually, I didn't want to leave him at all, given his current guardian. I dug out the ice bucket, filled it with bottled water, set it on the floor of the closet, closed the door for containment, and unlatched the carrier.

For a second, the striped puppy/kitten hovered inside. Then he sniffed his way out, finding what, for him, was probably the equivalent of a group Tiki drink. He balanced his miniature paws up on the edge of the bucket and started lapping. While he slurped, I tried to locate a gender indicator. All I saw was what looked like a pouch on his underside. A pouch. Like a kangaroo pouch. He wasn't a kangaroo, so what the hell was he? Or she? Didn't only females have pouches?

I was concentrating so hard on this unexpected development, that I didn't hear the door.

"Bloody hell!" I peered through the slats to see bow legs running to the semi-corpse on the floor, right in front of me. There was swearing in about six languages, three of which I understood, including Danish. I tried to pick up Howard, but he nipped me. I glared at him. He did it again.

Then, the closet door slammed open and Grey Hazelnut alias Ron Brazil, senior gigolo, still in his sweaty dance practice togs, switched to English.

"You! You, you bad penny bimbo! No, you're worse. Do you have any idea how many of my operations you screwed up in Tanzania alone?" He grabbed his hair. It slid sideways. "But not this time. Not this one. Oh, God. The Antichrist was supposed to be a man."

"That's incredibly sexist. Are you saying a woman isn't capable of destroying the world?"

"Have you been listening to anything I've said? Yes! Yes, there is a woman capable of ruining the entire world. You! You are the Apocalypse."

The puppy/kitten gave a whimper and nudged my hand.

"Hey, Hazelnut," I hissed. He flinched. "Stop it. I just got him calmed down. Or her. Is it a her?"

"Don't ever call me Hazelnut. Ever. For this mission, I'm Ron Brazil, period. Even in your head. Never say Hazelnut. Only Brazil. Ron Brazil. Say it."

I rolled my eyes. "Ron Brazil."

"Again!"

"Ron the psycho Brazil. Why should I cover for you?"

"It's not for me, it's for Sister Ellery. And for him." He pointed at Howard, who was curled up against my thigh. "It's important. Is he okay? He's not hurt?"

"No, of course not. So it's a he. Why does he have a pouch?"

Brazil squatted down and examined Howard, who nipped Brazil too. "There are two species of marsupials that have male pouches."

"But what for? Do they co-parent?"

"For God's sake, it's there to protect their penis from getting caught in, I don't know, spiky vegetation or something. Why are you in my closet and who is that on the floor?"

"I'm not telling you anything until you tell me why you are toying with my favorite nun."

"I'm not toying with her. She's the only reason I'm not bashing your head in right about now, which is what you deserve for stealing that rhino horn."

"I stole it for evidence. I may have messed up your little FedEx thing, but in the end, I'm the one who took down Bunty's boss in New York—that witch Eileen Fisher. I saved a lot more animals than I endangered, thank you very much."

He stood up and looked down at me. "No way. You don't have the skills."

"You know nothing about my skills."

"How then? How did you do it?"

"I trapped her with bird lime."

He actually stopped scowling, which I guess for him was smiling. "Poetic."

"Yeah, except that I got shot."

"Shooting is nothing. Try getting stabbed with a poison dart."

Drama queen. I rolled my eyes. "And, if I hadn't been here today, Mr. Bermuda Shorts would have taken Howard, so I'm two for one."

"Who is Howard?"

I held up the tiny marsupial. He growled a little. "Howard."

Brazil shook his wig. At least I assumed he was wearing the one from last night with pompadour potential. "What are you talking about?"

"He reminds me of Howard Banister in *What's Up Doc?* You know, Ryan O'Neal and Barbra Streisand?"

"If he looks like Ryan O'Neal, why don't you call him Ryan?"

"He doesn't look like a Ryan. What did you call him?"

"Patient Zero."

"No wonder he was crying. Come on, really? Even in private?"

He looked down for a long time. "Shackleton. I called him Shackleton." Howard gave a little yelp and looked up at Brazil. I looked down at the creature's pointy head.

"Seriously? You think he looks like a Shackleton?"

"It was more of a conceptual thing. Please put him back in the carrier so he's safe."

I opened the door and placed him in. He nipped me one more time with his razor teeth. I wanted to believe it was with affection. I stood up and looked at the guy on the floor.

"I don't know how much longer he's going to be out," I said.

"What did you hit him with?"

I held up the straightening iron. "Is this European?"

He grabbed it. "Did he actually see the tiger?"

"No. What do you mean, tiger?"

"Nothing. Did the guy see you?"

"I'm not sure. Back up."

I partially closed the door. "Can you see me?"

"No. But he must have seen you when you hit him?"

"I stilettoed his balls first, to make him bend over."

He nodded. "Give me the shoe."

"I'm not giving you my shoe."

"I just want to see how memorable it is."

"Memorable enough to cost five hundred retail. No fricking way."

"Give it to me."

"No." I aimed it at his head.

"Don't wear them. Hide them in your luggage. For your own safety. These guys don't mess around. If they know you can identify them or think you're involved, you're dead."

"Over a marsupial?"

"It's not just any marsupial. I'm serious."

I could still see Mr. Unfortunate Shorts going through my Balenciaga. I decided not to mention it. I mean, most women had a red purse, didn't they?

"Anything else you remember about his being in here?"

I told him what I'd overheard. He spewed a new list of Eastern European obscenities, then turned the man over and stared at him.

I came out of the closet. "Do you know who he is?"

"No. But I know what he is. And if he knew enough to find me, then Shackleton's not safe here. These guys usually travel in pairs. You're going to have to take him."

"Me? No."

"It's only for a couple of hours. I'm delivering him to a trusted associate as soon as we dock in Wineglass Bay."

"What are you going to do with him?" I pointed at the guy on the floor.

"Throw him overboard and hope for sharks. Which are endangered, by the way."

"You can't. Look, as far as accessories go, I'm strictly a purse and shoes girl. No murders."

"Well, we have to keep him tied up and quiet at least until I can get the cargo off the boat. You have any better ideas?"

"There's a morgue drawer available on the cargo deck."

He stared at me. "Too complicated." He moved to the dresser and pulled out a huge syringe—exactly the kind I wish I'd had last night—and jabbed it into the man on the floor. "Horse tranquilizer. He won't wake up for hours, and even if he does, he's not going to know your name or room number."

I considered this. I felt for poor Howard. And alias Ron Brazil had spent time with the Manzonis. And maybe Harriet. He was lunatic scum. But he might know something.

"This is the deal. I will help you. But you're going to have to help me too. *Quid pro quo* or nothing. Once Howard is safe, you're mine. Or I'll tell Sister Ellery. And Interpol. I have Graham Gant's personal cell number."

"You are the Antichrist."

"The AntiChristine."

We decided the pet carrier was a dead giveaway, so Brazil would keep it as a decoy and I would take Howard in my purse, then lock him in my bathroom until we docked. My priority then was getting my photos and blood samples back to Dr. Paglia.

"You can't let anyone see him. Or tell anyone you have him." He shook his head. "I can't believe I'm giving him to you of all people."

"Look, you chloroformed me. I can't believe I'm helping you either."

He took the carrier out.

"What have you been feeding him?" I asked.

"Rats."

"I beg your pardon?"

"In his natural habitat he eats rodents. Or wild pigs." That explained the bacon. Brazil handed me some beef jerky. "He'll probably be okay with this until I get him onshore."

"He'll be safer if you tell me what's going on."

"Nothing. Just be careful and meet me on Deck Seven by the photo shop at eleven forty-five. The busier it is, the less likely someone will notice."

"Does Sister Ellery know about this?"

"Of course not. What kind of arsehole do you think I am?"

"A huge one."

He shrugged and handed me Howard. I looked into my purse. It was a mess, post-molestation. I went into Brazil's bathroom, took two hand towels, lay them over the contents, then deposited Howard on top. I petted his head and hoped to God I'd tired him out, as that cough/cry was going to be hard to explain. At least we had a plan.

Until I got back to my room to find the door wide open.

Chapter Twenty-seven

I peeked around the door. At first I thought the place had been ransacked. The sheets were pulled off the bed and the balcony door was open. I heard whistling.

A tiny woman in a housekeeping uniform and a cleaning rag in her hand came out of the bathroom. I was mortified, because I hadn't taken the time to pre-clean the room like I usually did in a hotel. She smiled anyway.

"Hello, Miss."

"Hello. Cyd Redondo, Redondo Travel." I held out my hand, hoping it wouldn't provoke a yelp from Howard.

"Maria. Is there anything special you need today, Miss?" A shot of tequila, I thought.

"Just extra water bottles would be great, thanks. How long do you think you'll be?"

"Not long."

"Okay, I'll be back." I did an automatic dive for my wallet to tip her, and stopped myself just in time. "Will you be doing the room tomorrow as well?" She nodded. "I'm out of cash right now, but I will get more on shore and make it up to you then. Is that all right?"

"It's not necessary."

"Of course it is. I won't forget."

I had at least twenty minutes to kill. Part of me wanted to go straight to Sister Ellery, but I didn't want her more involved in this criminal enterprise than she already was. Where could I go where no one might hear Howard? I passed another room service tray with some untouched toast. I wrapped it in a napkin and headed toward the service stairs. Doc was coming out.

"Hi," he said. "I was just coming to find you." As usual, he was marginally gorgeous, this time in an untucked navy blue Cuban shirt over linen pants and Dockers. It made me wonder whether the thug in the bad shorts had woken up yet. So I wasn't paying attention when Doc pressed me against the wall and bent down to kiss me. With enthusiasm. And pressure. Enough to squeeze Howard. My stowaway gave a high-pitched cough. Damn. I started coughing in unison, to cover.

"Sorry. Think I might be coming down with something. Rain check?" I squeaked, as I bussed him on the cheek. He smelled like expensive aftershave and Herbal Essence shampoo. Even his half-kiss had made my knees turn to fresh burrata. I wanted to lean up against him for about five hours.

"I'll take you up on that." This really would have been a moment if there hadn't been a male marsupial under my armpit.

"The kayaking offer is still open."

The whole "I can't swim" thing on a cruise was as lame as the whole "I'm a travel agent who's never been farther than New Jersey" thing. I'd figure out a way to get out of it later.

"Great. I have to express something to the U.S., work stuff, first."

He kissed me again and left. I fell against the wall, then headed for the morgue.

"Esmeralda? It's me, Cyd." Howard started scrabbling and cry/coughing just as the teenager emerged. I hoped it wasn't from smelling Harriet.

Esmeralda stared at the moving bulge in my Balenciaga. "What is that?"

"I'd tell you but then I'd have to kill you."

"That's not a funny joke to make in a morgue."

"Right. I'm serious, though. Here." I handed her the toast.

"Thanks. What are you doing here? More forensics?"

I needed to stall. "Just wanted to check on you. Find out if I could help. Are you a refugee or something?"

"Or something."

"Come on. I just brought you sourdough toast."

"It's cold." She took a big bite. Howard was keening again and getting squirmy.

"I'll tell you if you tell me why you have an animal in your purse."

"You first."

"Fine. I am a refugee. From single-ness. I'm a fiancée." She held out her left hand, which bore the tiniest, sweetest engagement ring I'd ever seen. If you blinked, you'd miss it. With any luck, with the tips I'd been giving the Koozer, he could upgrade it to visible.

"How old are you?"

"Twenty-three."

"Come on, I have lipsticks older than you."

"Nineteen. I'm legal." This was a stretch, but I gave it to her.

"I mean he's cute, but do you really want to marry a man who stores you in a coffin? This is supposed to be the honeymoon period."

"We just wanted to spend our first Christmas together. We couldn't afford a ticket, and the staff can't have guests. So he snuck me on in one of the coffins. The crew and staff sneak things in that way all the time. No one checks. Usually it's liquor, drugs, or some other contraband."

"Which in this case is you?"

She nodded.

"So, what's in the purse?"

"A banned substance."

"Well, whatever it is, it isn't happy in there. Can it even breathe?"

She was right. Ron Brazil had made me promise not to let anyone know about or see Howard. But he really didn't sound happy.

"Look, I took an oath. Could you finish your toast in the coffin, so I can give him a little air? Please?"

She crawled back in. Just to be safe, I leaned against the coffin lid to keep it closed and unzipped the main compartment. Howard's pointy head jutted out. I went to pet him and he nipped me, then leapt out of the purse, just as the Koozer opened the door. The cabin steward froze at the door. Before I could even yell for him to close it, Howard was through it and gone.

Chapter Twenty-eight

I sprinted after Howard. How could something so little be so fast? I searched the hallway in both directions, then ran back to the morgue door and the Koozer.

"I know about Esmeralda. I won't tell. As long as you return the favor."

"What was that thing?"

"That's part of the favor. I can't tell you and you can't tell anyone that you saw it. Ever." I held out a five. "Are there rats on this ship?"

"What do think? It's a miracle they're not doing somersaults on the Oasis Buffet."

"Where's the best place to find them?"

"Are you doing an exposé?"

"God, no."

"Someone should."

"Alright, I'm doing an exposé. Where?"

"In the cargo hold or in the trash section next to the crew kitchen. They don't like stairs, so they tend to stay down here. It's just easier."

"Gag. So, if there were a kind of, well, rat hunter, it would gravitate there?"

"Rat hunter? Like a python? We've had three pet pythons go missing and never be found. Let me amend that, we've found skins a couple of times."

All I could see was a hangry python opening its jaws and Howard running right in. "Are either of those places on this deck?"

"The cargo hold." He pointed down the hall to a door propped open at the end. I went to the door and peered into the creepy cavern, stacked with crates.

"Howard?" If he weren't already embarking on a rat buffet, I might be able to lure him back out with food. I only had thirty minutes until I was supposed to hand him off to Brazil.

"Koozer. If you want me to keep tipping you the GDP of Tonga, I need bacon. Lots of it. Right away. Now!"

I took a deep breath, pulled out my emergency mini flashlight, and crept into the hold, closing the door behind me to limit the search area.

"Howard?" I turned on what was essentially a penlight. There was clanging and, just as I stepped into the dark, a jolt and a shudder. My seasickness came back with a vengeance. I grabbed a green apple I'd put in my purse and used it to "chew down" a seasickness pill.

It wasn't easy to squat in the INC skirt I'd gotten on loan from Debbie until she went back down a size. But squattage was necessary, as it was hard to imagine more crevices and corners where a small, rat-sized creature—or python—could hide. It resembled the warehouse at the end of *Raiders of the Lost Ark*, but dirtier.

There were cobwebs everywhere. In doing Australian research for my clients over the years, I'd discovered that, of the ten most lethal creatures in the world, ten of them were in Australia. Including the three most deadly spiders. I always included a "watch out for" newsletter for my clients, wherever they were going, and "AVOID COBWEBS!" was one of them for Australia. I looked on the bright side. Maybe I'd find Fredo and Sandra stashed down here. I chastised myself for my uncharitable thoughts and kept looking. Nothing.

Finally, the Koozer returned with a napkin's worth of bacon bits.

"Bacon bits! How am I going to lure him with those? They're too small to even smell!"

"I was thinking a Hansel and Gretel type of thing. It was the best I could do. The breakfast buffet's over. This was all they had on the salad bar. You haven't met those Balkan chefs. They hold grudges."

I took the napkin. "Okay, find Ron Brazil and tell him to meet me down here right away. You have to act like you don't know why. Don't mention bacon. In fact, let me write him a note. You can say I buzzed you in my cabin."

I pulled out my notepad and wrote. "Delay. Meet me in cargo hold. Deck Three."

"I'm supposed to be checking the cabins right now."

"Would you rather be checking toilets in prison?" This was pretty much an empty threat, but it worked.

I crept deeper into the bleak, pungent space, sprinkling bacon bits as I went. The hold was full of cargo for Hobart. I guessed the line made extra money for transport. Any island was screwed. Whatever they couldn't produce, they had to pay through the nose for, and everyone made money on the way, including, I guessed, Darling Cruises.

I looked harder to distract myself from vomiting. I wished Harriet were around so I could ask her about this freaky non-kangaroo marsupial. She'd been my guide to all things Australian and it was just one of the reasons I missed the hell out of her and resented Brazil for keeping me from tracking down her killer. Anyone who watched television knew that after the first forty-eight hours, the trail went cold.

I sprinkled more bacon around a large section where the cargo was addressed to a Pierce Butler and stamped The Fountain. Where had I heard that name before? I moved my light over the boxes. Most of them seemed full of eucalyptus candles, waffle robes, and massage oil—except for the one that was labeled Dolophine. That one looked partially open. But before I could investigate, the ship bounced, then made one final lurch and shudder, as did my stomach. When the motion returned to a gentler, vertical bob, my internal organs stayed on lurch. We were docking. Dammit. Even if I had Doc's number, I couldn't get any bars down here. Where was Ron Brazil? This was in the running for worst Christmas vacation ever.

I had just sat down on a crate of sporks when a slit of light appeared at the end of the hold. "Don't open it too wide," I yelled. "He might get out." A bullet whizzed by my head.

Chapter Twenty-nine

Okay, it was officially the worst Christmas vacation ever.

I ducked behind the stack of eucalyptus candles, as I thought they might slow the bullets, and prayed to God Howard's survival instincts had him low to the ground. Who would shoot inside a ship? Wasn't it like shooting in an airplane? I heard a scuffle, too loud for rats. Then, the sound of dragging.

My seasickness joined forces with my panic. I vomited beside a carton of cotton puffs.

"Hey, AntiChristine! You in here?"

"Over here," I yelled, "But I wouldn't get too close."

"Then come help me."

I followed the voice and found Brazil standing over another guy in shorts knocked out on the floor, this one with red hair.

"Don't worry about him. Give me Shackleton. I'm about to miss the handoff. And they won't wait. We agreed if I wasn't there, that meant it was too dangerous."

"I don't have him. I mean, he's in here. I just don't know where."

"*Me cago en todo lo que se menea!*"

"I understand Spanish, you know!" Sort of. It sounded like he'd said "I shit on everything that wiggles."

Brazil picked up a nearby hand truck and flung it against the wall, making a crash that could probably be heard in Melbourne. He swore again, this time in Italian.

"Do you have any idea what you've done? Do you?" He just shook his head. Then he sat on a carton of Metamucil and started to cry.

I pulled out a handkerchief and handed it to him. "You don't remember my name, do you?"

He blew his nose. "Why should I?"

"So that you don't scream out AntiChristine in public and get carted off to an insane asylum. Cyd Redondo, Redondo Travel." I started to tell him what had happened and he held up his hand like a referee to stop me. He picked up the bad guy's gun and put in his waistband.

"We look while we talk." He headed down an aisle, muttering. "Bimbocile! Leave it to you to lose the last thylacine, ever."

"The last what?" I ignored "bimbocile" and decided to save it for use on others in daily life. I ducked down with my penlight and shone it in a section I hadn't checked yet.

"The last thylacine. The last male anyway."

"Could you say that in English?"

"I am. Thylacine. Tasmanian tiger, you half wit. The last Tasmanian tiger."

"Tiger? I thought you said it was a marsupial. And how come I've never heard of it?"

"Because you come from a country where nobody reads or has a passport."

"Except Sister Ellery."

"Except Sister Ellery, exactly. People call it a Tasmanian tiger because of the stripes, but it's a marsupial. And a carnivore." He looked down. "Wait, those might be droppings."

"Nope. Bacon bits. It was all I had."

"You're just feeding the rats. The thing you don't understand, the reason that you have not only ruined my life and the entire planet, is that everyone thinks the Tasmanian tiger is extinct."

"Like Dodo extinct?"

"Yes. Like Dodo extinct. Well, technically, it's listed as "functionally extinct."

Like my love life, I thought, or Jello 1-2-3.

"The last documented one died in the Hobart Zoo in 1936. That's after the dimwit Australian government paid people to kill them because they were a threat to sheep farmers. Bastards. Like there aren't enough sheep. And we shouldn't be eating sheep anyway. So there are always 'sightings,' but no proof."

"Until Howard?"

"Until Howard's mom."

"Keep talking. It will motivate me." I shone the penlight down another crevice.

"About two years ago, one of my compatriots actually tracked a male and female in the bush in South Australia. He knew if he told anyone it would bring every psycho poacher and collector and news crew—especially since last year some *puta* magazine offered a million and a quarter dollar reward for anyone who came forward with evidence—so he hid them and by some kind of miracle, they bred."

Brazil got on his knees and peered into an empty box.

"The male died about a month ago, but the female produced three joeys, two females and a male. So this little guy is it. End of the line. There might still be others, but these are the only ones we know about for sure, the only ones we thought we could save. Until you showed up."

"Can I just remind you again that I stopped the Bermuda shorts guy from taking him, and who's that other red-haired guy, anyway?"

"Hench guys travel in pairs. He followed me down here."

"So now you have two unconscious guys to hide?"

He shrugged. "Details. Right now, we keep looking. Even if I miss the handoff, we have to find him."

I shone my penlight down a row of flower vases. "So if it was a complete secret, how did these guys know?"

Brazil walked over and turned on the lights. Various things scattered. "That's what worries me. Only three of us knew. That's why we're moving them. We all took one each and we're supposed to meet to take them to Maria Island."

"Why there?"

"It's a wildlife preserve and I have a compound." He looked at his watch. "I'm going to be too late."

So I'd just functionally killed a species by opening my purse. Now I was the one who felt like crying. Brazil moved toward the cotton ball/vomit area. "I wouldn't go over there," I said, following him around the corner.

We both stopped dead. There was Howard, lapping up the remains.

"No, Howard! Bad tiger!"

Chapter Thirty

By the time we'd cleaned up Howard (something I insisted on before he went back in my Balenciaga), tied up the second Howard-poaching hopeful, and gotten to the departure deck, most of the passengers were already on shore. I told Brazil I'd help him get Howard into a duffel, so we went to his cabin. Mr. Unfortunate Shorts was gone.

"I can't worry about that now." He packed up more beef jerky.

"What are you going to do?"

"The less you know, the less likely you'll screw it up."

"I never thought I'd say this, but good luck. Howard, you are a freaking miracle, so don't forget it. Mr. Brazil is a son of a bitch, but if anyone can save you, he can."

I kissed Howard's strangely scratchy head and watched the two of them go. Then, I went in search of Doc, but the Infirmary was closed up and the stewards said he'd already gone ashore. I stood, taking in the deep blues and greens of Wineglass Bay and wished I were taking a mini cruise past the white beaches instead of rushing to find a FedEx outlet because I didn't know how long blood would keep.

The shore crew directed me toward the town. The sign read Population 495. Given the gossip potential, I was surprised Brazil had chosen here for his handoff. I hoped he hadn't been too late. I tried my phone as I walked. The reception kept going in and out, even on land. I found a tiny sweet spot and sent Dr. Paglia the morgue photos.

Finally, I spotted a convenience/liquor store with a Post Office sign. The harried woman inside said my package—over which I'd written *Fragile* about fifty times—would get to Brooklyn before Christmas Eve U.S. time, as long as I was willing to pay one hundred fifty dollars. Along with fruitcake, holiday gouging seemed to be universal. Air miles, air miles, I told myself, as I pulled out my Visa card.

The post mistress said there was one pay-by-the-hour computer in the coffee shop on the other end of town, i.e., half a block down. The clerk there said I had to buy a flat white, whatever that was, to use the Internet. I hoped he didn't hear me gasp, or see tears pop up in my eyes when I found two emails from Harriet in my inbox.

The first one was dated while I was in the air between LAX and Melbourne.

"Hey sister. Peggy Newsome's been sending a lot of her folks on private excursions to this place called The Fountain in Hobart. So that's probably the first place we should check out."

The boxes I'd seen in the hold were addressed to The Fountain. They'd indicated a spa, except for the Dolophine, whatever the hell that was. I would have to go back in the hold. I could hardly wait. Leave it to Peggy Newsome to ruin my life even over the International Date Line.

Harriet's second email was more cryptic. "Don't mention the Manzonis to anyone until you talk to me. My friend Scott will get you to the boat if you're late. He's a serial dater, don't waste your time. Hang on to these until I see you and I'll explain. Hxx" At the bottom of the email were more numbers and letters like the ones I'd found on the paper in her room—all starting with CT.

My heart hurt. It seemed more and more likely that looking for the Manzonis had put Harriet in danger. I paid another outrageous fee to have her emails printed out, put out a few small travel agent fires, and was ready for another flat white, to go. I didn't understand why they didn't just call it a cappuccino, but it was damned delicious, in any language.

I hurried for the ship. I wanted to get back to those Fountain boxes and to the Koozer's friend, who'd been the steward for the Manzonis. As I got to the ramp, Doc and Lisa the hostess, both wet and grinning, ran up. Doc gave me a cursory nod and whispered something to Lisa, who looked back with a smug grin. I guessed I wouldn't be dining at the Captain's Table anytime soon. Or visiting the infirmary either. Damn.

I kicked myself. This was no time for romance anyway. I had one more night to pump the crew for info before I got to Hobart. And maybe by then, Dr. Paglia would get back to me. I really, really wanted to be wrong about Harriet's murder, but I was pretty sure I wasn't.

I headed up to my cabin. Despite my Do Not Disturb card, I got the sense someone had been there besides the houseckeeper. My lipsticks were in the wrong order and closet wasn't quite closed. I wondered whether the thug from Brazil's room had been looking for my nude heels, or revenge, or whether the Risk Management guys were still "investigating" the crime scene. Of course it might be that I'd just been asking too many questions and whoever'd killed Harriet was lying in wait to bash in my head too. I wished I'd stolen Brazil's straightening iron. My Balenciaga weighed forty pounds most days, so I held it up and rammed open the closet door.

No intruders, but someone had rifled through my clothes. I found shoulders off hangers and palazzo pants slumped on the floor.

I took a minute to evaluate my evidence. I had the photos of the Manzonis with the Captain and with Ron Brazil. Damn, in all the horror of the last few hours, I'd forgotten to ask him about them. And I'd forgotten to try to open Elliot's flash drive in the computer cafe. Was I ever going to get my Brooklyn brain back?

I had a bruise, an injection site, blood, fingerprints, and khaki fabric. I had a half-opened box for The Fountain labeled Dolophine. I had a Captain who was first and foremost trying to save her job, and a Staff Captain who would probably welcome a scandal on board so he could take over. I had a fake photographer, who could be a creep, a criminal, or just desperately single. I had Harriet's scrunched up note, her emails, and her illusive real or faux husband. I hit the "steward" button. I had some questions for the Koozer.

Chapter Thirty-one

I barely heard my favorite steward knock. If he was afraid of me, I was going to work that to my advantage. When he entered, even his preppy haircut looked stressed.

"I like Esmeralda, by the way. When a woman is willing to go into a coffin for you, don't screw it up, okay?"

He nodded.

"Now, I need three things and I don't have any more cash until we get to Hobart, so you're going to have to give me a line of credit."

"There are ATMs on Decks Ten and Twelve."

"If you think I am going to pay a five-fifty fee on top of the bank charge, you're insane. And before you say it, I'm not using my one chance to cash a personal check when we have four days left. The way things have been going, I might need another helicopter."

"Advance on your sea pass?"

"Koozer, seriously."

"Okay."

"First, you need to give me a better description of the man you saw with Harriet"

"How much credit is it worth?"

"A kick in the balls." I flexed the Stuart Weitzmans I'd barely saved from Ron Brazil.

"The type of guy who sells life insurance and reverse mort-gages. Very white, trim, tall, blondish hair. Black eyebrows. He was wearing khakis and a purple checked long-sleeved shirt. He didn't tip."

"And you're sure you haven't seen him again, anywhere, since then?"

He shook his head. I pulled out Harriet's list. In the legible version, all the items started with CT, followed by numbers and dashes. I didn't recognize the numbers as dates until it hit me. Everything was backwards in Australia. If the days came first, then the months, it could be dates. But what did that mean? And what was CT? Cat Scan? Customer Transport? Cruise Terminal?

If it meant Cruise Terminal, maybe I could put the dates together with the times the ship was in port. Could that have something to do with the disappearances? I held out the list.

"Koozer? Is that a ship term? CT?"

"Sure. It means Captain's Table. It's the list of the guests who've been invited, how many times, etc. The cruise line keeps a record, and it helps the Captain and her staff keep track of who's been where, who's due for an invitation, etc."

"And this number?" The extra numbers were always 1, 2, 3, or 4.

"I don't recognize those. What is that, anyway?"

"Nothing. I need to talk to your friend, the one who took care of the Manzonis' cabin."

He looked at his watch. "Well, you can't wear that. You look like a passenger."

Ten minutes later we were headed down the back stairs. The Koozer was remarkably spry. I barely kept up, mostly because the Housekeeping uniform he'd borrowed was tight on me. Honestly, how could anyone clean a bathtub in this? We moved lower into the metaphoric and literal bowels of the ship. I got a waft of alcoholic sweat, rotting trash, basement, disinfectant, and fresh paint. It was a beehive of activity, the way I'd imagined the tunnels below Disneyland. As a travel agent, I knew any paradise featured an underbelly.

I watched as the Koozer nodded to a series of other crew members in various jackets and uniforms. I got a few stares, but everyone seemed too busy to stop me.

I followed him down a hall to a place I'm not sure qualified as a room. Or even a closet. Maybe half a closet. There were bunk beds with about one foot between them and the desk. I thought I glimpsed a bathroom, but the toilet was in the shower. That couldn't be right.

"Wow," I said. "I'm not tipping you enough."

"Yeah. That's why we all spend our time in the dining hall and the bar."

"Yeah, it makes the morgue look like a suite." He stared at me. "I'm not going to tell. What is the deal with that, anyhow?"

"What do you mean? With Esmeralda?" We stood outside the nautical hovel. "What do you think? Love. I was on a cruise with my family in the Caribbean. Esmeralda was a singer on the ship. But they fired her because she got too many piercings, so she had to come back here. Neither of us can afford to fly to see the other, so I wrangled a job with Darling and finally got this route. We only get four days a month in Melbourne, and they can move you to another ship or another route anytime they want, so we try to see each other while we can. That's what the tips are for. So we can get married."

"Koozer, you are either the best con man in the world, or a total sweetheart." I felt like hugging him, but instead, wrote out another IOU. What the heck. It was Christmas. "What now?"

"Nylo must be in the dining room," he said. "You can't go in there. I'll get fired. Just hide behind the door until I get back."

Once he closed the door I was already in the crevice behind it, the headboard of the bunk bed digging into my back. I stepped forward just as he smashed the door into my head, which was fine. I didn't already have a headache or anything.

The Koozer stood there with a small man in his early twenties with the straightest, thickest, blackest hair and the most serious expression I'd seen since Catholic school. He was holding a loaf of white bread and a bowl of rice, looked like he hadn't been to bed since Thanksgiving, and reeked of rum. Koozer punched his arm.

"Nylo. Ms. Redondo wants to know about the Manzonis. Do you remember them?"

He groaned, then caught himself. "I apologize, ma'am."

"No apology necessary. They're my ex-in-laws. I groan every time I think of them too. They're loud, messy, and unless they've changed, terrible tippers. The thing is, they've gone missing, and though they probably deserved it, I need to find out what happened to them."

I pulled out a notepad and wrote an IOU for twenty bucks. "The Koozer's already taken me for all my cash, but I'm good for it. Right?"

The Koozer shrugged.

"Hey!"

"Yes, she's good for it."

"Would you mind if I asked you about them while you're eating? I know you have to get to work."

He shrugged too. I guess the crew had to conserve their energy, and saved politeness/ass kissing for above-board. Fair enough. I was invading their world, after all.

"Did you notice anything weird about their behavior?"

"All Americans are weird."

"Yes, well, besides standard American weird."

"They fought a lot."

That didn't surprise me. "Bickering or yelling?"

"Both."

"Do you remember anything at all they might have said?"

"Yeah. They acted like I didn't exist. That happens a lot." He chewed bread for a while. "They were talking about uptown

and downtown? How there was no way in hell he was giving
her half the traveler's checks. She said he was in for an ugly surprise. That's about all I remember, except for their asking for the
cheapest Riesling. What's the problem? The Staff Captain said
they decided to stay in port."

"Did he say why?"

"He just said don't worry about their cabin."

"That's strange. Did you pack them up?"

"Not really. Pretty much all their stuff was gone. There were
a couple of things hidden under the mattress." I stared at Nylo.
"We always check. Passengers leave cash under there and forget
it when they leave. We wait a week to spend it."

"A whole week. How Boy Scouts of America of you. What
else?"

"Bad ties. Really bad. And a cell phone."

I looked back and forth between them. They had me pegged
as a sucker, that's for sure. "How much? There's no way it was
a new model."

After a negotiation, I wrote out an IOU for fifty bucks. They
made sure the coast was clear, and took me down a long, thin
corridor where all the smells—fried rice, motor oil, Coppertone,
spilled Planters Punches, and teenage boy—intensified. It got
darker and louder as we went. I hoped I could trust these buf-
foons. I jumped a couple of times, due to the python-colored
water hoses on the walls.

Finally, we came to a door labeled "Lost and Found." Nylo
pushed on the door, knocking over an oversized bin of half-used
toiletries. The room held every size and shape of luggage, from
backpacks to trunks, single flip-flops, tuxedos, bathing suits, pool
noodles, Mardi Gras masks, *Star Wars* Storm Trooper costumes,
and a few toupees, among a million other things, were hanging
and stacked everywhere.

"Oh, my God. People leave all this? Do they ever claim it?"

"Sometimes. But they have to pay the shipping and, depending on where the ship goes next, it could be months before they get it."

"Wow. What happens to it when it's unclaimed?" Silence. Nylo took out a piece of bread, balled it up, and put most of it in his mouth. I walked around, filled with luggage envy, jealous that these people were so well-traveled that leaving their luggage was a mistake, not a tragedy.

Nylo finished chewing. "We wait two months if it's the next of kin claiming it."

"This is dead people's stuff?"

"Some of it. Or missing people. I mean they usually don't pack to go overboard."

Koozer punched Nylo in the elbow. He bent over and dug around in a trash can and came up with a creamsicle-colored flip phone. "I think this is it. I remember because it was so ugly."

If the phone was here, that might explain why Sandra hadn't answered Barry's calls, but it could also mean she wouldn't need it anymore. Ever.

"Anything else?"

"Maybe this?" It did look like one of Fredo's polyester suits. I checked the label. Third Avenue Big and Tall. Bingo. I folded up the suit, and put the phone in my bag.

"Thanks, Nylo."

Then I stopped. "Over there. Isn't that the Manzonis' luggage?" I'd loaned Margy a piece of luggage and put a Redondo Travel globe sticker on it so she wouldn't forget to give it back. It hadn't worked. "I thought you said they took their luggage onshore."

"That's the first time I've seen it since I moved them in. This is bad, right?"

While the stewards retrieved the bag, I grabbed a couple of Mardi Gras masks and some Jimmy Choo sandals and tucked them into my Balenciaga. It's scary what stress can do to a person. What was I going to tell Barry?

Chapter Thirty-two

As soon as the bags were in and Koozer was safely out the door, I put Sandra's suitcase on my bed. Had Fredo pushed her overboard, then dumped her bag? He was probably capable of it, but Harriet and the Cruise Director said they'd gone ashore together. It made no sense.

I thought about the woman who'd been my mother-in-law for three months. She was first and foremost a social climber. She'd pushed Barry to do Cotillion, learn golf, run for student body president. Maybe that was why he wound up on fire, in a pirate suit, at the top of an escalator in Caesar's Palace.

I'd never been good enough for her and she'd made sure I felt it, evaluating every outfit with a head-to-toe sweep of her eyes, then an exaggerated sigh. She rushed to serve Barry at the table before I could, despite giving me *How to Be the Perfect Housewife* for my birthday. She made sure to add an over-the-top, extended shake of salt into anything I cooked, and always brought Barry a hot water bottle or Ovaltine, just as we were going to bed. You can imagine what her being in the next room did to our sex life, which was opportunistic at best, even from the beginning.

I'd comforted myself with the thought that no one was good enough for her Barry—until she started inviting Angela Hepler over for dinner. And here I was, still trying to please her, or show Barry she'd been wrong. She was wrong. About fashion, at least. The suitcase confirmed it.

She'd always dressed like she'd gone to have her colors done on Opposites Day. Her toiletries weren't there, though, which gave me hope, unlike the phone, which sat like a fat toad in the middle of her Soft Surroundings tunics.

I tried to turn it on. It didn't have much battery, but the good news was, she'd maintained the "no locked doors" Bay Ridge policy on her device and I didn't need a password. She wasn't much on texting. Meaning there were no texts. I found a few phone numbers she'd dialed with a Tasmanian area code, though, and wrote them down. And of course, there were a few calls to Barry. Barry. God, I hadn't even called him. What was wrong with me?

It was too early in Brooklyn to call him now, his insomnia notwithstanding. I was meeting Sister Ellery for dinner, then Cruise-In and a Double Feature Night. They'd be projecting *It's a Wonderful Life*, *National Lampoon's Christmas Vacation*, and *Die Hard* against the wall on Deck Ten, complete with popcorn, hotdogs, nachos, artisanal ice cream, and Raisinets. It would make up a little bit for not watching *Mr. Magoo's Christmas Carol*, with my nephews and Uncle Leon.

I needed to dress for dinner. I'd already used up my good black dress, so I went for a simple leopard print chiffon, swing style. It hit just above the knee and, though the nude heels I'd had on earlier really elongated my short legs, I took Brazil seriously for a millisecond and went for my "borrowed" Jimmy Choo sandals, just in case the henchman was still at large, instead of overboard, which is what I secretly suspected. I knew Brazil was slightly unhinged, particularly when it came to poachers. It made me worry about Sister Ellery. I still hadn't told her about him. I focused on getting ready instead, hoping it would cheer me up.

I looked at my hair and almost burst into tears. Obviously, the humidity here required extra styling gel. At this rate, my travel size would be empty in two days. And there wasn't a concealer on earth that could take care of these jet lag/homicide stress circles under my eyes. I put on a bright red lipstick, to draw attention away from my blue eyebags, spritzed a little Chanel No. 19, grabbed my Balenciaga, and headed to Deck Ten via the Staff Captain's office.

Staff Captain Bentley's assistant said he could be found on the bridge. I headed up in the elevator, then chickened out a floor below. My bravado/adrenalin from the morning had deserted me and I didn't feel tough enough to fight for my life without at least two appetizers. Maybe it was better to wait until we were in Hobart, where I had an escape route that wasn't the Tasman Sea. We would be there in less than eight hours. What could happen between now and then?

I could still check the flash drive, but the only desktop I knew about was the one in Doc's office. He wasn't pleased with me at the moment, but it was worth a try.

I headed down the stairs toward the Infirmary. On the landing, I found Elliot Ness, splayed out in a bad forest green and navy plaid jacket.

"Elliot?" No answer. I dropped my Balenciaga and fell to my knees. No pulse. I slapped him. Nothing. I caught my breath so I could try CPR for the second time in forty-eight hours. It didn't work this time either. People fell down cruise ship stairs all the time. Hence, resort torts. Still, like with Harriet, it didn't feel like an accident. I remembered there'd been a defibrillator in Doc's office and ran down the last two set of stairs. I heard a door slam above me, but didn't have time to run back up. The Infirmary door was open.

Doc sat at his desk. I careened through the door. "You, defibrillator, stairwell, now!" It took him a minute to detach it from the wall, but finally he was running behind me up to the Deck Six landing. I arrived, breathless, my calves cramping.

The body was gone.

I stood, pointing at nothing. Doc panted. "If you wanted to get me alone in the stairwell, you only had to ask."

"That's not funny. Honest to God—and I know I'm jet lagged and I accidentally stood you up—Elliot Ness was lying here four minutes ago, not breathing. Right there." I pointed again at the landing floor. No stains, no evidence, no body.

"Elliot Ness? The G-Man?"

"No, the guy pretending to be the ship's photographer. That's who I was meeting last night. He had pictures of Harriet and the Manzonis. When I found him, I thought he might have just fallen down the stairs, but it might be murder."

"Two murders in two days on one cruise ship? Come on, Cyd. Be rational."

"What good did that ever do? The best people are always irrational—Newton, Einstein, Harriet the Spy, Elvis. I could go on. I didn't imagine it. Look at my lipstick. Would I ever go out in public like this?"

"Okay, okay. It probably took two people or a hand truck to get him out of here, so they can't have gone far."

He put down the defibrillator. I picked it back up and glared at him. As we moved toward the door, I saw a wad of paper just inside.

"See?" I said. "Someone did this to get back in."

I handed it to him, hoisted the heart machine on my hip, and opened the door.

"Cyd?" I turned back. "These are your business cards."

I almost dropped the defibrillator. Thank goodness for the sure-grip handle.

"I can explain that," I said. "Come on."

We ran out onto the deck. There was no one in either direction. We could hear laughter and dishes clattering and then, a faint but unmistakable splash. I stared at Doc. We both ran in the direction of the sound and saw two figures hurrying into another stairwell door.

"Follow them," I yelled. "I'll check for Elliot."

I ran to the railing and peered into the water. Even from Deck

Six, it was a long way down. I went all dizzy and blank for a minute. I thought I caught a flash of plaid, but by the time Doc returned, it was gone. There was nothing but dark.

To his credit, he scanned the water for a whole minute or so. "Cyd, I'm not saying you imagined all this, but maybe you imagined all this."

It was all I could do not to brain him with the defibrillator, but the way this night was going, I might need it.

"Okay, give the code for overboard." I grabbed his walkie-talkie. "Felix! Felix! Felix!"

"Feliz Navidad to you too," someone croaked in response.

Doc rolled his eyes and took the instrument back.

"It's not Felix?" I felt dizzy again.

"Oscar."

"Okay, Oscar, Oscar, Oscar!" I yelled into the salt air. Doc took me by the shoulders, and moved me to a damp deck chair. On the deck above, I could hear James Stewart's George Bailey getting ready to jump off a bridge in Bedford Falls.

"Breathe." He took my pulse. For the first time, that particular event felt erotic. My GP, Dr. Kevekian, usually hacked Turkish cigarette smoke into my face during this activity. Doc just kept his thumb steady on my wrist. It made my heart beat faster, but I didn't tell him that.

"You don't believe me."

"It's not that I don't believe you, exactly. But it's a very big deal to turn the ship around and hunt for someone. The Captain will want to know what happened and how and, right now, you're the only person who's actually seen this person. We didn't see him go overboard, right?"

"But you heard the splash, too, right? I'm not insane."

"I thought I heard a splash, yes, but that could be a lot of things. And we were listening for one. The mind can play tricks on you. When was the last time you ate?"

"Breakfast."

"And how many seasickness pills did you take?"

"Four?"

"Four!"

"Three didn't work."

"You're supposed to take one every twelve hours. And you haven't had any food?" He just shook his head.

"We have to do something. Please, Doc. Don't you have that whole Hypocritical Oath thing?"

"Hypocratic, though that's probably more accurate. I have a passenger list in the office. Let's go look him up and go from there."

"But we're losing valuable time. We could still save him."

"How long did you do CPR?"

"Three minutes?"

"I hate to say it, but if he wasn't breathing and his heart wasn't beating then, the chances of him being alive in the water now are pretty much zero. Even if he was just unconscious, the fall probably killed him."

He was right. I just didn't want to believe it. Elliot Ness was a con man, but he'd given me his handkerchief. That meant he had a mother who taught him manners. I knew my mother would want to know my fate, no matter what. I felt a stab of homesickness and responsibility.

"Even so, we can't just leave him there. He might have family." He put his hand behind my head and pulled me forward, kissing me on the forehead. Finally, I let him help me up and followed him back downstairs into his office. He pulled out another one of those cruise ship clipboards I coveted, and flipped through it.

"Ness, you said?" I nodded. He kept flipping, then shook his head. He handed me the list. He was right. Elliot Ness wasn't there. No Elliots at all, even under another last name.

"Maybe it was an alias?"

"Maybe." He wasn't buying it. He had that "you're more attractive when you're crazy" look in his eye. He got up, unlocked his drug cabinet, and took out a vial. I stared at the stock of pharmaceuticals.

"Doc? What's Dolophine?"

"It's a form of methadone. Why?"

Wow. I guess The Fountain offered deep relaxation. "No reason. I didn't imagine Elliot Ness. No matter how many pills I took. Wait! I have evidence. I have his flash drive. Here, I'll show you." I plugged the flash drive into his desktop. That's the last thing I remembered.

Chapter Thirty-three

I hadn't pegged Doc as the love bite type, but there were some not entirely unpleasant teeth gnawing on my neck when I came to. It took about three seconds to realize I was back in cabin 710 and they weren't human.

"Howard! What are you doing here?" He was shaking himself on the bed and, in addition to my neck, had been at the down pillows. The bed and half the room was dusted in a soft white. At least it finally looked like Christmas.

"Thanks to you, we missed the handoff. I figured we were safer here."

I jumped, spooking Howard. "Sorry, buddy."

It was Ron Brazil, complete with pompadour, a yachting outfit, and a pistol in his lap. At least it was pointed at the door instead of me.

"How did you get in?" He rolled his eyes. "Wait, how did I get in?" I looked down. This time I was still dressed. Thank goodness chiffon was tougher than it looked. My Jimmy Choos were in front of the closet. Oh, God. My Balenciaga. Where was it?

I did not like to be separated from my bag. The last time it happened, I'd wound up imprisoned in a damp hotel room in Dar Es Salaam preparing to have snakes inserted into my bra. Now, if anyone expected me to check it, anywhere, I insisted that I needed my medication. "My condition could strike at any time," I would say, my condition being the need to have my bag on my shoulder. I looked around, starting to hyperventilate.

"Looking for this?" Brazil held it aloft.

"Yes! Yes. I am looking for that. Give it here! And don't throw it." He did, of course. It seemed intact. I saw the chewed pillows by my head and put it on the side away from Howard.

I tried to sit up. Everything was hazy. Where had I been before here? Doc's office. The flash drive. I dug through my bag and didn't see it.

"What day is it?"

"The twenty-third." That meant it was the twenty-second in Bay Ridge. Dr. Paglia wouldn't have the samples yet.

"How long have you been here?" I sat up and let Howard nuzzle under the covers.

"Since about four."

"Four in the morning? And I was here, then?"

"Yep. Zonked. I need to leave Howard with you so I can get rid of the guys who've been following me."

"They're both loose again?"

"I think there may be three. Somebody untied the other two."

"Great."

"They still don't know who you are, or they'd be in here. Once we're in Hobart I can get a boat to Maria Island. But I need you to disembark with him, because they'll be waiting for me. Also, because this is all your fault."

"That seems pretty harsh, considering."

"Considering that you lost him and then he was drawn back by your vomit? The 'Circle of Life' defense?"

"I hate the Circle of Life."

"Tough shit. Get over it. The planet is a ticking bomb. You actually have a chance to do something about it for once."

I looked at Howard. His eyes were still sad. He shook his little behind, and his stripes shivered. Then he yawned and I got my first full view of his razor sharp teeth. I touched my neck, amazed I hadn't bled out.

As he pounced on a feather, I wondered whether he missed his mom. And whether he knew he was the last of his kind, an honest to God miracle—the kind of once in a millennium thing that terrified me. I didn't have the skills to save a species. It needed expertise. It might need violence. It needed the lunatic fringe figure sitting across from me.

"Look, as you said, I keep screwing up. This is too important for me to be in charge of. What if I screw up again? I'm a travel agent, not a secret agent. I've never even had a pet. Why don't you just wear one of your five hundred disguises? You're a trained eco-warrior, right?"

"It's too risky. Help me fix it, or I'll tell the Hobart Police you broke into my room."

"Who is going to believe that?"

He held up his own digital camera. "It's always on."

"And if I do this, you are going to help me find out what happened to my in-laws, right? And to Harriet? I have to go to this place, The Fountain. I think they might have gone there."

"Fine. Once he's safe."

"What's Sister Ellery going to do while you're at your compound?"

"She said she's going to rest a little."

"Why? That's not like her. Is she okay?"

"She's not in her seventies anymore."

"I know. It worries me." Sometimes I forgot that. I think the first person who reads you *Dick and Jane* seems invincible, if not immortal. I could still see her whipping her wimple out of the way and settling in to hold the book backwards so we could all see.

"You're going to let her down easy, right?"

"What makes you think she won't dump me?"

"Yeah, you're right. When she sees those wigs."

There was a knock on the door. And another one, louder. I threw up my hands.

Brazil grabbed Howard and got into the closet. These closets really weren't designed for repetitive subterfuge.

I looked through the peephole. It was Doc. Part of me was glad to see him, but part of me heard alarm bells. Was he a good guy or a bad guy? The last thing I remembered was putting the flash drive in. I leaned my forehead against the door, then cracked it open. I smelled Gillette aftershave and breakfast cooking somewhere. I was starving.

"Morning. I just wanted to make sure you were all right. Are you?"

"I'm not sure. What happened?"

"You keeled over in my desk chair. I'm guessing from an overdose of Dramamine and an underdose of food. I didn't want to get slapped again, so I left you in your clothes this time."

"Thank you. I think."

"You're welcome. You had a rough night." Oh, God. Elliot Ness. Had I dreamed all that?

"Can I come in for a minute? I have a couple of things for you."

"I'm not really presentable."

"Don't worry, I'm a doctor."

I hear Brazil cough "Don't" under his breath.

"Come on, Cyd. I brought breakfast. And your flash drive."

I needed that flash drive. I shot a look at the closet and undid the chain.

"Is no one ever sick on this boat? You seem to have a lot of free time."

"Yeah, they're not too happy this trip, as they aren't getting to charge enough for medical services. Someone's bound to sprain something on the waterslide. In the meantime, here. You may not feel like eating, but you should."

He had a massive room service tray and the whole works in his hands—the covered plate, silverware, a tiny flower vase.

I realized I was hungry, really hungry for the first time since I'd arrived. He handed me the flash drive and sat down on the chair by the balcony. I walked onto the balcony to keep his eyes away from the closet.

"There are a few shots on there you should see."

"Of Harriet?"

"I'll show them to you later. You should eat before it gets cold."

He got up and took off the room service lid to reveal eggs, toast, hash browns, and bacon. Oh God, no. Not bacon.

I heard the yelp of a gigolo imposter being nipped by a mythical creature, and tried to cover by dropping the serving spoon. Onto carpet. Needless to say, it was ineffective.

"What was that?" Doc said. "Is there someone in here?"

"Now you're the one imagining things. I didn't imagine Elliot Ness, by the way."

"I know."

He started to walk toward the closet. "Look, let me just check, because there have been odd things going on and I want to make sure you're safe."

"Don't be ridiculous." I moved in front of him. Right in front of him. I mean, I had to. And then my mouth was on his and his hands were in my hair and I didn't want it to stop. He moved his hand to my shoulder, then lower. My hips pulled towards his and the kiss got deeper.

Dammit, why did I have to have a "Peeping Ron" in my closet at this moment? Or a baby Howard? The longer the tiger was stuck in the closet with bacon in proximity, the more likely he was to yip again.

I pulled away before I wanted to. Way before I wanted to. And I think before Doc wanted to, too. "Sorry."

"No apology necessary. This is crazy. Eat your breakfast. I'll see you when we dock."

"Right. Thanks for, you know."

He nodded and left. I redid the chain.

The closet flew open. "First Aid kit," Brazil yelled, as Howard made a bee-line for the bacon. I snatched one piece and the toast and put the rest on the floor for him.

I dug into my purse for Band-Aids and Neosporin. "He's not rabid, is he?"

"No. You, maybe. Why did you let him in? It was moronic." He looked at his watch while he slammed a Band-Aid on the tiny bite marks on his hand. "Okay, here's the plan."

Chapter Thirty-four

Unfortunately, Brazil's plan involved Howard's returning to my Balenciaga. I still hadn't had the nerve to tell him the bad guys might recognize it, though if they did come after me they would have to tear it, and the tiger inside, from my cold, dead hands.

If I was transporting Howard, I needed to make provisions for him and for my vintage bag. A tiger had a slightly larger "carbon footprint" than a chameleon and he'd already left a few of those pungent "footprints" in the closet. Thankfully, I'd put all my clothes and shoes up on the wooden shelf for bedbug protection. Still. Bullet holes and cobra venom notwithstanding, there were some things a purse couldn't recover from.

I headed into the bathroom. Thank goodness he was still tiny, as I managed to fashion a diaper with a large make-up sponge, dental floss, and two crisscrossed shower caps. At least he was used to having his privates in a pouch. I leaned down, looked into his little eyes, and apologized for his impending humiliation. Then, using a combination of bacon, patience, and lightning fast kickboxing reflexes, I triumphed.

I figured I would let him run around and get used to his new look before cooping him up. I checked that the sliding balcony door was secure and pulled the curtain. I was too afraid to take a proper shower, but I sluished as best I could, put on my "onshore" outfit of a pale pink gauze tank top over a white poplin miniskirt.

Again, my nude heels were designed for this outfit, but I erred on the side of strappy white sandals. Stuart Weitzman, of course.

The room still looked like a chicken coop but I didn't have time to clean up. I called housekeeping to say I didn't need service. I didn't want Maria or the Koozer to have to deal with, or ask about, Howard's antics.

If it was the morning of the twenty-third in Tasmania, it was the night of the twenty-second in Bay Ridge. Smack dab in the middle of the ptomaine potluck. I trusted Eddie and Frank to make sure Mom and Aunt Helen made it through the yuletide ordeal. I would call later to see how it went. Then I remembered. It was Thursday. I had missed my weekly visit to Uncle Ray. I was sure, given his octopus-like network, he knew where I was, but it was the first time I'd missed a visit since he'd gone to prison.

I sat on the bed, fluffing feathers onto my outfit. Although I was really here because Uncle Ray had broken the law, part of me had to face that I'd also come because I was a coward.

It was true I didn't want to ruin things for Ma and Aunt Helen, and that Barry needed my help, but the real reason I'd jumped at the chance to flee was because I just couldn't stand the idea of a Christmas without Uncle Ray. So, I'd done a runner. It was selfish. As I used my mini lint brush on my behind, I renewed my vow to find the Manzonis, find Harriet's killer (and Elliot's), and save Howard, to make up for it.

I had two more things to do before I left the ship—check on Sister Ellery and ask Storr Bentley about the Manzonis. I wished I could leave Howard in the room, but it wasn't safe. And I couldn't have him jumping out of my Balenciaga and blowing our cover, either.

I put everything in my bag into various Tupperware containers, or secure pockets, then lay a towel over them. I dug out the seventh-grade friendship bracelet I kept in my purse for luck and loosened it until it fit over Howard's head. Then I tightened it just enough to stay there, tied it to a navy blue J. Crew sash, and tied that to the handle of my Balenciaga. At least this way, I'd have time to catch him if he bungee jumped again.

Then, the final indignity. I hated to do it, but I reached in my bag for a scrunchie. I petted Howard's head as I whipped it over his nose and mouth, hoping it might work as a gentle muzzle. I figured if it was soft enough not to break off sun-damaged hair, it wasn't going to hurt him. I hoped not, anyway. I looked around, grabbed the flash drive and my collapsible sun hat, then sat on the part of the bed with the least feathers. Howard scrambled up. I petted his head, secured his training pants, and patted the Balenciaga. He jumped in.

"Good tiger," I said.

Chapter Thirty-five

I could hear passengers in the hallway. I'd been on the boat for two days and I hadn't met any of my neighbors/potential clients. I guessed now wasn't really the time, given what was in my purse, so I waited until I heard four heavy treads fade away. I put the Do Not Disturb card in and Howard and I ducked out.

I went by Sister Ellery's room and tapped on the door. I didn't want to wake her if she was sleeping. No answer. I left a note under her door with my BlackBerry number and headed up to corner the Staff Captain. As I reached the elevator, I heard my name. Kind of.

"Cyd Gepetto. Would Miss Cyd Gepetto please report to the Staff Captain's office on Deck Eleven? Miss Gepetto." I felt Howard stir in my purse. Was this a passive aggressive, pre-emptive strike? Could Storr Bentley be Harriet's murderer? Technically, I could ignore the page, given the name snafu, but I needed to find out what he knew. I had to risk it.

When I reached Deck Eleven, I passed Margy, who gave a cheery wave. "Did you find a driver, sweetie?"

"Yes, I'm all set, thanks for the numbers."

"Great. I signed you up for dinner at the Drunken Admiral tonight. It's a Tasmanian tradition and it's right on the dock. You'll love it. Eight o'clock!" Her verbal exclamation marks were exhausting, but they were part and parcel of her job. She might be as tired of them as I was. As a person who worked in sales and service, I tried to be perky, but there was a limit.

I found the door which read "Staff Captain Storr Bentley." I'd left my purse slightly unzipped so Howard could breathe. His tiny nose was pushing the zipper open. "Howard!" I hissed. "Stay down, okay? It's not safe. Seriously." I let him sniff my hand, then pulled the zipper most of the way, careful not to snag the scrunchie and leaving just enough room for air and for the sash. I threw my linen scarf over the top of the purse and knocked.

"Enter," Bentley said.

I cracked the door. "Hello, sir. You paged a Cyd Gepetto, but I think you meant me, Cyd Redondo?"

He rose, stiff as a board. His face was red. "Hmmm. Redondo. That sounds incorrect. Are you sure that is your name?"

This was going to be torture. "Yes. I am sure of my own name. Sir."

He shrugged. "Names are unimportant."

"As long as you don't feel that way about navigational coordinates," I said, trying to lighten the mood.

"Ah. A joke. Harriet said you were humorous. Sit." It was like he couldn't speak without making it sound like a command. It worked. I sat.

I kept my Balenciaga on my lap and tried to pet/soothe Howard through the leather, as though I had a nervous tick. Now that I was closer, I could see that it wasn't so much that Bentley's face was red, as his eyes.

"So, Harriet mentioned me?"

"She did."

"You spoke to her on the first day of the cruise. How did she seem to you?"

"Angry," he said. "We argued."

Then he threw his head into his hands.

Oh God, was this a murder confession? My BlackBerry, with voice recording, was somewhere under Howard. So were my tissues. I reached over and patted him on the shoulder. He finally looked up.

"I loved her. You knew her. You know how wonderful she was. Too good for me, of course. She could never love me, I knew that. But to bring that man, that cretin, onto the boat, after everything. It was just too much."

"So. So, you killed her?"

"No!" He jumped to his feet. "You are appalling to suggest such a thing! You lower onto the ship in a most discourteous manner, you force me to see my beloved dead on the floor when I am in an official capacity and cannot show emotion, and now accuse me of hurting the person I loved most in the world? How dare you! Get out!"

"Oh God, I'm sorry. Wait! I apologize, Staff Captain. For all of it. I had no idea you two were, well, involved." Actually this was a lie. I guess once I met him I couldn't see it being true.

"So, she never mentioned me?" When men cried, it was either really fake or scarily real. As his outburst including gasping and snot, I figured it was real. It was like when nice people finally snapped and wound up taking someone out with their car. Apparently, when repressed Marine officers let go, they just unhinged all the way. I grabbed paper towels from the wall and handed him a stack. He took them without looking up.

"Harriet was very discreet." I eased back down so as not to frighten Howard. "In fact, she never even told me she'd been married. And her husband was on the boat? Who is he?"

"He's a monster." He gave a shudder, then started a sharp, hiccoughing sob. "A profiteer."

Wow. I didn't think I'd heard that word since *Gone With the Wind*. It was a good word.

"So who is he?"

"Butler. Pierce Butler."

No way. He was a profiteer and his last name was Butler? What were the odds? Pierce Butler. Wasn't that the name on the packages for The Fountain? Harriet was married to the man who ran The Fountain? Where all the seniors flocked when they went onshore? Where the Manzonis might have gone?

"Do you think he murdered her?"

"I thought it was an accident."

"I don't think so. I'm trying to find out. Do you want to know what happened? Really know?"

"Of course I do. It will allow me to kill the person who did this. People say Swedes are cold. I am not cold. I am a Scorpio." He looked up. I looked at my watch.

"Then can you tell me why you told Cabin Steward Nylo that he didn't have to worry about the Manzonis' things?"

He stared at me. "I was told they wouldn't be returning."

"Who told you that?"

"I do not recall. I will look back at my files. I have a request, as well," Bentley said. "You were Harriet's friend. I do not want her taken to this strange place alone. Will you assist me and accompany the body onshore?"

It was no more than Harriet deserved, though it was going to make my Howard handoff tight. "Of course," I said. "It's very kind of you to include me."

"I am going now to the morgue to see her moved and brought up properly," Bentley said.

Oh God, I thought. Esmeralda. "Would you like me to handle that? It could be very upsetting for you. You've been through enough."

He rose. "That is very thoughtful of you. Yes, I was dreading it, seeing her in that awful room. If you are truly willing, I will meet you on the deck."

Howard, please be asleep, I thought.

I needn't have worried. The Koozer was in the morgue. He'd stashed Esmeralda somewhere else, or she'd already disembarked for what I hoped would be an illicit romantic getaway. They were just lifting Harriet's coffin when I arrived at the door.

Doc was standing outside and shook his head when I tried to go in. "There isn't room. I made them promise to be careful." I wondered whether he'd checked the body before the move and noticed the new needle marks.

I'd grabbed a handful of one of the multiple flower arrangements in the lobby, and placed a small bouquet on top of the coffin. It was a sad procession, the Koozer and a contingent of what he had called "the Filipino mafia" stewards as uniformed pall bearers, the sad flowers on top, the noticeable odor of morgue, and the crunch and grind of the service elevator when the door opened.

Doc and I waited as the stewards went in, then squeezed in behind them. As the elevator jolted, the flowers went flying. Doc caught them and handed them to me, then leaned against me in a junior high move, which I appreciated.

By the time we arrived on the departure deck, most of the passengers were already moving down Macquarie Wharf. The ship had docked next to the peeling, wooden, warehouse-esque Cruise Terminal. The rest of the city, however, didn't disappoint, even from this angle.

Hobart had a charming harbor, with piers and wharves of various lengths fanning out from its center. I could hear the slap of fiberglass against wooden pilings, as fishing boats and yachts anchored and shivered there, amidst the restaurants and pubs. Hobart's equivalent of the food truck, a deep, squarish blue boat with a bright yellow banner, bobbed to my right, promising fish and oysters right out of the water.

The city itself started at the sea and climbed uphill all the way to Mount Wellington, which seemed close enough to touch. Stately Victorian buildings scaled the incline, stuffed beside harbor warehouses and newish restaurants and hotels with an excess of glass. Directly in front of us was the Hotel Grand Chancellor, where I had sent my favorite Tasmanian travelers. Dorcas, in sales, always helped me out. I would have to stop in and say hi.

I was obsessing over the scenery because I didn't want to think about Harriet in that box. We started down the ramp where Staff Captain Bentley, in full whites, stood waiting. He saluted then fell in with me, behind the procession. I replaced the flowers and he gave me a grateful look. Doc had run ahead to a waiting ambulance. He signed the paperwork and, as Bentley and I stood behind, the stewards lifted my friend into the back.

"I will take it from here. Thank you for your kindness, Miss Gepetto. And you, Doctor," the Staff Captain said, and climbed in.

It drove away without a siren. Howard was awake. I noticed his nose poking out of the zipper again, probably sniffing for wharf rats. I eased it back in when Doc wasn't looking and dropped in a piece of bacon I'd been saving in the outside pocket. It would help distract him from the rats and, besides, he deserved it. It was heartening to know his survival instincts hadn't been bred out of him.

I needed to find Brazil and get the thylacine out of my purse as soon as I could. How could I ditch Doc without looking suspicious? I decided on the Manzoni excuse. Which wasn't really an excuse. I needed to find them as much as I needed to get Howard, undetected, to safety.

"What happens now?" I asked Doc.

"She'll go to the city morgue."

"For an autopsy, hopefully?"

"If there's no evidence of anything but accidental death, no. They'll contact the family and, depending on their preference, will either deal with a funeral home here, or arrange to have the body flown back. The ship isn't equipped to deal with a body that's more than a few days old. Sorry," he said, "I know she's not just a body to you." The ambulance turned up the hill.

"Has this happened to you a lot? Bodies?"

"Define a lot."

"Every other cruise?"

"Not quite that often, but you're a travel agent, you know the statistics."

"Yeah," I said. "From my reading, two murders per five-day cruise is high."

"Cyd, I know what you think you saw. But last night you were pretty manic. And I talked to the department heads. None of them remembered an Elliot Ness."

"But you said there were pictures on the flash drive I should see. Isn't that proof?"

"That might be proof that he existed. But not that he's dead. The Captain was pretty upset that you'd even suggested it. I think she feels like you've been put on board to sabotage her."

"Oh, God no. Why would I do that? I'm all for female captains."

"She's had a hard time." There was something in the way he said it that made me wonder whether they'd been involved. Or were still involved.

"The pictures?"

"There are a few people looking like you described, having an argument. Near the railing."

Maybe Fredo really had pushed Sandra overboard, then had Nylo get rid of her things.

"I have to go," I said. "I'm going to check in with the Hobart Police and then meet the Manzonis' driver. Thanks for helping with Harriet."

"My pleasure," he said. "Sure you don't want company?"

"I appreciate the offer, but this isn't your problem." He looked down and I felt awful. "Are you going to the Drunken Admiral dinner?"

"If you are," he said. "Otherwise, I wouldn't be caught dead there."

"Well, that's an endorsement. I'll see you there, if not before." He gave me a look, but I could feel Howard wiggling so I started backing away.

"The police station is about four blocks up," he said.

I waved and headed down the dock. I passed The Drunken Admiral, which did in fact look like a tourist trap with its whitewashed brick, and elaborate, extended sign. I happened to look up toward the hotel and thought I saw the two thugs who'd been after Howard walking down the next wharf over. Brazil had said he thought there were three. Where was the other one?

And where was Ron Brazil? I couldn't keep carrying Howard in my purse. It was too hot, for one thing. He would need water and, although I didn't like to think about it, another diaper.

The Grand Chancellor would have a lobby restroom suitable for my needs. I'd just headed that way when someone grabbed my arm and jerked me behind a tattered warehouse.

Chapter Thirty-six

My years of self-defense, kickboxing classes, and brawls with my brousins had all been channeling me toward this moment. Of course, I didn't anticipate having the last male, and sperm, of a species in my purse, but my reflexes kicked in anyway, happily with my heels rather than my Balenciaga. I landed a half-round-house-strappy-sandaled kick right in my attacker's jaw, forcing him to loosen his grip. I turned, about to give him an extra kick in the balls.

"For the love of Christ! No!" It was Ron Brazil. I stopped mid-kick. Years of pummeling an imaginary Peggy Newsome in stilettos helped me keep my balance, as planned. He stumbled back and leaned against the wall. "That hurt!" His Travolta wig had spun sideways, creating Cousin It bangs.

"It was supposed to. Why did you do that? Why couldn't you just say 'pssst' like a normal person? You scared the shit out of me."

"I didn't want the shorts twins to see me."

"So what did you think I was going to do, blindly follow some random arm? I'm responsible for Howard."

"Is he okay?"

"He was until that. Let's see." I eased the zipper open and Howard's nose immediately popped out, then his tongue.

"Oh, thank God," I said. "Hi, Howard." I petted his nose, but kept the zipper mostly closed. I was a girl who learned her

lessons, at least most of the time. "Are you going to take him?"
He nodded. "In what?"

"That." He pointed at my purse.

"Oh, hell no," I said. "This purse and I do not part company,
ever again. Why didn't you bring a duffel bag or something?"

"Because I didn't want to look like I was carrying anything,
you nimrod." I wondered how old Ron Brazil actually was.

"Let's head to the Grand Chancellor. I'm sure they have a gift
shop. I'll go first, then you meet me in the women's bathroom
in five minutes."

I exited the alley as though entering it had been my choice,
then waited for the walk sign, crossed the busy street, and climbed
the front stairs of the hotel.

It was twelve stories high, boxy, and like most hotels, didn't
quite look like its professional photos. That didn't diminish my
relief at the possibility of entering a four star lobby restroom. The
lobby was hopping, full of tourists and locals having excessive
holiday drinks. You could feel the family tensions that would
explode two days from now, resulting in burned roasts, smashed
wineglasses, tears, and the lifelong emotional scars that went
with them.

The hotel had floor-to-ceiling windows looking out on the
harbor, with wreaths and fairy lights around them. Even the
berries on them looked exotic. Dammit, I wanted to see Tasmania. But for now, I'd settle for the gift shop. First, I headed
to Reception.

"Hi," I said, holding out my card to the receptionist, who
was too tired, or too hungover, to be perky. "I'm Cyd Redondo,
Redondo Travel. Is Dorcas around, by any chance? She's helped
countless times with clients coming to Hobart. I wanted to thank
her in person."

"She helped you, did she? How lovely. She's on vacation for
the holidays. That's why I'm doing double shifts."

When it came to other people, you never knew when you
were going to hit a landmine.

"Oh, how awful, you poor thing. Has it been insane?"

She nodded toward the bar, where two large brothers were shoving each other in an increasingly hostile way. "Those are the nice people. They're not staying here. People are so picky during the holidays."

"People are picky all the time in America," I said. "It's exhausting."

That finally got a grin. "I'm actually here on the *Tasmanian Dream*, I just wanted to wish Dorcas happy holidays. But I was going to ask her about shopping. I wanted something hardier than this for trekking around." I held up my Balenciaga. "Do you have any backpacks in the gift store?"

"A couple. There's a sporting goods store on Elizabeth Street, but the Market's going today, down in Salamanca. That would be the best place."

The Market. I couldn't let myself think about it yet.

I found a Hello Kitty school backpack, which seemed just ironic enough to throw people off, plus seeing a grown man with one should serve as a repellant. I headed into the women's bathroom. By the time Brazil showed up and it was empty, I'd already given Howard a drink and transferred his leash, his towels, his bacon, and extra "diapers" to the backpack.

"It's too sad to keep saying goodbye to him," I said as Brazil allowed me one last look. "Let's just say *au revoir*, Howard. Live long and prosper. That's the first time I've ever said that, much less meant it."

Brazil shook his head. I let him go first, then used the five "cover" minutes to fix my makeup. Then I headed for the Hobart Police Station. Probably my only stroke of luck in the last few hours had been to find out that my go-to Tasmanian limo driver, Gary, was the one the Manzonis had booked. Although it did disturb me that Peggy Newsome and I recommended the same one, I decided to ignore that particular worry. Gary was supposed to meet me outside the station in fifteen minutes.

The sun was higher and the cool morning air was starting to turn full-on Tasmanian summer. The complete change in season and time wasn't helping my headache or my looks. Between the hotel and the street I could already feel the humidity collapsing my hair and melting my eyeliner. I went over, for the fiftieth time, what I was going to tell the police so that they would take me seriously. I wanted a proper autopsy on Harriet before someone moved her to a funeral home, and I needed to find the Manzonis so I could find her killer. It was tough to figure out which thing to bring up first. As I agonized, I noticed tan-colored Uggs in a thrift shop window and passed The Hope and Anchor Tavern pub, "The Oldest in Australia," promising Captain Bligh ale, which seemed an unfortunate name if you knew your *Mutiny on the Bounty*.

The sky was clear, then cloudy, then crazy bright. The light here changed every three seconds. It felt like an optician's visit where they kept flipping the lenses back and forth. Clouds darting by completely changed the lights and shadows and transformed the air in a way that just flat out didn't happen under the industrial canopy of the Bay Ridge sky. It was a revelation to see what purer air might mean to the way you looked at things. I decided to appreciate it while I could.

I tried to refocus on my talk with the authorities. Should I point out the coincidences? The fact that Harriet had been asking about the missing Manzonis right before she was killed, and that as far as anyone knew, she didn't have any enemies? The fact that several other couples had gone missing, or at least missing temporarily, on cruises to Tasmania, specifically Darling Cruises? That Harriet was the ex-wife of Pierce Butler, who ran a spa and resort for seniors where the Manzonis might have visited, and was getting a huge shipment of pharmacy grade methadone? Maybe "resort" was a euphemism for rehab, but how many senior heroin addicts were there? And how many of those went on Christmas cruises?

Argyl Street was a mixture of Georgian and Victorian build-ings, so the Hobart Police Station stood out, with its seven stories of rectangular white concrete and its glass ground-floor window. The building was early utilitarian, but the Tasmanian government seal was ornate and beautiful and featured two Tasmanian tigers on either side. It gave me hope that it wasn't totally soulless inside. That lasted about thirty seconds when I saw the look on the woman's face who sat behind the desk. Her hair was brighter than might be completely natural, and she had gauged how much hairspray the climate required, then added more for good measure.

She checked out my outfit and sighed. "May I help you?"

"Yes, I hope so. Cyd Redondo, Redondo Travel," I held out my hand. She didn't take it. "I'm looking for two of my clients who have gone missing from the *Tasmanian Dream*. I believe their son, Barry, filed a missing person's report from the U.S.?"

"Randy!" she yelled at cheerleader volume into an intercom microphone, then gestured me to the plastic chairs against the wall, where she continued to stare at me. After smiling for an unnaturally long amount of time, I reached for the local papers to avoid her curiosity.

And there he was on the front page—Pierce Butler. The lead article featured a smiling man with light hair and a summer suit at a podium, holding a plaque. The headline read "The Fountain's Pierce Butler receives Tasmanian Humanitarian Award." The article went on to explain how Butler had revolutionized senior care and had just received a huge government grant for research on aging. Perhaps I shouldn't mention Pierce Butler as a possible murderer right away.

Before I could read more, I heard "Randy! Front!" There was mumbling, then footsteps, and a short, red-headed bruiser, about two inches taller than me, smashed through the door with a cheeky grin.

"A little courtesy, missie, if you please. That's Inspector Randy to you."

"That's dead Randy if the Chief finds out you and 'Inspector' Ed were wrestling again."

The officer straightened his clothes, brushed his hair off his face and gave her the finger. I guessed that particular gesture was international. The receptionist pointed at me and he turned. "Missing person," she said, then sat back down and opened her magazine.

He tried the grin on me, less effectively, and moved forward. "Who's missing? Not your husband, is it?" He winked. Really, winking at a bereaved person?

"My former in-laws. Cyd Redondo, Redondo Travel. And you are?"

"Randy."

"I know that, I heard her. You're an inspector? What does that mean?"

"Why don't you come back with me and fill out the paper-work?"

"There should already be paperwork."

"No need for hysterics is there, love? Calm down and just come with me." I gave a "rescue me" look to the woman at the desk. She rolled her eyes. I followed Inspector Randy down the hall. He grabbed a clipboard and gestured me into a tiny, unlovely room which smelled of Diet Coke and feet. He started to close the door.

"Could you leave that open, please, just to get some air in here?"

He shrugged and left it cracked. He pulled out a chair, and turned it around, so he could sit across from me with his legs akimbo. This was a fifth grade move and a favorite of Jimmy's. This guy had no idea the kind of trouble he was in if he started anything, since he left himself wide open for attack. I took him through the Manzoni part of the story. He shook his head.

"There's no file. If there was a file, I'd know."

I looked through my notes from Barry. "Well, the son said he spoke to a Chief Hanson."

"The Chief tells me everything." To his credit, he got up. He came back with his head down and a file in his hand.

"Maybe you were wrestling," I said. He shrugged then held the file out of my reach.

"Well, any news? Who's been investigating? Where have you looked?"

"The usual places."

"What does that mean? Are there regular places people disappear in Hobart?"

He looked at the file. "We've checked all the hospitals, all the accident reports, all the homeless shelters."

"Homeless shelters?"

"Well, if one of the geezers has an episode, sometimes they wind up there. Or in a church."

"Have you checked to see if they were on any flights out?"

He stared me. "What do you think we are, Interpol?"

"No. Is there anywhere I can check on private charters or anything?"

He dug through his papers and went off to copy a list of private boat charter companies. I wasn't sure whether I believed anyone had really checked or not. Was I going to have to recheck all these places myself? I looked at my watch. The driver, Gary, should be outside. I hoped he would wait for me. Inspector Randy returned.

"Here's our list of boats—I can't guarantee it's complete. Look, they're probably fine."

"They're in their eighties, they're in a foreign country, they don't have their cell phones, they're probably not fine. They might be dead."

"Don't overreact." If one more man told me not to overreact, I was going to. Big time.

"Well, has anyone else gone missing around here? Is there a kidnapping ring operating here?"

"This isn't America."

"Fine. Where's the Embassy?"

"Sydney."

"Well, can I at least have your card so I can call you if I find any leads? I am the representative for the family and a travel agent. I'm sure you don't want it getting around that people come to Tasmania and disappear."

"Well, that's hardly news, is it? That's what the English settled it for. To make people disappear. It's our specialty. Let me know if you want a beer?"

"Right, Randy."

I thanked the receptionist, who ignored me, and stepped onto bright street, and looked for a town car. A polite toot turned me in the right direction. I approached the car from the back and, given how the trip had been going, took a quick photo of the license plate number.

Just as I finished my photo, a tall man in an impeccable suit, dark hair gelled off his forehead, and the world's best poker face emerged with a sign in his hand which read "Ms. Redondo." I smiled in relief.

"Gary? Cyd Redondo, Redondo Travel."

"Lovely to meet you, ma'am. I appreciate the work you've sent me over the years."

"Cyd, please. My pleasure. I've only heard fabulous things about you from my clients." We were practically colleagues and I remembered about the front seat vs. backseat thing in Australia. "Where would you like me to sit?"

"I would be honored to have you in front, ma'am."

"Thank you. It does always feel weird to be in the back. Who started that anyway?"

"The British. It reinforces the class system and the oppression of the masses."

"Gotcha. We have that in America too. We just don't admit it."

As I settled in, my Balenciaga at my feet, Gary offered me a bottled water. "You've booked a private day tour. Do you have anywhere special in mind?"

"I did ask for you for a specific reason Gary. My former in-laws are missing. And I believe they used you for a private tour about a week ago, the last time the ship was in port. Fredo and Sandra Manzoni? Terrible dressers and probably wretched tippers too? Any chance you remember them? I'm hoping they're just still in Hobart and just decided not to go back to the ship, so I thought maybe you could take me where you took them, if you don't mind?"

He looked like he did mind. "You don't want to go to Port Arthur?

"Did they go to Port Arthur?"

"No. It's really worth a visit, if you have time, though."

"I would love to see it, but I need to follow their itinerary first, then we'll see how much time we have left, okay?"

He logged into his phone, then into his GPS. "I took them to New Norfolk."

Just as he started the town car, I jumped at a knock on the window. It was Doc.

I buzzed the window down. "Hi?"

Doc leaned in. "Day trip?"

"Yep."

"Solo?"

"That was the plan. Why?"

"Just wondered if you wanted company."

"It's kind of a work thing."

"I don't mind."

"It will be boring for you." His showing up vaguely creeped me out. Did he want to date me or keep me under surveillance?

He put his hand on the open window. "Look, you're looking for the same people Harriet was looking for. And you think she was murdered, right? I'm not sure you should be out on your own. No offense, Gary." They knew each other? Was this even more disturbing or not?

"None taken. It will be an additional hundred dollars, though, for another passenger. And for the threat of violence."

"Thanks a lot, Doc."

"I'll pay for myself. And any weaponry." Doc got in the back. Even though we were separated by a leather seat, his proximity was distracting. I could feel my cheeks heat up.

As we headed out of town, I turned to Gary. "Do you remember where you left them in New Norfolk?"

"Of course, ma'am. At the insane asylum."

Chapter Thirty-seven

"I beg your pardon?"

Doc laughed. "It's not an insane asylum now. Well, not officially, anyway." He and Gary shared a look in the rearview mirror. "It used to be. Actually, it was women's prison for the criminally insane."

Gary chuckled. "It's been what they call gentrified. You'll see. That's where we're headed. It's up the Derwent River, about half an hour out of town."

"Great. And, Gary? I know you're not paid to be a tour guide, but this is my first and possibly only trip to Tasmania, so if you'd like to catch me up on local history, I'm all ears." Doc and Gary rolled their eyes. "I saw that."

Still, they offered a few things as we headed down Elizabeth Street and back toward the harbor. Doc said the Tasmanian Museum and Art Gallery—a unique combo, in my experience—and the Maritime Museum were not to be missed. We passed the Botanical Gardens and headed out of town.

The rolling hills offered glimpses of beautiful colonial and Victorian buildings and some uninspired cookie-cutter structures. This pretty much seemed like the way the world was going. Something gorgeous and magical next to something soulless and hideous. It made me feel that Brooklyn wasn't as far removed from the rest of the world as I'd thought. This was comforting in a perverted way.

Gary explained that most of the historic buildings and sites around Hobart were originally prisons, asylums, or breweries, which made sense, given the island's history. The English had used Tasmania to deal with prison overcrowding, and to establish residency so the French wouldn't snatch it from under them. They used the convicts to construct the buildings and wharves. "Of course," Gary said, "they needed beer and confinement to make that work."

I spotted a triangular yellow sign with something black and plump on it. "What the hell was that?" I jerked around to keep it in sight.

"Wombat crossing." Doc shrugged. "They're low to the ground, so you have to be careful."

"I want to see a wombat before I die." If they needed a sign, it upped my odds.

As we traveled farther up the river, Doc and I share a few significant looks. I still questioned his presence. At least I had Gary as a chaperone. Then we passed a building that looked like a thatched English cottage, with a shiny, pointed cap on the top, like an upended ice cream cone, dipped in white chocolate. We passed another. I stared at Gary.

"Oast houses. For beer. Most of the hops on the island's grown out here. You know we make a mean craft beer."

"I've heard. So how do they work, anyway?"

"I'm a driver, not an engineer, love."

"As the hop dries, the moisture rises and it needs a way to escape. So it rises through those upside down funnel tops," Doc said.

"Why are they white? If they're for drying the hops and there's a hole in the top, what happens when it rains? Are there Oast umbrellas?"

Doc gestured to Gary, who threw out his hand. "Let's move on to New Norfolk, which we're approaching. Third oldest settlement in Tasmania. Settled when the Norfolk Island prison was abandoned. It had one of Australia's oldest pubs and its oldest Anglican Church. And our destination," he said as we rolled in a gorgeous valley, ringed by gentle mountains and cut in half by the river, "Willow Court, one of its most notorious asylums. Now a resort and spa."

He pulled up in front of an impressive complex. It had a central stone building in the Australian/Victorian style, then additions to each side and behind, with cast iron balconies and tin roofs and courtyards. I think even without the heads up, I might have felt its chilling history.

By the entrance, a subtle sign in white cursive lettering read "The Fountain Foundation." Underneath that were the words, "The Fountain of Youth is Respect."

Wow. Respect. Or maybe, methadone. This was the last place the Manzonis had been seen, the place that was run by Harriet's mysterious ex-husband, the waffle robe repository. I really hoped the Manzonis were in there, in waffle robes, right now.

We got out of the car. I turned to Gary. "Did the Manzonis mention why they wanted to come here?"

"Probably, but I wasn't listening. Certain customers, I tune out." I couldn't blame him. I'd made a job out of tuning the Manzonis out myself. "I didn't anticipate their fugitive status. I dropped them off right here, where you're standing."

"But they didn't want a drive back? They didn't arrange for you to pick them up?"

"No. They paid four hours and said they'd call if they needed me. They didn't call. The Fountain receptionist did. She said my clients were returning with friends."

"Friends? Where did they make friends?"

"Sauna? Sometimes it works for me. I reminded reception they needed to be back at the ship by five and had another cup of tea at the inn over there, where I have an arrangement." He pointed to one of the outbuildings with fresh paint and a porch. "After the four hours were up, I headed back into town."

"But you'll wait for us, right?"

He nodded, beeped the car locked, and headed for the inn.

"An arrangement," I said. "What the hell does that mean? Never mind, I pretty much know what it means."

Doc put his hand on my back. "You want to tell me exactly why we're really here, before we go in?"

I wasn't telling him anything else, in case he was keeping an eye on me. "To find out if the Manzonis ever left here, and if so, where they went. It doesn't really make sense that they dismissed Gary, does it?"

"It is a spa. They might have decided to stay."

"Let's see, shall we?"

We headed for the large middle building, passing signs with arrows that read "Hot Springs," "Relaxation Center," "Library," etc. It all looked well-organized and harmless, except for the asylum for the criminally insane vibe. "Follow my lead," I told Doc, as we walked up creaky wooden stairs and entered the airy reception area, dominated by soothing pastels and predictable Impressionist prints. Most baby boomers were imprinted with Monet's "Water Lilies" in their youth, I figured.

More soothing cursive pointed to Reception, where a serene-looking woman with a loose white updo and a long turquoise shift dress, smiled. "Welcome to The Fountain," she said. "I'm Marion. Are you here on behalf of one of our visitors?"

"Maybe. Cyd Redondo, Redondo Travel." If I started out acting like the Manzonis had disappeared here, I might not get maximum info. "I specialize in senior citizen travel. I've heard rave reviews about your foundation, so I'm considering putting it on my list of Tasmanian destinations."

"Are you listed with the Australian Travel Agents' Association?"

"No. I'm from the U.S. Brooklyn. I have a long-standing relationship with Darling Cruises. Even with strong recommendations, I feel a responsibility to my vulnerable senior clients to see the facility myself."

"It's quite interesting, what you did there." A tall man with thick gray/blond hair, a pink button down Oxford shirt, and khakis appeared. His accent was about as Oxbridge as it was possible to fake.

"Mr. Butler? I'm Cyd Redondo, Redondo Travel." Did he go a tiny bit pale when he heard his name, or did I imagine it? "I just read an article about you in the local paper. Congratulations on your research funding."

"Well, thank you, Ms. Redondo." He had a low, evangelical tone to his voice. He turned to Doc. "And you are?" He wasn't the only one waiting for this answer, since I realized I still didn't know Doc's first name.

"H.A. Mathis. I'm the ship's doctor. I believe we may have met before on board?"

"Ah, yes, I have been known to do a seminar or two for them, over the years. We may well have crossed paths. You see, Ms. Redondo, my research is all about the effect of the infantilization of senior citizens. If they are your focus, you must value them, and yet you called them 'vulnerable,' like children or at-risk youth. You attempt to screen their accommodations for them as if they are toddlers. You may feel it is caring, but it is insulting and reductive. Here at The Fountain, we treat seniors like the capable, competent, highly skilled, and experienced adults they are, rather than as creatures who need to be coddled. They make their own decisions, they are never talked down to."

It would have been nice if he'd treated me like a competent adult rather than a pre-teen as well, but I took his point.

"Yes. The Fountain of Youth is respect. Got it. I agree, Mr. Butler."

"Dr. Butler."

"Oh, I apologize, are you an M.D. as well?"

"I have a PhD in Gerontology."

Of course he did. "Well, I agree with you, they are tougher and smarter than any of us, but of course some of them are physically frail and I need to see whether the facility can handle any type of physical problem my clients might encounter while here. So, would it be possible for us to have a tour of the facilities?"

"May I see your AARP card? That's the American version of our ARPA, correct?"

"I'm thirty-two." Both he and Doc weighed that statement, damn them.

"Well, then I'm afraid not. We have a strict rule for employees, guests, and visitors, of a minimum age of fifty. That way, none of our clients are patronized and they don't have to feel self-conscious in the sauna, the pool, or elsewhere. It's horrible how modern culture judges older bodies."

"Yes, absolutely. But I can't recommend the facility if I haven't seen it."

"Well, that is your choice. Where did you say you were from?"

"Brooklyn," the receptionist said.

"Brooklyn? I believe we have a Brooklyn travel agent who does referrals already."

"Let me guess? Peggy Newsome at Patriot Travel?"

The updo woman ran her finger down a ledger, then nodded in agreement. "Yes! She's recommended a large number of clients. Is she a colleague of yours?"

"Peggy Newsome would recommend a tick farm if she got a kickback."

Pierce Butler moved forward and shook his head, as though to a three-year-old. "And again, see how patronizing your tone is, when talking of a middle-aged woman? Perhaps you feel threatened by her greater experience? Youth is a brief gift. It is not earned." No, it's not, I thought, but often a stiletto to the balls is.

I could feel Doc's hand on my arm. The phone rang. The receptionist answered it, then gestured to Butler. He gave a curt bow. "Lovely to meet you both," and backed into his office, closing the door.

I considered how to handle the receptionist. "I love the color of that shift. Did you get it in Hobart?"

"Actually, a day trip to Melbourne. They have the most fabulous clothes in Melbourne."

"That's what I've heard. Any chance you'd share the name of the store?"

"You know it's probably in my phone. Would you allow me a moment?"

"Absolutely." I turned the guest book around and took pictures of the last five or six pages as fast as I could. "Block her!" I hissed to Doc, who moved between me and the hallway.

I pretended I was finishing up a call when she returned. She handed me a card that read Christine's. "It's too expensive for me, really, but they have sales twice a year."

"Thank you so much. Just one more question and we'll be out of your hair. Could you tell me how long the Manzonis stayed here?" I spelled the name for her and told her the day they arrived. She did a quick look and I could tell by her face she was lying. "They must have taken a quick tour without checking in," she said. "It was nice of them to recommend us on such a short visit." She looked back toward the office, then set a smile on her face.

"Thanks, Marion. Give our regards to Dr. Butler." I shoved Doc out.

I'd just texted Gary when a figure sprung from behind the building. It had a pompadour. Ron Brazil stopped just behind a shrub and gestured to me. Doc hadn't seen him. I said I was running to the ladies' room and ducked behind the building.

"They're onto me," he said. "They're about four minutes behind. I'll try to distract them, but you have to take Howard. I'll text you when it's safe to meet up."

He lifted Howard out of the Hello Kitty backpack and handed him to me.

"Have you changed his diaper?"

"I've been running for our lives. Get the hell out of here!"

He put the backpack on and kept running toward the road. I patted Howard's head, rearranged the towel again. "Sorry,

Howard. You're going to have to be quiet even longer." I found a new scrunchie and eased it over his nose. He curled into my purse and I zipped it up.

Gary pulled up just as I returned. This time, I insisted Doc take the front seat and I slipped into the back, putting my precious cargo on the floor, where no one could see it wiggle.

"So, more sightseeing?" Gary said. Doc looked at me.

"Is there still time to get to the Salamanca Market before it closes?"

"Just. It's Christmas. Most of the vendors will stay late today."

As usual, the trip back seemed shorter. I developed a dry cough, just in case I had to cover for Howard. At one point, there was a thud. I hoped it wasn't a wombat.

I asked Gary to stop in front of the Grand Chancellor and told Doc I was going to run in and cash a few traveler's checks, then head to the Market.

"Want company?" Doc asked.

"No thanks, I'll be more efficient on my own. I'll see you at the Drunken Admiral?"

Gary rolled his eyes.

"I saw that." I got out, keeping my bag and Howard behind me.

"Let me know if you need a ride anywhere else?"

"I will, thanks, Gary."

I waved bye to both of them and ran for the Grand Chancellor lobby, eager to get Howard some water. For an animal activist, Brazil wasn't very nurturing. I stuck a mini water bottle into Howard's mouth as soon as I got into a secure stall. I was pretty much out of bacon.

As I held him, I worried that he didn't look so good. I hoped Ron Brazil would text me soon. With Howard securely back in my Balenciaga, I stepped into the lobby and saw the Unfortunate Shorts guys, enemies of all endangered animals, casing the lobby.

They must have figured Brazil handed Howard off to me

and followed the town car. Was there a back way out? I headed toward the underground garage, but one of them spotted me.

"Hang on, Howard." I ran out the side door, toward what, I had no idea.

Chapter Thirty-eight

I could practically feel the goons breathing down my neck as I ran down the hotel steps and considered trying to jump on one of the dozens of small boats in the harbor. Then, out of the corner of my eye, I saw a museum. Uncle Leon pinged into my mind. He knew someone there. I headed to the parking lot, serpentining, then ducked behind a Jeep. I heard footsteps go by—the wrong way. I pulled up the notes section of my BlackBerry, found Amanda Heep, taxidermist, Tasmanian Museum and Art Gallery, and made a dash behind a brick wall and into the sandy courtyard.

There was a sign for holiday hours—the museum was closing early. Damn. A security guard with the most contagious grin I'd ever seen was headed toward the entrance with a padlock. Careful of my Balenciaga, I slipped in before he got there.

"Happy Holidays! My name is Cyd Redondo. I'm looking for Amanda Heep. Any chance she's still here?"

"Maki, nice to make your acquaintance." He chuckled. "Our Mandy? She never leaves. Hold on a tick, I'll give her a ring."

"Great. Maybe I should I wait out of sight, so I don't confuse anyone?" I moved behind a rack of art cards in the gift shop while he picked up the phone. I glimpsed ugly shorts flapping outside the door. "You can go ahead and lock up if you want, I'd hate to disturb your schedule." I ducked down further.

He did. "You're too polite for an American. Canadian, are you?"

"I wish. We're not all bad."

The red-haired thug banged on the door. Maki pointed at the hours, shooed him away, then went back to mumbling on the phone. By the time he gestured me up the stairs, my pursuers appeared to be gone.

Ever since I'd read *From the Mixed-Up Files of Mrs. Basil E. Frankweiler* I'd wanted to be in a museum after hours. I wished I were on my own, without the weight of an entire species in my handbag, but I needed to hurry for Howard's sake. Maki walked me past Tasmanian devils, snakes, roosters, wombats, and kangaroos and straight into the Tasmanian Tiger Gallery. I gasped.

"They're something, aren't they? It's a feckin' tragedy what happened."

Howard wiggled. Could he smell his ancestors, or was he was just sick of being squished? I patted him through the red leather.

"So they're really extinct?"

"Enh. That's what they say. I say maybe, maybe not. You hear rumors now and then, spottings and such. Remote areas. We live in hope. It's our tiger you know, Tasmania's. Mandy's the one to talk to. Her mother lived in a zoo with 'em."

"You're kidding."

"I never kid. She'll be right down."

As soon as he disappeared I took a real look at the room. The full grown, stuffed thylacine in the middle looked fierce and hyena-like. Two skeletons with their jaws extended, showed what Howard's teeth would grow into. I was glad I'd met him in infancy.

There was a video playing of "The last thylacine in captivity." That's what they thought. The tiger, pacing back and forth in that tiny, confined space, was maybe the saddest thing I'd ever seen. Howard starting wriggling in earnest. I couldn't let him see this. He'd be traumatized for life. Then I found a picture of four babies, huddled together in a cage. They were the spitting image of Howard. I felt like crying and slumped to the floor to stop myself. In that moment, not even Ron Brazil aka Grey Hazelnut wanted to save Howard more than I did. My awe of what he was and what he meant, and my terror of letting him down shot up exponentially. How could I handle this responsibility all on my own?

"Ms. Redondo?"

A slight woman who might have been fifteen, if not for the laugh lines around her gray eyes and the dark circles under them, was at the doorway. Her hair was the same reddish brown color as mine, but perfectly straight and pulled back in a ponytail halfway down her back. She had better cheekbones. She was wearing a dark green smock with muck all over it, over cuffed jeans, boots, and a sleeveless blue cotton shirt. She looked like a cross between a fairy and a blacksmith.

It takes practice to rise from splayed despair to four-inch heels, but I collapsed on the floor a lot, so I managed to rise without killing Howard. My head popping up from behind the skeleton display must have startled her. She backed into a glass case and shook her head.

I came around and held out my hand. "Cyd Redondo. Redondo Travel. Thanks so much for seeing me."

She hesitated, then gave a solid handshake back. "Amanda Heep. Mandy."

"I hope you don't mind. My Uncle Leon gave me your contact info."

"Leon Redondo?"

"Yes. He said you were someone I could call if I got in a jam."

Maki poked his head in. "Everything all right, Mandy?"

"Yes, absolutely. You can lock up and go home, I'll take Ms. Redondo upstairs."

"Thanks so much, Maki. Happy Holidays!" He waved at me and ducked out. Amanda motioned me forward. At that moment, of course, Howard decided to do one of his keening things. She froze. I froze. She stared at my purse, which was bulging a little. I pulled it closer, Howard side in.

"Seasickness. I have no control over my bowels, apparently."
She was still frozen. "Are you okay?

"It's just I've heard about the Redondos all my life. It's like
seeing a mythical creature, I guess. I apologize." We were both
still aware of my crying, shifting Balenciaga. Then Howard started
pushing his nose against my Spanx.

"What do you really need?"

"Asylum," I said. "And bacon."

Chapter Thirty-nine

Howard let out a howl. Mandy jerked me toward the back stairwell. "Come on."

After a breathless three floors, complete with an extinct marsupial soundtrack, we arrived in her office, which was half diorama and half torture chamber. Partially finished animals stood amidst bits of feathers, fur, screwdrivers, and jars of tiny glass eyeballs. I grinned.

Mandy closed and locked the door. "It doesn't creep you out?"

"No way. My uncle used to take me with him to work at the Natural History Museum. It's one of my favorite places in the world."

"I did all my homework here, too. Please. Sit down." I grabbed one of the wooden spinning stools and she sat on the edge of her desk. She took a deep breath. "That really, really sounds like a creature that doesn't exist. So it can't be, right? Because if one did exist, no one would keep it in a purse. Would they?"

My purse leapt into the air. I barely caught it before it hit the floor. Howard was making it harder and harder for me to keep my promise.

"Can I show you something?" Mandy reached into the bottom drawer of her desk and pulled out a huge photo album. It was less dusty than the other books in the room. She wiped it off anyway and eased it open.

"My mum grew up in the keeper's cottage at the Beaumaris Zoo."

"The one in the video?"

She nodded, then pointed to a picture of a teenaged girl with a ponytail and a leopard on a leash. And there the same girl was, inside the thylacine cage. "She was the one who broke into the zoo to try to keep them alive. Later she became the taxidermist for the museum. That's how she met Mr. Redondo, at a convention in Paris. 1966. It was her first time out of Tasmania and she fell in love with, well, with Paris. She never got back. It was her one adventure. Here's a picture of her and your uncle."

It was a black-and-white snapshot. The two were standing with a group of undernourished men in glasses and worn suits in front of Montmartre, beside a peacock which looked real, but considering it was a taxidermy convention, might be stuffed. Mandy's mother sported an Audrey Hepburn bob and Uncle Leon had, as ever, a sharp-looking, tight-fitting suit. They were laughing and leaning against each other.

Of all the Redondo boys, Uncle Leon was the one who looked most like my late dad. Seeing him there in '66 made me realize my dad must have looked a lot like that when he married my mom. I got a knot in my throat. Amanda had the same look on her face.

"It always changes things, seeing them when they were younger than we are, doesn't it?"

She nodded. "So all of this is just to say, it's okay to open the purse. I fully understand the gravity of the situation. And my mother is watching me."

I examined the room. "Anybody else? Are there cameras in here?"

"On a museum budget?"

"Right. He's likely to be a bit of a mess. I had to improvise." I eased the zipper open and Howard's nose emerged, then his whole head. He yawned with his relatively enormous jaw. The scrunchie was long gone.

"Howard? This is Mandy. She's here to help us. Be good." He gave me a tiny nip and propped his paws up over the edge.

I looked at Mandy. She was crying.

She couldn't have been much of a crier normally, as there was no tissue box on her desk. I handed her the handkerchief that had belonged to Elliot Ness. She didn't need to know that.

Howard was halfway out, but still sitting in my bag. At least he seemed to like it there. She couldn't take her eyes off him. She reached across and grabbed my hand.

I spilled the parts of the story that were mine to tell.

"Ron Brazil? Are you sure he's legitimate? I thought I was up on all the animal warrior types. To be honest. Grey Hazelnut is the only person I know of who could possibly pull this off. But no one knows where he is."

Well, not no one. But I couldn't blow his alias, as much as I wanted to.

Howard climbed out of the purse, revealing my improvised diaper. I shrugged. "Desperate times."

I could tell she wanted to touch him, but gave him space to explore first. It made me like her even more.

"Can we get him a bowl of water? And anything to eat?"

As she put out the inside of a chicken sandwich, she stole looks at me.

"Your uncle told my mum, there were only boys in the family."

"Yeah, well there was, until I showed up. And ever since."

"Do you see him very often? Your uncle?"

"He lives with us. Him and his wife, my Aunt Helen."

"Oh. That must be nice."

"It is. Kind of." I got up to pace, worried that the bad guys knew I was in here. Would it be safer for Howard if I were parading my purse elsewhere? I asked her. She agreed and offered to stay with him.

"What about Christmas?"

"I hate Christmas." Amanda got out a spacious cage. "Acceptable?"

"I thought all your subjects were deceased."

"I've been known to rescue a few live ones." She brought out a blanket for the bottom of the cage and put his water bowl inside. Howard liked her. I admit, I was a little jealous. I gathered up my Balenciaga. It felt empty and a little sad.

"Is there a back way out of this place?"

Chapter Forty

Howard was safe, at least for now, but I still hadn't found the Manzonis and I still had too many suspects for Harriet's murder—I'd crossed off Storr Bentley, but added Pierce Butler. I needed something to clear my head.

I was three blocks from the Salamanca Market, famous for affordable opals. It was open 'til three every Saturday. I had an hour.

Perfect. I preferred markets late in the day, when sellers were more apt to reduce the price rather than have to cart everything back home. I arrived on the wharf to see plenty of white tents still standing. Last time I'd been in a market, I'd innocently, but stupidly, bought an ivory necklace. I wanted to be responsible today. I hadn't heard anything on NPR about "blood opals," so I donned my barter armor.

I moved down the first aisle, past grilling meat—I hoped it wasn't kangaroo—local honey and tea, hand-loomed scarves, and necklaces with silver so fine they seemed spun by a Tasmanian spider. Multiple stalls featured handmade stuffed animals—wombats and Tasmanian devils. And Howards. I froze.

Tasmanian tigers were everywhere—on magnets, tea towels, coffee mugs, coasters, and carved into cutting boards. Howard's ancestors might be extinct, but their image was very much alive. I hoped this boded well for Howard and his siblings, but the rampant commercialism made me happy that, right now, the last male thylacine was safely in the basement of a well-guarded, alarmed museum with a woman who understood exactly what endangered meant.

I was negotiating for a pair of drop opal earrings when I spotted a head of hair that not only screamed American, it bellowed Bay Ridge. In fact it was classic Sandra Manzoni.

My former mother-in-law always looked as if someone had poured a bowl of noodles on her head and then squashed it. It had put me off ramen for life. I could never comprehend why certain women worked so hard to make their hair do something that was not only alien to its nature, but ugly. There was nothing more desperate than a bad perm. Accept your hair, people. It's here to stay. End of story.

It had to be her. No one else had that hair, the leaning, breast-forward walk, the plumber-esque calves, and the lack of consumer control indicated by the ten shopping bags she was struggling with. I veered between relief that she was alive and absolutely fury that I had put Harriet at risk for someone's shopping spree. I stalked her down one aisle and two alleys, knowing she would not be happy to see me. I didn't think she'd actually scream, as she was too worried about appearances, but she was a fast waddler.

So, when she ducked into a store the size of a phone booth, I blocked the doorway with a deft placement of my Balenciaga. I watched her in the jewelry mirror. She wore a top featuring her cleavage, probably in hopes no one's eyes would descend to her muffin top or Silly Putty-colored leggings. I noted, for my own eventual menopausal self, that it was ineffective.

She cantilevered her cleavage toward the shop owner, who held out a particularly lovely opal necklace. "Are you looking for anything special, Miss?" Even in Tasmania, they knew the power of calling women of a certain age "Miss."

"Yes! Something that says 'Available!' 'Back on the market!' I just got divorced."

I tried to keep the gasp in, but it had a mind of its own. Sandra swung around and turned OxiClean white, completing her early Raggedy Ann look.

"You!"

I smiled at the shopkeeper. "Hello, how are you, sir? Please find something lovely for my former mother-in-law. She doesn't have many nice things."

If a look could slap someone, I'd have wound up in the necklace case. As it was, I took out my phone and snapped a shot of her horrified, furious face.

"That's for Barry." Before she started, I held up my hand, the only way to slow down a Manzoni. "He sent me, by the way. Once you were declared missing."

"What are talking about? I'm not missing. I'm right here."

"Yes, now. But you were missing enough for me to fly halfway around the world looking for you. Where's Fredo?"

Her shoulders fell. "I don't know."

I hit her arm. I knew it was juvenile. I didn't care. She was lucky I didn't punch her. "What do you mean you don't know?"

"He's not missing. He's just not with me. At the moment."

"So you're pretending to be divorced?"

"I'm not pretending."

"Right." The shop was so small, the owner didn't have anywhere else to look. "Fredo is her husband of forty years. They were on their anniversary trip before she lost him. Guess I better let her only son know about this." I reached for my BlackBerry.

She grabbed my hand. "Cyd, please."

It was the first time my ex-mother-in-law had ever used the word please with me. She was desperate.

"Perhaps it might be a good idea for you to buy me these opal earrings before we sit down and talk." Sandra Manzoni had gone out of her way to reinforce every insult my family had ever pummeled me with. I was not going to miss Christmas with them for nothing.

Half an hour later, I admired my new deep brown opal ear-rings—with flashes of purple, and turquoise—in the mirrored door of the Hotel Grand Chancellor, until Sandra arrived with my Jack Daniels and what looked like an anemic Cosmopolitan. "They don't even know what a Grasshopper is," she sighed. "And I could use one."

She sat down with a thud, rustling all her shopping bags. I sipped my bourbon. I needed to keep my wits about me.

"All right, spill."

"Fredo and I hate each other. We have for years."

"Everybody knows that. So?"

"So, we both turned sixty and we said, what are we doing? Let's split up so we can both find happiness before it's too late."

That seemed very evolved for them, but okay. "Fine. Classic mid-life, or in your case, late-life crisis. It happens. But why on earth would you go on a vacation together?"

"For cover. So no one would know. Nobody can know, Cyd."

"Of course people are going to know if you split up, vacation or not."

"No they won't. That's why we went to Guam."

"You went to Guam? Guam? Even I've never sent anyone to Guam. When?"

"Three days ago. You can get a quickie divorce there. We figured we'd cruise to Tasmania, fly to Guam, then get back on the next ship that came in. The Cruise Director knew all about it. She said she'd cover for us." She certainly had, the lying witch.

"So you went to Guam to get a divorce no one can know about? Why not just separate?"

"Catholic guilt."

"But if you don't get divorced, you don't have to feel guilty."

"Not about the divorce. Adultery."

"Oh." I took a longer sip of my bourbon. "I mean no. I still don't understand. Why?"

"Angie got pregnant. We wanted the baby to have proper

grandparents. Plus we couldn't upset Barry. He's been having a hard time."

"Well, that didn't work. He's tearing what's left of his hair out."

"Peggy Newsome said she would let him know we were extending the trip. She didn't?"

"She didn't. Barry stalked me at Chadwick's, asking for help. Why didn't you call him?"

"Something happened to my cell phone." Well, that part was true.

"That's not an excuse."

She took a sip of her own. "I thought he might hear something in my voice."

For a second I almost felt sorry for her. Almost.

"How is this going to work? You're going to go on living together?"

"We have separate bedrooms anyway. We'd come home. We'd know we were divorced. But Barry and Angela and their baby would think everything was the same as it ever was."

"That makes no sense, but putting that aside, how the hell are you going to keep dating a secret in Bay Ridge?"

"We've got that all sorted out. We'll only date people in Manhattan. He gets the East Side, I get the West Side."

I shot the rest of my drink. "But wait, Peggy knows about all this? Guam, the divorce? She arranged it?"

"God, no. That would be like putting an ad in the paper. She only did the cruise."

"Well, who booked you from here to Guam?"

"Fredo." Sandra up-ended her Cosmo and gestured for another. "It was all working until you. You always ruin everything."

"What exactly have I ruined?"

"I missed Barry's wedding. I didn't get my mother-of-the-bride dress, I didn't get to pick the cake."

"Best case scenario, the groom's mother doesn't pick the cake."

"And you never called me mom."

"You told me not to!"

"And I didn't get to glower over Mrs. Carpaccio."

"So this is why you hate me so much?"

"I don't hate you. You're a Redondo, so I'm never going to like you, but I don't hate you. It's because you weren't in love with Barry."

That stopped me. She was right. I was fond as hell of Barry, but I hadn't been in love with him the way you needed to be in love to make something last for more than three months.

"I thought I was."

"Any idiot could see you were just friends."

"Is that so bad?"

"Not so bad is not good enough for my Barry. He's a prince."

"Yeah, he is. Angela Hepler, though? She's awful."

"She's not going anywhere."

I thought about the Lanz nightgown and her terrible aim with the seven iron. "I guess you're right. I mean she has no skills."

Sandra shrugged, then did her breast-forward lean. "Cyd. Is there any chance you might consider keeping this a secret? I mean, I did get you those earrings."

"That was a start," I said.

Sandra and I came to an agreement about the Masonic Lodge's business returning to Redondo Travel and the Manzonis mounting a rehabilitation offensive for the travel agency's reputation, starting with letting my mother host Angela's baby shower. I had one final condition: I had to talk to Fredo and make sure he was okay, to save Barry's Christmas.

"Where's Fredo, really?"

"He's at this place called The Fountain. It's a spa. We went there together first and he liked it."

"But I was just there. They swore up and down they had never heard of you two."

"They're probably just protecting our privacy. They said our privacy was paramount. Fredo stayed to talk to that man, the handsome one."

"Pierce Butler?"

"Yes. About some hair treatments."

I rolled my eyes. "He fell for that?"

"Why do you think we're getting divorced? Mr. Butler mentioned some investment opportunities too." This didn't sound good.

"Call him. I need to be able to tell Barry you're both okay."

"I don't have my phone."

I reached into my bag, found it under some Tupperware, brushed Howard's hair off of it, and handed it to her.

She made the call. It rang for a long time.

"Fredo?" She sighed. "I don't care if you're about to go into the isolation tank. Peggy Newsome never called Barry, he thinks we're missing. Just say 'Hi, I'm fine' and you can float and bloat, until hell freezes over." She handed the phone to me. I never got a chance to identify myself.

"Barry? I'm fine, don't be a worrywart, it's not manly." Fredo hung up.

"Okay." I handed her back the phone. "Call your son."

"It might be the middle of the night."

"If he hasn't heard from me, he's not sleeping. Call. Now."

"What about my voice?"

"Your voice is fine and you're going to have to practice keeping it that way." I gave Sandra some privacy so she could lie through her teeth in peace, and finished off my Jack Daniels, worried that Ron Brazil had not been in touch. Where was he?

When my former mother-in-law hung up, I told her to pay the check. I still wasn't sure what to do next. I didn't want to go back to the museum until I had to, in case the thugs were still around. I checked with Mandy. She said all was quiet on the critical species front.

Sandra came back from the bar. "Do you have any cash?"

"You've got to be kidding."

"They said my credit card was denied. It's probably some dick move by Fredo, but it's the only one I have." She looked back at the bartender, who glared at her. "You owe me," she said.

"I owe you for what?"

"The earrings."

I gave a deep sigh and handed over my last emergency money. "This negates my promise of silence on the divorce." She hesitated.

I made her write out an IOU, then relented and gave her a twenty for emergencies. "Have you arranged berths for the two of you heading out on the twenty-fifth?"

"We paid for a round trip. Peggy said we could just jump back on the next one."

Peggy fricking Newsome.

"Well, you can't. This is a completely separate cruise."

"We paid for it."

"It doesn't work like that. Do you want me to see what I can do?"

"Would you?"

"Not for you. For Barry. Don't make me put a tracker on you, because I will."

"Where am I going to go? I'm landlocked," she said. In more ways than one.

I left with a newfound pity for Sandra, if she thought she was going to get another man, anywhere, much less the West Side, with that perm. Still, stranger things had happened.

I shook her damp hand. "Hey? What if one of you falls in love?"

"You don't have to be married to be in love. In fact, sometimes it doesn't even help."

She was right. I was still in love with Roger Claymore and I didn't even know where he was. I would keep her secret if I could. That baby was going to have enough to deal with, having a spoiled Junior Class Secretary as its mother, without geriatric divorce trauma too.

Go with God, Sandra, I thought, or in this case, go with Guam.

Chapter Forty-one

I'd given Sandra the last of my cash and at the rate I'd been tipping, I'd need hundreds more for the rest of the trip. With unknown assailants after me, I was too vulnerable at an ATM.

I always carried at least three hundred dollars in traveler's checks in the bottom compartment of my purse, where I also found an Australian ten dollar bill. I used it to buy a double shot of bourbon for the hungover receptionist. She dumped it in her coffee and gave me the cash I needed. When professional courtesy failed, try alcohol. Then shoes. I was happy in this case that it hadn't gone that far.

I also got Sandra a bad room at the hotel, right beside house-keeping. It was the holidays, what can I say?

Now, I had just over an hour to try to figure out what was going on before I had to meet Doc at the Drunken Admiral. The Manzonis were alive. At least I could check that off my Christmas list. But I still hadn't convinced anyone that Harriet's death was a homicide. Maybe it wasn't. Dr. Paglia was the only person who could put my mind at rest, if he wasn't down five hundred by now. I looked up his itinerary on my BlackBerry, then made a stupidly expensive international call to Atlantic City.

"Trump Taj Mahal, this is Aaron from Winnetka."

"Hi, Aaron. Cyd Redondo, Redondo Travel. May I have Dr. Paglia in 1571 please, and if there's no answer, can you come back to me?"

"Absolutely." The phone rang and rang. I tried not to think about how much it was costing. Aaron came back.

"Any chance you could page him in the casino?"

Another fifty bucks in telephone charges and two times through the extended version of "The Morning After" later, I heard a familiar growl.

"Hi, doll. I was gonna call you. I just got the labwork back a couple of hours ago."

"But you were up at the time?"

"Naturally. Now I'm down. So much for the holidays. Your friend, was she in rehab?"

"Not that I know of. I highly doubt it."

"Well, she had a crazy amount of methadone in her system. It's not really used for anything else. I can't be sure it was the cause of death because I don't have the body, but from the amount of blood around the wound, I'd still say she was dead before the head wound. If she had a methadone overdose, that would make sense. First one of these I've seen though."

"Methadone? You're sure? Can you tell which brand?"

"Yeah, that pops right up on the vial."

"Don't be a smart-ass. I'm serious. I saw a box of Dolophine in the hold. The ship's doctor said it was a brand name for methadone."

"Can you link the box to your suspect? Methadone makes it suspicious, but as I said, your nail polish blood container isn't admissible."

"Can't you make a call to the coroner's office here and ask them to do a proper autopsy? Don't medical examiners have a secret code for something's fishy?"

"Yes. It's called vodka. Your best bet is to have a next of kin request it. Sorry, kiddo."

"Thanks so much, at least I know I'm not crazy. Hope you win big."

"From your mouth to, well you know. Hey, by the way, who took your mom's picture for Catholic Blend? She looks hot."

"You're on Catholic Blend?"

"I'm a fifty-five-year-old man who looks sixty-five. I'm on everything."

"Bullshit. You don't look a day over sixty. Love you. Merry Christmas."

I needed to call my mother or at least get my IT guy to take her "hot" Catholic Blend profile down. But family obligations would keep her occupied for the next couple of days, so Pierce Butler was my priority.

As Harriet's ex-husband and a pillar of the community he might have pull with the M.E.'s office. Then I remembered that the methadone I'd seen was addressed to him. Had he killed Harriet? How contentious was their breakup? Certainly Margy had sounded shocked that Harriet was seeing him, and Harriet herself had lied to me about it. And he did wear khaki, I thought, remembering the tiny piece of fabric caught on the balcony I'd sent off to Frank.

But still, why kill Harriet? Why would a person so visible in this world do something so risky? Jealousy? Could she reveal a secret he wanted kept? Did it have something to do with The Fountain? I had been so sure her murder had to do with the Manzonis' disappearance, but if they were fine, it couldn't, right?

If Butler were the murderer, asking him to request an autopsy might get me killed too. Still, he wasn't the only suspect— no one could actually confirm he'd been on the ship. Since the door to the cargo hold had been open, as had the box of Dolophine, pretty much anyone on the crew could have gotten to it.

What would the killer need? A syringe? Did the drug come in pill form? Could you put methadone in soup or a hot beverage? I would have to ask Doc. Maybe now he would talk to the Hobart Medical Examiner. Except then I would have to tell him that I'd gone behind his back and taken the blood sample. That didn't seem smart. I looked at my watch, hoping Howard and Mandy were safe. I had another half hour before I needed to meet Doc.

I decided to look at my photos of The Fountain guest book. If Butler was involved, maybe there was a clue there. I still didn't know why every guest had a number circled beside their name. I grabbed the printout of Harriet's email and looked at the numbers again. What did the Captain's Table have to do with The Fountain? Why did Harriet want me to have this code?

I found the Manzonis on The Fountain sign-in sheet. There was a "two" circled by their name. What did that mean? And then I saw a name that made my blood run cold, someone who'd checked in not fifteen minutes before Doc and I'd been there: Sister Ellery Malcomb. She hadn't been asleep in her cabin, she'd been on her way to the methadone spa. And she was, apparently, a "four." Dammit. Why didn't she tell Brazil she was going?

I thought about the Captain's Table photos. The Manzonis had dined at the Captain's Table. So had Sister Ellery. I wondered whether the other couples who'd gone missing had too. But what could that have to do with anything? I pulled up their names on my BlackBerry. The first couple was in the guest book from two weeks ago. There was a "three" by their name. But that was as far back as the pages I'd photographed went.

I didn't like the idea that Sister Ellery might be there. Since the desk clerk owed me, I had her find the fax number for The Fountain, and then send a quick fax from me, addressed to Sister Ellery care of the spa, saying I hoped she'd had a good day and I was looking forward to seeing her at eight at the Drunken Admiral. At least they'd know I knew she was there, in case anything strange was going on.

I understood why detectives had a sidekick. They could talk all their crazy ideas through and have assistance for things like breaking into The Fountain for the rest of the records. It was time to meet Doc. Maybe I should reconsider him for the position.

The restaurant was just across the street. I stopped on the hotel steps and looked at the harbor. This time of year in Bay Ridge, it got dark around three in the afternoon, so I wasn't used to the combo of Christmas lights and daylight both bouncing off the water. It was gorgeous, with no snice in sight. No thugs either, as far as I could tell, though I looked both ways about fifteen times as I crossed the street and walked onto the wharf.

The Drunken Admiral was the sort of place you passed and told your friend or family member, "we have to go there!" The long, whitewashed, three-story stone building had a fourth story jutting up just at the end. The square, wooden windows were trimmed in a weathered Chinese red, and above the door a painted wooden torso of a sailor in a blue jacket and tri-cornered hat saluted to everyone and no one. Flanking the massive oak door were a black cannon and a black cauldron, large enough to boil several children, or a hell of a lot of grog. With the thick, jet-black antique serif font sprawled across the building (I printed a lot of brochures, I knew my fonts), the overall feeling was comic and a bit sinister.

I was going to inch open the door, but it weighed about eight hundred pounds. I had to shove it with my hip instead and stumbled into what I could only describe as a room where Disney's "Pirates of the Caribbean" ride and one of the more upscale Red Lobsters had been shackled together in the belly of a nineteenth-century ship.

If you adored rust, men in yellow fisherman slickers hiding in barrels, unsubtle painted joke signs, and a skeleton skittering back and forth at the helm, the Drunken Admiral was the place for you. Massive platters of fish, oysters, and lobsters passed by, garnished with muskets and rusty keys. This was the place to take your nephews for their ninth birthday, if it weren't so expensive. I was glad my trip was all inclusive.

"Can I help you, matey?" a pert blond woman yelled. "Just kidding. We don't have any tables until two weeks from Friday, but you could eat at the bar."

"Thanks. I'm from the *Tasmanian Dream*? I think we have a reservation or something?"

"Oh, absolutely. They're in the back, just push on through. Mind your head."

As if I weren't doing that already.

I elbowed my way through the four-deep crowd at the bar. It was not a place where you could make a quick getaway, I thought with a shiver of panic. It was too late to tunnel out, so I kept going until I parted the passengers around Margy.

She had her hand on the shoulder of a handsome, oversized white-haired man in a billowy yellow linen shirt which hinted at his beer belly. He was sitting with Mary Lou and Jack, my British friends from the Captain's Table. The man threw his hands in the air at the end of whatever story he was telling. Everyone laughed. Mary Lou gestured me over and introduced me to Cal Langston.

"Cal is the friend we told you about. He's flying to Sydney tomorrow for the yacht race."

We exchanged a mutually impressive shake. "That's so fabulous, Mr. Langston."

"Cal, please. Have you been on a lot of boats, Ms. Redondo?"

"Call me Cyd, please. No. I actually don't know how to swim, so it would be like booking a ski vacation when you didn't have health insurance."

"But worse." He grinned. "I bet you'd do okay if someone just threw you in. You look like a scrapper."

"I'm scrappy as hell, Cal."

"I'll bet you are. You could come with me, you know, give up this whole tourist business and fly to Sydney with me."

"That's a very generous offer. But I'm looking for a friend of mine and can't really abandon her. I may take you up on your offer someday, though."

"Good. If you fall overboard, just give me a ring and I'll swing by and pick you up." He handed me his card. Everyone laughed. I tucked his card into the "dry bag" I kept in my purse in case of hurricanes or puddles. It had been too small for Howard.

"Margy, have you seen Sister Ellery? I thought she was going to rest today, but then I heard she might have gone to The Fountain."

Margy frowned. "She must have done a private ride hire. I'm surprised. Ron has a problem with Pierce Butler. I'm sure he wouldn't be happy to hear that."

"Have you seen Ron?"

She shook her head and handed me a small printed menu. "Pick one from each category and order at the bar. The lobsters go fast."

"Thanks." I said my goodbyes to the table and went in search of Doc. But it wasn't until I stood on a chair that I finally spotted him, talking to Lisa Callahan, the Captain's hostess.

Were Doc and Lisa an item? If so, why was he blatantly flirting with me? Maybe I should "mind my head," as the perky blonde had said. But the Koozer was sure CT meant Captain's Table and Lisa was in charge of that, so I stuck out my elbows and headed into the fray. She saw me coming and arranged her face into a cruise-worthy smile.

Doc gave me a real one. "Hungry?" He held out an oyster. Fine, I thought, torture me. I tossed it down without incident and took a second one.

"Hi, Ms. Callahan. It must be nice to have a night off from hosting."

"We're always hosting, even here."

"Oh, of course you are, sorry."

"Let me get you both a drink. House specialty okay?"

"Perfect, thank you."

I watched her make her way to the back bar. "She hates me, right?"

Doc laughed. "She likes me and I like you, that's all. How was your afternoon?"

"Complicated. You haven't seen Sister Ellery or Ron, have you?"

"No."

"She was on The Fountain register. Weird, right? I'm a little concerned about her. She doesn't have a cell phone."

"Let's get out of here, it's too hard to talk." I still wanted to talk with Lisa, but this probably wasn't the place. Then she arrived with our holiday drinks and it was rude not to share them with her. Once we'd knocked them down, Doc cleared a path for me and we made it out to the wharf.

Just then, my BlackBerry beeped with a text from Mandy:

SOS

"Shitfire," I said. "Hang on a minute." I walked away and called her.

"Howard doesn't seem well. Really listless. He's panting a little. I'm not sure what it is. He might just be dehydrated. I've tried to make him drink but he won't. Have you heard from Mr. Brazil?"

"No."

"I know it's too risky to call a vet, even if I could find one tonight. I'll see if I can find any info online."

Doc was watching me. "Mandy? Hang on. I'm on my way."

She gave me the code for the basement door. I walked back to Doc.

"Hey? The vet thing. Was that a joke? Seriously? Was it?"

He looked down. "No."

"You're a vet? A real, qualified vet?"

"I went to medical school too, most of it. I'm sorry, the cruise line doesn't encourage honesty in this situation." He looked up, ready for a slap or something.

"No. No, it's great. Theoretically, if a young, dog-like animal is listless, is that normal?"

"Dog-like?"

"Yeah. Dog-like. Just no energy. A little panting."

"I can't really say without an exam, but it sounds like dehydration." Of course, the one thing my Balenciaga didn't have. A water fountain.

"That's what we thought."

"Who is we?"

"It's not important. Do you just give it more water?"

"Usually by that stage it needs an IV of fluids. What is this about? Have you acquired a pet in the last few hours?"

"Sort of. I can't really explain. I just need your help."

"Well, I have all the stuff on the ship. Do you want me to get it?"

Howard, and any potential offspring he might have, were my responsibility. If it were a choice between Doc knowing or Howard dying, I'd pick Howard every time.

"Yes, get it. Please. And bring a blindfold if you have one."

Chapter Forty-two

"Okay, put this on," I said. We were standing outside the basement door of the museum. Doc had a proper doctor's bag. Or maybe it was a proper vet's bag.

"Cyd. I already know we're at the museum. Are you really expecting me to put an IV in a small, dog-like creature with an eye mask on?"

I considered his point. "I have to think about it. Wear it for now."

I took his arm and helped him up the first three stairs. He promptly tripped.

"Sorry. Are you okay? All right, we'll put it back on when we get there."

We got to Mandy's office door and I put the eye mask back on Doc, then knocked.

"It's Cyd. Don't open the door yet." I could hear her moving toward it. "Is he better?"

"Not really." I could feel her stress through the door.

"Okay. I've got a vet with me. He's blindfolded. Should I bring him in?"

There was a long silence. Footsteps moved across the room, then back. Mandy eased the door open and evaluated Doc, who, even I had to admit, looked pretty silly. He'd forgotten the blindfold, so I'd resorted to the signature brown-and-white-striped Henri Bendel sleep mask from my purse.

"Hi," Doc said. "I have no idea what is going on, but if there's a sick animal in there and I can help him—it's a him?" We nodded, forgetting he was blind. He waited.

"Yes," I said.

"I feel compelled to help him. It's that Hypocritical Oath thing, Cyd."

Mandy gave me a questioning look. I nodded. She opened the door. I helped Doc in. I could hear Howard doing tiny little pants. They made my heart hurt. I ran over and put my finger through the cage. He looked at me, but didn't move.

"Is there any way you can tell one of us what to do?"

"I'm a taxidermist," Mandy said. "I'm pretty handy."

"I'll bet," Doc said. "You'll be a great assistant, but if you've never put in an IV on an animal, do you want to take that chance?"

I had a flash of splattered thylacine blood on the half-finished emu. "Okay." I took the eye mask off and put it back in my purse.

Doc moved toward the cage. Then stopped.

"Bugger me. Is that a...I mean what the hell?"

We nodded. "Don't ask," I said, "just help him. His name is Howard."

"Cyd, seriously. If I'm right, that's not a dog-like creature, it's a marsupial, so it's more kangaroo and possum-like. That might make a difference in treatment."

"It's marsupial-like."

He sank into the nearest chair. "I don't know if I can do this. What if I mess up?"

"Like you said, better you than us."

Mandy had a sink where we could all wash up and everyone decided, since Howard knew me best, I was the one who should hold him while Doc delivered the fluids. I would have to keep my eyes closed, so my needle phobia didn't end the species with inadvertent crushing.

Poor Howard. I understood why Mandy had been concerned.

He could barely hold his pointed head up. I'd dragged him around in a pocketbook. This was all my fault. I picked him up and held him to my chest. For the first time, he snarled. He really didn't feel well.

"I'm so sorry, Howard."

Doc let Howard get used to his smell before he started his examination. "It's going to be fine, Howard. I'm going to make sure it doesn't hurt. You'll be fine, you've already survived that purse of hers." I fell in love with Doc a little just then. "I think it really is just a lack of fluids. He seems fine otherwise. This should fix him up."

Mandy and I let out the breaths we'd been holding in. Doc got out the equipment and was just sterilizing Howard's little front leg, when my phone beeped.

Mandy held up my phone. It was Ron Brazil.

"Crap." I was really hoping we could get Howard back on his feet and back into my purse before Brazil found out any of this. With any luck, he was far away. I stroked Howard's head with one hand while I took the phone with another.

"Finally. Where have you been?"

"Trying to steal a boat. Everyone has security now!" I pulled the phone away from my ear and Doc and Mandy heard cursing, then "What the hell have you been doing?"

"Trying to keep Howard away from the guys who were following me. I'll be very happy to get him safely back to you."

"Good. Buzz me in."

"What?"

"I'm downstairs. At the back entrance."

"How the holy hell do you know where I am?"

"I dropped a GPS in your purse."

"What?"

"Trust no one. Unlike you, I'm a professional." I missed being able to slam down phones. Tapping a keypad was just sad. And unsatisfying.

"Who was that?" Doc put down his swab.

"How long will this take?"

"About an hour," Doc said. I couldn't stall Brazil for an hour. My phone was already beeping again.

This was just getting worse and worse. Now Doc would know Ron Brazil wasn't a gigolo and Ron Brazil would know Doc wasn't a doctor. Well, at least mutually beneficial blackmail was a possibility. We had to help Howard. There was nothing to do but face the music. Even if it was Philip Glass music. I handed Howard to Mandy.

"He has a temper," I said. "I'll go get him. It'll give you time to hide anything that's breakable." Mandy gestured around her. The whole room was breakable.

As I made my way back down the stairs, I hoped at least Ron could tell me Sister Ellery was okay. I was emergencied out for one day.

I cracked the door. "Have you lost those guys?"

Brazil was in all black, including a balaclava bunched over his pompadour wig. "Do I strike you as a half-wit?"

"No comment." I opened the door.

"He's here?" I nodded. He punched the stairwell wall. "Why?"

"It's a long story. There have been some complications."

"I don't like complications."

"Bullshit. You live for them," I said. I talked as we headed up. I'd only gotten to the part about resorting to Uncle Leon's "contact" for help when we got to the office door.

"But she doesn't know, right? She hasn't seen him? No one's seen him?"

I sighed. "Like I said, there have been complications. Don't throw anything, you might scare Howard." I opened the door.

Ron Brazil took in Mandy, Doc, the IV bag, and the medical supplies. He shook with fury, his bow legs trembling like two terrified apostrophes.

With those legs, the disguise was useless. Doc would know exactly who this was.

To Ron Brazil's credit, he started in a low voice. "This was a sacred, vital, and above all, secret mission. Do you not understand the concept of secrecy? How difficult is that, really? I leave you for a few hours and you turn a solo assignment into a bloody book club! I was right. You ruin everything!" He reached for a jar filled with tiny eyeballs and I barely got to it before he did.

"Hey! Ron!" Doc held up his hands. "It is you, Ron, isn't it? This animal is seriously dehydrated. He could die in the next hour if we don't get fluids in him. Cyd's just trying to keep him alive. She's tried to keep the secret the best she could. She even tried to make me put in the IV with a blindfold on. None of us are going to say anything. We understand what the stakes are, okay? Now will you let me help him?"

Brazil walked over and looked at Howard. He let out a long breath. "You can do something?"

"If you'll let me. Cyd?"

I sat down and took Howard back in my lap. He felt even lighter. I kissed him on the head and held him by the belly while Doc took him by his paw and prepared the needle.

"Hang in there, Howard, this might sting a little, but you're a fricking tiger. It's nothing for you." To distract myself, I groped for social niceties.

"Ron this is Amanda Heep. She is the taxidermist at the museum."

"Taxidermist? Oh my God, woman, they're murderers. Taxidermists are murderers!"

I looked at Mandy and rolled my eyes. "You're an idiot. I live with one and he's a pussy cat. Plus, Mandy's mother took care of the Tasmanian tigers in the Hobart Zoo, she cried when she saw Howard, and she saved all our asses today. Mandy, this is Ron."

"No, it's not," she said. "It's Grey Hazelnut."

This time I wasn't close enough to save the eyeballs.

Chapter Forty-three

Howard yelped, which I hoped meant he was closer to his old self. When the tiny eyeball marbles stopped rolling, Brazil lunged for my throat.

Mandy stepped in the way and grabbed his arms. "Stop! She didn't tell me. I knew Grey Hazelnut was the only person who could possibly pull this off. Besides, I've seen you before. I was at the echidna protest. Don't worry, you're my hero."

Brazil slumped into Mandy's desk chair. "I can't even steal a bloody boat."

"I have a boat," Mandy said.

An hour and a half later, Howard was his old self, pacing the length of the room and ferreting out the last shreds of bacon bits from my Balenciaga, and Doc had given Brazil a special powder to mix with Howard's water for the next few days. Though we wanted to help make sure Howard made it to the island, two people were less conspicuous than four, so Brazil insisted Doc and I say goodbye to Howard and let them head to Maria Island on their own.

"What should I tell Sister Ellery? If I can find her?"

"What do you mean, if you can find her?"

"She went to The Fountain and I haven't seen her. Have you talked to her?"

"No. How could you let her go there? That creep Pierce Butler is a con man. Watch out for him. Can I trust you to find her while I do this?" He started to pace. "Of course I can't. You'll just screw that up too. Do I have to do everything?"

"You think I can't handle that pompous preppy ass?"

I was about to deliver a roundhouse kick to his head when he started laughing.

"Pierce Butler's a dick but you're right, he's no match for the AntiChristine." Mandy and Doc stared at each other. "Tell her to wait for me in Sydney. Time to go."

Mandy and I had only known each other for a few hours, but it had been an intense few hours. I couldn't cry. That would be ridiculous. Still, I felt a strange kinship with her, and Black Friday sales-level gratitude. How could I ever repay her for what she'd done for me, and more importantly, for Howard and his whole species?

My response felt totally lame. "Sorry about the eyeballs. I'll get Uncle Leon to send you some." She didn't strike me as a hugger, but I tried.

"Anything for a mythical Redondo." She hugged back. I was right, hugging was not her strong suit. "Hey," she said, moving to her desk, "any chance this might make it back to Brooklyn in one piece? I'd love for your Uncle Leon to see it."

She lifted a tiny, exquisite stuffed hummingbird with a shimmering green chest.

"Absolutely," I said. I'll make sure it does." She bubble-wrapped it and lowered into a sturdy box. I put it in my purse. "He'll love it. And thank you. Really." I handed her my card. "If you ever need travel help, or come to Brooklyn, you'll let me know, right?"

Brazil gestured to his watch, then the tiger.

I squatted down and looked at Howard—magical, mythical beast—with his long face and stripes that could have been drawn on with a calligraphy pen. He gave me a particularly nasty nip, then, for the first time, licked the bite on my hand. I did tear up then. I couldn't help it.

"Good tiger."

I was loathe to let him out of my sight, but if there was anyone who would fight to the death for him, it was Grey Hazelnut aka Ron Brazil. He scooped Howard up and gave Doc a grudging nod.

"Thanks for the privilege, Brazil."

"I'm glad you know that. People are a dime a dozen. There's only one of him."

Brazil was right. There was only one Howard, the hope for a whole species in a world which didn't seem to care what disappeared, only about how much profit they could make for what was the most rare. God, I hoped they made it okay and, as scandalous as it sounded, I hoped Howard had lots of little thylacine babies with his two sisters.

Mandy waved goodbye, then followed Brazil.

As the door closed, Doc put his arm around me and I turned my face into his chest, so he wouldn't see me crying. He let me stay there awhile, then pulled me around to face him.

"Hey, no one may ever know it, but tonight, you're the most important and beloved woman in Tasmania."

"As long as I get on a magnet," I said. "Tea towels are impractical."

He brushed my tears away, then put his hand on my hip. "Want to play night at the museum?"

We didn't get very far. Before we were one landing down, Doc had my hands pinned above my head and was kissing his way from my forehead down. With the day I'd had, I didn't have the strength to resist him. Who am I kidding? I didn't want to. I was still in love with Roger, but he hadn't trusted me enough to tell me the truth. Doc might be lying too, but he had saved Howard, at least. When he got to my mouth, I insisted he stay, tangling my fingers in his hair and pressing my lips (and everything else) against him. When I couldn't breathe anymore, I let him continue down. He'd just gotten to my clavicle when his beeper went off.

"Are you on duty?" I gasped.

He pulled back, I'd like to think reluctantly, looked at the beeper, then called in. "I'm three minutes away." He grabbed my hand. "Come on. It's Sister Ellery."

Chapter Forty-four

Thank God I didn't have flats slowing me down as I sprinted with Doc down the cobblestones and across Davey Street, toward the ship. He had his bag with him, which I hoped had human stuff too, so we went straight to Sister Ellery's cabin. Margy Constantinople was there with her. She looked worried.

I wanted to run straight to Sister Ellery, but I held back and let Doc in first, then pulled Margy aside.

"What happened?"

"Lisa was leaving the Drunken Admiral party and found her wandering on Davey Street. She didn't know where she was and couldn't tell us how she got there. She doesn't seem to be physically hurt, but we were worried she might have had a stroke."

My old friend looked miniscule, even on a cruise ship bed. She had been there so many times for me: when I skinned my knees, when Herbie Mankowitz decided to jerk out my first front tooth, when I didn't understand the pluperfect tense. At least I was here. But it made me question this whole idea of perpetual cruise versus nursing home. If she'd been in Greece and in trouble, she might have been all alone. I moved closer to the bed, but I wasn't close enough to hear Doc's whispered conversation with her, only to see him shine a light into her eyes, then take her pulse and her temperature. I saw him reach into his bag for a bottle shaped like it was giving everyone the finger. He held it for a minute, took her pulse again, and put it back.

He rose and waved me over. Even asleep, she looked confused. My stomach made a fist. I bent down and kissed her forehead. "I'm here, Sister Ellery. And Ron will be back soon."

Her eyes popped open. "Who's Ron?"

Oh, God. What had happened? I sat beside her on the bed. Doc settled into the chair by the balcony.

I turned to him. "Did she say anything else?"

"Something about a money market account? She wasn't making much sense."

"Is it a stroke? Alzheimer's?" He shook his head. "What? I can take it."

"No. She'll be okay tomorrow. She's been drugged."

"Drugged? Drugged with what?"

"An opioid. I can't tell exactly what kind unless I do blood work, but I don't want to put her through that tonight."

"Then how do you know?"

"Her pupils are the size of walnuts. Even a vet knows what that means."

"She was at The Fountain." I told him about the box of Dolophine and my suspicions. "Could that be it?"

He considered this. "That's a pretty serious accusation, but yes."

"It's nothing to what I'm going to do to them if I'm right. Can't you do anything for her now?"

"There is a drug that will bring someone out of an overdose, but it's like using epinephrine for anaphylaxis. It's a real shock to the system. Given her age and condition, I'm inclined to let her sleep it off instead."

"Was that the weird bottle you took out of your bag? The antidote?"

"Yeah. It's called Narcan. It's a brand of naloxone. They use it on opioid addicts. It's a nasal spray."

"What? You save someone from an overdose with nasal spray? How is that possible?"

"Clinical trials."

"Haha. Can I see?"

He pulled it out of the bag. It was a short, squat bottle, with three nozzles—two short ones and a long one in the middle, hence the obscene gesture reference.

"How weird." I held onto it. "I always thought if someone overdosed you had to do that *Pulp Fiction* needle in the heart thing."

He grinned. "Yeah, like most things in the movies, it's absolutely true." He leaned over to check Sister Ellery's pulse again. While he did, I palmed the bottle and tucked it into my Balenciaga. He didn't know Harriet had methadone in her blood when she died, but I did. There was entirely too much methadone floating around this ship for my liking.

"You used to have to, but this is a lot less stressful. For the administrator, at least. Like I said, it's traumatic to the patient. They can jerk awake and become immediately violent, for example."

"She would hate that. She's a pacifist," I said.

"I figured, given her former profession." He lay her hand down gently, like he had Howard's. Then he reached for mine. "Do you want to come back to my cabin?"

I did, but I couldn't leave Sister Ellery.

"I'd better stay here."

"That's what I thought. I'll take the floor." He grabbed an extra pillow and blanket from the closet and arranged it at the foot of the bed.

I threw him an inflatable neck pillow from my purse. "Will you be able to sleep?"

"I got through the 'staying up for seventy-two hours' part of med school. I can sleep through, and on, anything." He proceeded to prove it.

I didn't want to crowd Sister Ellery, or frighten her. I found the chenille dressing gown I'd helped her pick out in Bay Ridge.

I figured she wouldn't mind my draping it over myself in the chair. It smelled like home.

I felt a sharp, sudden desire to eat eggplant Parmesan, while being guilted by my mother and chastised by my aunt. I hoped they'd had fun at all the holiday parties, though that seemed unlikely. Once it was a decent hour there, I'd call them. As I looked over at my favorite junkie nun and impostor veterinarian, it was hard to believe it was Christmas Eve.

Chapter Forty-five

"Good King Wenceslas looked out, on the feast of Stephen."

"Ahhhh!" Sister Ellery started the groan, then Doc and I joined in.

"Christ on a bike!" she threw her alarm clock at the door. "There is no feast of Stephen! Shut the hell up!"

We heard the thump of carolers high-tailing it down the hall.

Sister Ellery noticed us, started to sit up, then reversed back to the pillow. "What happened to my head?"

Relieved she was back to her old self, I ran for a water bottle. By the time I'd made her drink the whole thing, Doc had a couple of pills out as a chaser.

"Hi, Sister," he said. "You're going to need these. Do you mind if I do a quick check for vital signs?"

"Did I die or something?"

"Not yet." Doc checked her pulse. "There's always time."

"I told you he was a keeper, Cyd." She grinned at me. "Now what in blazes is going on? Why did you both sleep in my room? Don't sugarcoat it."

We didn't. She listened, then nodded.

"What's the last thing you remember?" I handed her another bottle of water, which she drained. I could understand why opioid users might wind up bloated.

"So many people had told me about The Fountain, and Ron

was busy, so I thought I would ride with Mary Lou and Jack out there."

"Mary Lou and Jack from the Captain's Table went too?" I liked them. I hoped they weren't pimps for Pierce Butler. Or tied up and drugged somewhere.

"I didn't see them after we arrived. That Butler guy took me in first. He said he never wanted a single person to feel less important than a couple, that so many widows feel invisible."

That was probably true. Yet another reason not to get married. Ever.

"What a load of crap he was. But I was there, and they offered a free sauna. Afterwards they gave me some lovely tea. I think they said it was African. I was feeling sleepy, and they said they had a Relaxation Area. The next thing I knew, I was freezing and I woke up here."

Doc and I looked at each other.

I got up. "Can I talk to you in the hallway?"

After we were outside the door, I thought maybe telling Doc about the blood samples was a bad idea, but on the other hand, this could mean that Harriet was murdered, and maybe by someone from The Fountain. It made whatever happened to Sister Ellery and what might happen to any other Darling Cruise Line passengers who visited a much bigger deal. And telling the "Howard" secret had saved a species. I hoped.

So I told him. About taking the medical supplies and the blood samples and mailing them to Dr. Paglia. And about the results. The only thing I didn't spill was Esmeralda.

The affection on his face turned pretty instantly to disgust.

"Dammit, Cyd. How could you break into the Infirmary? Why didn't you ask me? How could you take supplies? You didn't take any of the drugs, did you?"

I started to say no, then I remembered the seasickness pills. "Just one bottle."

He fell back against the wall. "That's a felony. And I'm responsible. I have to account for all that stuff. Every bit of it. Oh, God, they're going to think I took it." He turned and ran down the hall without another word.

Great. I wanted to sink into the ugly carpet. I banged my head against the door.

"Come in and stop all that racket."

Sister Ellery was sitting up. Her color was almost back.

"More water?" I reached for another bottle.

She shook her head. I sat on the edge of the bed.

She took my hand. "What is it?"

"I did something stupid. Actually, about fifteen things that were stupid."

"I doubt that. I want you to tell me all about it and I'll see if I can help. But first, did Ron get to Maria Island?"

I froze.

"Well, did he? I thought you were helping him."

"You know about all this?" I couldn't believe that Brazil would put Sister Ellery in that kind of danger. I reminded myself to castrate him later.

"He didn't give me any details. Said it was better if I didn't have them. He had to get 'important cargo' to one of the islands. I assume it's an endangered animal. I'm pretty sure that's what he really does. You must know that by now."

"I do know that. I just can't believe that you do. And you're still going to marry him?"

"Oh, God no. He's not my type. I mean, come on, those bow legs?" She laughed as I put my head in my hands. "I like a man with a little beef on him. But Ron's doing something important, isn't he?"

"Yes." I thought of Howard's stuffed ancestors in the museum. "Very."

"That's what I thought. When we met on the *Santorini Dream*, we hit it off right away. He cracks me up. Of course, I could tell in about five minutes he wasn't who he said he was."

"How?"

"Really, Cyd Elizabeth Sarah Redondo? Was there ever a single thing that happened at school that I didn't know about?" There hadn't been.

"I'm a nun. We're all-seeing. And, you know, the wigs." I snorted. "I have mentioned it to him, but he's a little sensitive about it. Anyway, aside from being all-seeing, nuns have good instincts about people. I knew he was all right. I offered to give him money to help out with whatever he was up to. He turned me down, but when I insisted, he said if I came on this cruise and pretended we were engaged, that would be a huge help. It would keep the other senior piranhas away from him. I said absolutely. So, did he get there?"

"He got on the boat at least."

"Good." She got up. "I have got to brush my teeth. Give me a second, and then you can tell me about the other thing."

Chapter Forty-six

I woke Gary the driver. He had the same reaction to me that Sister Ellery had to the carolers. After I'd agreed to double his fee for working on a pre-holiday, he said he'd pick me up at the end of the wharf. The harbor was quiet, except for preparations for the Sydney to Hobart Yacht Race. Mary Lou and Jack had said most of the yachts would arrive midday on the twenty-seventh. I hoped Cal would get lucky and come in second to last this time.

It was sunny and seventy-five degrees. I was in my newly-freed nude heels, a sleeveless forest green silk shell, and a dark brown silk miniskirt, as they were the closest things to camouflage in my wardrobe. I was sweating through them both by the time Gary pulled up.

The passenger door un-clicked. I'd brought him a fruitcake from the ship gift store. He tossed it into the backseat, where it joined four others. Some holiday traditions were universal.

"I'm not in a talkative mood." They could probably smell the scotch leeching from his pores in Antarctica.

"No problem."

"Coffee?"

"Please."

He handed me a mug and filled it from his thermos. It was pretty bitter, but Australians were touchy about their coffee, so out of politeness, I sucked it down.

As we drove, I reviewed my plan. I'd gotten as much information about The Fountain as I could from Sister Ellery—including what she could remember about the layout—and checked that Mary Lou and Jack had gotten back safely. I'd found the Koozer and arranged for him to keep an eye on Sister Ellery until I got back. I was happy to see he had "I spent the night with Esmeralda" written all over him, chapped lips and all. I hoped it hadn't been in the morgue.

Then I'd gone to see Margy at the Cruise Director's office, to let her know that Sister Ellery was improving, and asked her what I should do on our last free day in Hobart.

Although she'd seemed genuinely concerned about the former nun, I was now following Ron Brazil's policy of trusting no one. I threw in a question about The Fountain in the middle of my conversation and she mentioned that it was closed between now and Boxing Day. Perfect.

Now that we were docked, my BlackBerry had erratic reception. I called Sandra to see if she'd heard from Fredo. She said no. I needed all the info on Pierce Butler, so I risked calling Frank.

Eddie answered. He said he'd been crashing there for a few nights. Being gone for the holidays made me feel awful enough, but it was especially brutal to think I couldn't be there for my brousin when it looked like his marriage was falling apart.

"God, Eddie, you can stay in Mrs. Barsky's if you want. The keys are in the lockbox in my bottom drawer."

"Um, that's nice of you. But thanks, anyway. I need to be distracted." More guilt. I could hear my nephews, David and Louis, screaming in the background.

"Do you want to help Frank help me catch a guy who's drugging senior citizens with methadone?"

"You bet," he said.

After the call, I made sure I had the Narcan. If I didn't use it, I would sneak it back into Doc's cabinet. I'd tried to find him and apologize, but he wasn't in his office, his cabin, or any of the other places I looked. It was just as well. I'd involved him in enough illegal activities.

"So it isn't a date this time?" Gary growled.

"It wasn't a date last time."

"You could've fooled me."

"I'm not in a talkative mood, either, Gary. May I?"

I reached for a fruitcake. As usual, it took five minutes to unstick the cling wrap. Just as I'd broken off a piece, Gary slammed on the brakes. The seat belt kept me from pancaking on the windshield, but the fruitcake didn't make it.

"One down, three to go," Gary said.

"What just happened?"

He pointed. To the right of the road, a chubby brown creature waddled toward the trees. I jumped out of the car and tried to snap a picture, then noticed the wombat crossing sign I'd missed, due to cling wrap. I felt dizzy from the wonder of it. I climbed back in the car.

"Wow. I've actually seen a wombat. I can die now."

"Good to know," Gary said.

"I thought they were nocturnal."

"They usually are. Holidays don't count."

I saw The Fountain ahead. "You can just drop me off here. I feel like walking. I'm assuming the holiday doesn't screw up your arrangement at the inn?"

"No, it doesn't." He didn't stop, or even slow down. At the same moment that I started to wonder what was up with Gary, I started to feel even more dizzy. Also spacey and weird. Drugged, in fact.

The coffee.

I bent forward and shielded my Balenciaga as I went through it.

"Problem?"

"Allergies," I was careful to hide the logo as I sniffed up my special Narcan nasal spray and shoved the bottle back into one of my secret compartments.

Gary pulled up beside Pierce Butler, who was waiting with a wheelchair. I didn't know what the methadone or the Narcan would do to me, or how long either would take to do it, so I decided to "play marsupial" and let them think they'd tricked me. I anchored the strap of my Balenciaga across my body, thankful I'd worn a Chantelle minimizer bra, and held it with one hand as I got out of the car. They got the wheelchair under me just in time.

Chapter Forty-seven

I didn't remember being wheeled into the "Relaxation Center." The Narcan had weakened the effect of the methadone, but not completely. I felt dizzy but not crazy, at least to myself. That might not count. I cracked my eyes long enough to see I'd been tied to the wheelchair in a room filled with human-sized, white objects laid on their side, like mutant maggots. Were those the isolation tanks? Were they going to put me in one? I heard someone moving behind me and slammed my eyes shut, in fear my normal-sized pupils might give me away.

I could smell Ralph Lauren cologne. Pierce Butler was in the room. It was the natural cologne accessory for a condescending ass. I could also smell whiskey sweat. Gary.

"Get these new bank details entered, Gary. We need to take a breather here and push the opening of the facility on Macao. We'll move the money there."

"Do you want everyone's financials?"

"Just the fours. No reason to take a chance on curious heirs at the moment. Lele's marked the single ones over eighty with at least million in stocks and hedge funds. From those, pick the ones at high risk for heart attack or dementia. The medical assessments are in the blue folder."

God, that was what the numbers meant. The seniors were rated one to four. Ones were a bad risk—too young, too many kids, or not rich enough—and fours were the best bets—no family, in bad health, with trust funds. Like Sister Ellery.

The other numbers on Harriet's list must be financial accounts. How diabolical could you get? And who the hell was Lele?

"Actually," Butler said, "hide the one through threes in that travel agent's cabin. She services seniors, she's the perfect fall guy. We'll uncover the scam ourselves and be heroes."

I beg your pardon, I thought. Fall woman.

"So we're letting her go back?"

"I haven't decided yet."

I should probably figure out what to do before he decided. I wondered whether "Lele" was on the property, or if it was just Pierce and Gary. Gary, at least, was hungover.

"And what about him?" Gary said. "Did you get his cashier's check in the bank?"

"They closed early. Holidays. I'll do it on the twenty-seventh. He got the cashier's check in town. It's his signature. The courts don't have a lot of sympathy for buyer's remorse in these cases."

"We can make sure. He's got to be close to cooked by now."

I got an awful feeling. Investment opportunities. Isolation tank.

"Not worth it. We're responsible for doing the timings on the tank. We don't want a lawsuit following us to Macao. His wife strikes me as the litigious type."

"Nah," Gary said. "If she were, she'd have sued that hairdresser." They did a convincing sportscaster's laugh.

The wife had to be Sandra. Which meant it was Fredo who was medium rare. Greedy moron that he was, he must have invested with Butler. It served him right. But there was Barry. And Barry, Jr. Or Angie, Jr. Dammit.

I had two advantages. No, three. I was awake. My arms and legs were tied to a chair with wheels. And the idiots had left my purse in my lap. Then, I got a fourth. I heard Gary leave.

I couldn't see what Butler was doing or whether he could see me. My bonds felt like yoga straps, not that I knew what yoga straps felt like—I found yoga undignified. The fabric was strong, wide, and thick. It couldn't be tied that tightly. I also couldn't undo it with my teeth. I pressed against the straps. They weren't tight. I guessed Gary assumed I was drugged, so they'd just tied me to keep me from slumping out of the chair.

I heard a zipper behind me. I pushed my luck and managed to work the strap on my right hand all the way off the arm of the wheelchair. I had no way to know if Butler noticed. I freed my hand and felt for the wheelchair brake—when you represent seniors, knowing where the wheelchair brakes are is part of your training—and undid it, then put my hand back where it had been, with the strap lying over it.

Footsteps moved my way. I let my head loll down enough to crack my eyes one more time. Butler walked to the tank beside me. I saw a floor-to-ceiling column on my right.

How did an isolation tank work? Was Fredo completely submerged, with mask and oxygen tank so he could breathe? Or was his head above water? I clearly needed more time at the spa. Or in clinical trials.

I was pretty sure, at the very least, I should wait until Butler showed me how to get the top off. As soon as he hit a button on the side of the machine and I heard a low hum, I managed to untie my left hand and sneak it into my Balenciaga. When the top was unlatched, I was ready.

Chapter Forty-eight

I used the column to push off and hurtle toward Butler. As soon as I'd rammed him up against the tank, I jerked on the brake, trapping him there. Then, I used the last of Doc's stolen syringes to inject him in the thigh with the Dolophine I'd snagged in the hold.

I had no idea how fast it would work.

Not fast enough.

He was as adept with wheelchairs as I was. He unlocked the brakes, shoved the chair, and bashed me into the wall before I could brain him with my Balenciaga. The chair spun, throwing my forehead into the concrete wall. I saw cartoon-grade stars, while he ran to the table for what looked like a Taser. Dolophine, a head injury, and Tasing was not a good combo. I had to stay out of range.

Luckily, I had spent the greater part of my youth trying to ram my brousin Jimmy at the bumper cars on Coney Island—I understood the physics of impact. I hurled the chair toward the table at a forty-five-degree angle, knocking it sideways. The Taser flew off, just out of his reach.

As he dove for it, I ran over his arm with the chair, suddenly grateful for that extra ten pounds I was carrying. He cried out and I thought I had him, until he used his free hand to jerk out a pen knife and slash the wheelchair wheels. I sank to the floor, immobilized. In knife range. One jab to my femoral artery and that would be it.

"I've already reported you to Interpol."

He chuckled. "Right. I'm sure they put a two-bit travel agent right through." His tone was pinched. I hoped I'd broken his forearm. To make sure, I did a little jog up and down on the wheelchair seat and heard something crack, hoping he was smart enough to know my dead weight would be harder to move. He curled up on the floor.

"Look Ms. Redondo, I understand it's your rage as a professional woman that's brought this on. It's so hard for women in the workplace."

"Seriously? No wonder Harriet never told anyone she'd been married to you. Is this why you killed her? She found out what you were doing?"

He went still. Was the Dolophine finally kicking in? If my feet hadn't been tied together— and to the chair—I could have done an easy roundhouse kick at the knife.

"Killed her? I didn't kill her. I was trying to get her back. That's why I met her in Melbourne. We were trying to reconcile."

"Bullshit."

"Seriously. She was the best thing that ever happened to me. I was devastated when she left."

I eased myself a little sideways. "Harriet wouldn't reconcile with a murderer."

"I told you, I'm not a murderer."

I managed to reach the side pocket of my bag. "What, technically? You don't get your hands dirty, Gary does?"

"What Gary does on his own time is not up to me. I'm a con man, doing the easiest con in the world. You work with seniors, you know." He was still waving the knife, but slower. "They're lonely, most of their children ignore them. They have money, but not the sort of security measures they need for their investments. They're just looking for anyone who'll listen to them. To see them. I see them. And, in poker parlance, I raise them."

"Bastard."

"Businessman. But not a murderer."

"What about the methadone?"

He jerked a little at this. "The government sends it to me. It's standard for treating opioid addiction, and by the time people are in their eighties, lots of them are on permanent pain medication. It's responsible to have it on hand. Gary convinced me I had to neutralize you today and suggested methadone syrup as an easy way to make you pliable. I don't usually need it. Between my bedside manner and the isolation tanks, I can usually work anyone who drops by." He grinned up at me.

I untwisted the top of the travel-sized bottle of Listerine I always had with me and threw the minty germicide into his eyes. He stabbed himself with his knife as he reached for his face.

That gave me time to untie my feet, plant a four-inch heel in his back, and bind his hands with the plastic handcuff ties policeman Frank insisted I always carry.

Suddenly, there was banging. From inside the tank. Fredo.

I dug my heel further into Butler's back. "How do I get him out of there? What do I do?"

Butler slumped down, out on Dolophine.

Chapter Forty-nine

I turned to the isolation tank. Peeking out of it was my former father-in-law's bald head, in a hot pink bathing cap. I turned off the mini-cassette tape recorder in my purse, grabbed my BlackBerry, and made sure to get a blackmail snap before I helped him out. His orange, overstuffed Speedo clashed with the cap. I handed the dripping idiot a fresh waffle robe.

"What are you doing here?"

"Barry sent me to find you and Sandra. Clearly you need keepers."

He tried to give a dignified tug on his bathing cap. It slid partway off. "I most certainly do not. And what have you done to Pierce? We're business partners. Untie him immediately." Fredo drew himself up and went toward Butler.

I grabbed the belt on his robe and jerked him back. "Listen to this."

I played him the recording I'd made of Butler and Gary. His face provoked the same kind of faint pity I'd felt for Sandra the day before.

"The other guy is still here. Will you watch Mr. Butler while I go try to save our lives?"

He gave me the nod of the defeated, as the pink bathing cap slid off and onto the floor.

I assumed Gary was in the office. I needed to immobilize

him and get the papers he was going to plant in my cabin, then call the police.

I was too late. Gary and the town car were gone.

At least he'd left a working landline. I dialed the Hobart Police, then hung up. I remembered Inspector Randy's scorn and Pierce Butler's face on the front page of the paper. I knew how small towns worked. People protected their own and no one wanted to hear bad news, especially at Christmas. Also, I'd reported two people missing who weren't missing.

I remembered Scott, my valiant helicopter cop. I dug his card out of my purse and dialed. I had to tell him about Harriet. That was awful. After we reminisced about her, he said the Melbourne Harbor Police only had jurisdiction when they had evidence that the crime had occurred in harbor waters. I didn't have that. Yet.

"It sounds like this Butler guy and his partners have definitely committed fraud, but Interpol's only going to pursue that, or the murder, if it happened in international waters. Be careful on that ship. If you can get in a twelve-mile radius, I'll come pick you up."

We wished each other happy holidays and I programmed his number into my BlackBerry. I made one more toll-free call, courtesy of The Fountain—to Interpol. Graham Gant's voicemail said he was away for the holidays. Wasn't everyone?

So I tried Frank.

"Geez, Cyd, enough with the conspiracies already. You sound ridiculous." He'd had some eggnog. "You come from a family of law enforcement, it's embarrassing."

"Will it help with the Precinct to arrest the man who's been running an international fraud ring, using and selling senior identities, including lots of people from Bay Ridge?"

"Probably."

"Okay. Here's what you need to do. Just make sure I get enough credit to keep the business going, that's all I ask."

"You've got it, Squid."

"In return, you have to call Interpol for me."

Now, if I could just get Pierce Butler into international waters. In a wheelchair. Or force him to commit a crime twelve miles or fewer from Melbourne. How was I going to do that?

It turned out it didn't matter. He was gone too.

It was all I could do not to slap Fredo in astonishment. "Wait until the Bay Ridge Masons hear about this," I said.

•• • ••

Half an hour later, we were on an overcrowded bus full of holiday revelers headed into Hobart. Fredo had been so mortified, he wouldn't even speak to me until after I'd located the ride and found us a seat in the very back. Of course, then, we had to shout our conversation over an out-of-tune, communal version of "The Twelve Days of Christmas" involving an emu up a gum tree.

I kept at Fredo until he admitted he'd heard footsteps and hidden behind the isolation tank. When he thought it was safe to come out, Butler, the wheelchair, and the duffel were gone.

"Did you at least look around to see who it was? Was it Gary?" Had I just missed him?

"You played me that recording. I thought my life was in danger."

"Actually, your life is in more danger now. You realize I managed to get your money back and you've given it to him again, right? The check was in that duffel bag or his wallet."

"Don't overreact. I'll cancel it. We can go to the bank when we get back to town."

"No, and no. First, the banks closed at noon for the holiday, and you can't cancel a cashier's check. It's the equivalent of cash. That's why people ask for them."

Fredo went even more gray than usual. "That was the down payment for Barry and Angela's house. He said he was going to double it." He'd looked better in the bathing cap.

The bus made a lot of stops and got rowdier as we went. We

finally reached the middle of Hobart at three. I left Fredo at the hotel. I told him he needed to find Sandra and start pretending to still be married. And that her credit card had been declined, so he would need to pay for the hotel.

"You didn't by any chance give your credit card numbers to anyone at The Fountain?" He wouldn't look at me.

"Get out." I gave him a fifty. It was Christmas Eve.

I dreaded going back on the ship. Doc was furious with me, and Sister Ellery expected me to catch Butler. I thought I knew who'd killed Harriet, but I still wasn't one hundred percent sure. Even if I had been, I didn't have enough evidence to go to the authorities.

I went to a bench by the harbor and let the waterworks loose, just to get it out of my system. So I didn't see Doc coming my way from the center of town.

Chapter Fifty

He didn't say anything, just sat down beside me and handed me a sleigh-shaped cookie the size of my hand.

We both looked straight ahead while I ate it.

"When I was a medical student, a friend and I got drunk one night and broke into the hospital pharmacy for a lark. We didn't take anything, but they threw me out. That's why I didn't finish." He took my hand. "I overreacted."

I turned to him. "No you didn't. It was an inexcusable thing to do. I was an idiot. I'll go straight to Captain Lindoff now and tell her it was me."

"You don't need to do that."

"I do. I put you at risk. And for nothing. None of the evidence is admissible."

"It wasn't quite for nothing." He pulled out a reindeer cookie and split it in half.

I took my half. "What are you talking about?"

"I just convinced the local ME to do an autopsy. He likes cookies too."

Despite my mouth half full of icing, I grabbed him and kissed him. He kissed me back, smearing icing and lipstick everywhere, then put his arm around me. We looked out at the ships.

"How about you? What have you been doing?"

I told him.

"You mean those two are loose?"

"As far as I know. They're probably already on a charter to Macao."

"I liked Gary."

"Me too. Until, you know."

"Any word from the island?"

"Not yet."

"Eggnog bar?"

We liberated Sister Ellery, who was recovered and starving. We stuffed ourselves, then went up to the deck. Red and green holiday lights jumped on the water. The wharf was tasteful by Bay Ridge standards, but there were a few houses and neighborhoods that floated and glowed in familiar, over-the-top glory. I leaned against Doc and tried to figure out what I could do. Get Fredo and Sandra on the boat, for one. I knew there was at least one small, messy cabin available, if they didn't mind that it had belonged to a missing dead man.

My cabin, on the other hand, had a very live man in it that night. Doc said he'd walk me to my room, but we only made it to the elevator before his hands were around my waist again. He was persuasive and imaginative, even finding an erogenous zone I didn't know I had, on the inside of my knee. As a doctor, he knew his anatomy. Just like Roger had. Roger. Just to convince myself he didn't matter, I made sure Doc and I finished what we'd started on the museum stairs. Twice. As Gary said, holidays don't count.

On Christmas morning, we pulled into Port Arthur. Doc, Sister Ellery, and I had a huge buffet breakfast with Mary Lou and Jack, and then retired to Sister Ellery's cabin, where we exchanged our Secret Santa presents. I'd found the tackiest possible Tasmanian tiger tea towel for Doc and a new electric blue halter for Sister Ellery. She agreed to call my family with me.

Aunt Helen wasn't available, as she'd succumbed to a case of food poisoning from the Pinskys' "figgy pudding." What did she expect? I told my mom I would call again tomorrow, when it was Christmas Day in Brooklyn.

Then, we got our real present—a text from Ron Brazil:

The eagle has landed.

We went back to the Castaways Bar to celebrate. As we raised our glasses, Sandra and Fredo walked in. Even in the dark, I could see Sister Ellery straighten her bony spine.

"The Fountain wasn't all bad."

Oh God, Fredo.

He kept darting looks her way. Who was I to interfere with the course of true love? Absolutely the right person. But I didn't get the chance. I got my call back from Graham Gant.

It cut out immediately, so I went up on deck, hoping for better reception. I stared at the gorgeous, sinister Port Arthur. It seemed a strange place to dock for Christmas, but there were plenty of passengers wandering the grounds. And town cars parking. Where was Gary?

It was too hot in the sun and Gant still hadn't called, so I returned to the bar. No Doc. Someone had complained of a dodgy stomach and he had rushed them to his office, and away from the other passengers. Norovirus, just what we needed. Sister Ellery thought it had been a mistake for the cruise line to hang mistletoe in all the bars. I agreed.

I told her we'd both be better off in a sterile area and I would meet her at the disco later. I wanted to rest, then change into something appropriate, maybe from the lost and found. I was so used to taking the stairs by now, it was second nature. If I hadn't, I wouldn't have surprised Pierce Butler and Lisa Callahan making out on the Deck Five landing.

Chapter Fifty-one

"Ow!" Butler's right forearm was in a splint. Good. "Careful, Lele."

Gag. Even Butler's pet names were patronizing. But now it all made sense. Lisa Callahan aka "Lele" was in on the scam—she was the one who organized the "CT" part of the equation. She knew when someone was at the Captain's Table, so their rooms could be broken into undetected. That must be how she got all the personal information. And if she'd spirited Butler onto the ship last night, she could have gotten him on and off the day Harriet was killed.

I cracked the door again to find his tongue down her throat. Slimebag bastard. He'd obviously lied about wanting to reconcile with Harriet. She must have threatened to report him to the cruise line, so he killed her, then worked me with a sob story.

I was just getting my phone out to take a picture of them when Gant called back. They heard the phone and whipped my way. I slammed the door, levered a nearby trash can in front of it, and ran, ducking into a housekeeping closet to take the call.

Of course Gant kept breaking up. Through the static, he said he'd been on Butler's trail for years, ever since he was operating as a *faux* chiropractor in Greece under a different alias. When Gant got the call from Frank, he'd gone straight to the airport and was on his way to Melbourne. He would use local law enforcement (with any luck, Scott) to helicopter him to the ship while it was still in international waters—that way Butler couldn't escape in the chaos of disembarking and there wouldn't be any issues with jurisdiction.

"I'll be there by..." I lost the call. I inched out of the closet into the empty hallway.

The ship was beginning to reek of bleach. Two more people had fallen sick, and every housekeeper on the ship was disinfecting railings and door handles. I heard the whistle. The ship was leaving the harbor. Would Butler stay or go?

I ran to the deck and took my mini binoculars from my Balenciaga. Passengers poured up the ramp, but no one went the other way. I tried Gant again. No answer. It was going to be up to me to keep the ship in international waters until that helicopter got here. I calculated Gant's potential travel time, factoring in holiday delays. I figured he'd be cutting it close, and might arrive late afternoon the next day. Boxing Day. The day of the yacht race.

Neither Doc nor Sister Ellery was around. I had a sad, single person's buffet—with crab legs—and headed to bed early, knowing in the morning, I'd need help.

I didn't want Sister Ellery at risk again and, since I passed a woman in a tropical muumuu projectile vomiting over the railing on my way to breakfast, I figured Doc was going to have his hands full. After two short stacks for energy, I went back to my cabin and buzzed for the Koozer.

While I waited, I searched for the documents Butler had threatened to plant in my cabin. Had Gary done it? Was he on the ship? I'd pulled out everything I could by the time the Koozer opened the door and looked at the mess.

"Do you want me to get Housekeeping?"

"No." I crawled backwards out of the closet. "It's a very long story, but someone might have planted evidence in the cabin to frame me. I have to find it before we get to Melbourne."

"Any chance this is it?" The Koozer held out a package addressed to me. "It was left for you last night, with directions to leave it in the cargo hold until your departure. That seemed weird, so I thought I should let you know." Over-tipping—never a mistake.

I took the package. It was full of the financial and medical information on Butler's "ones through threes." I hoped it would help Gant prosecute. I hid it under the chair cushion.

"Koozer, Esmeralda is one lucky girl. In fact, if you can help me with a few more things, I'm going to gift you guys all my air and hotel miles so you can have a proper honeymoon." He gave me a questioning look. "You'll get an IOU."

"And positive cruise line evaluations for me and Nylo?"

The Koozer had told me promotions and bonuses were all dependent on passenger recommendations. "That goes without saying." It did.

"These are the things I need. Two life jackets, two of those pool flotation toys you put on your arms, a flashing red light that will work in the water, a wet suit—I thought I saw one in the lost and found—and a vintage polyester wrap-dress in a size six, preferably Diane Von Furstenberg."

"You got it," he said, and left.

There were only three reasons a cruise ship stopped: if it was sinking, if it was on fire, or if someone went overboard. At least with option three, I'd be the only one who could get hurt. Of course, not being able to swim made it more complicated, as did the need to know exactly where international waters stopped and Australian waters began. To be honest, it gave me a headache just thinking about it, so I tried to avoid my terror of death like most people do—by frantic, pointless organizing.

I hoped Gant would get here before I had to stop the boat, but in case he didn't, I wanted to increase my risk of survival by entering the water from the lowest point possible. I would need the Koozer's help with that. If I managed to fall while people were on deck cheering on the yacht racers, I'd have witnesses. I didn't want the cruise line to cover it up and leave me there to sink, like they had with Elliot Ness. And, being a non-swimmer, I wanted assistance as fast as possible. Preferably instantly.

Keeping an eye out for Pierce Butler, I went to the ship's library and got out a nautical map. It looked like I would have to jump at least an hour out of Melbourne. They started slowing the ship a half hour before then, so at least the wake wouldn't be quite as bad.

I could put my BlackBerry and satellite phone in a dry bag. Then I had a terrifying thought. My Balenciaga. The idea of leaving it was much more terrifying than jumping off the boat. I couldn't do anything without my purse. It was too big for a dry bag.

I was going to have to entrust it, and my father's compass, to Sister Ellery. If I drowned, I would leave instructions that it was to be buried with me, King Tut style, so I would have all the vital things I would need in the afterlife, like Tupperware, emergency cash, and dental floss.

Just then, there was an announcement that, due to an over-abundance of caution, there would be a mandatory quarantine for all passengers. Everyone was to stay inside their cabins until further notice.

Great. There went my witnesses. I tried Gant one more time. Nothing. Then I tried Scott. He didn't answer either. This plan was starting to seem stupider and stupider. And more likely.

At least the crew was still allowed to move around. The Koozer eventually returned, sporting a surgical mask and rubber gloves. He said the "flotation toys" were too bulky to carry, but he had everything else. The dress was a knock-off, but it was unlikely anyone was going to be dancing anywhere but to their toilets tonight, so that was fine.

I explained what I wanted to do. To his credit, he really tried to talk me out of it. In the end, he admitted that he and Nylo could probably lower me on one of their ropes or even with a small inflatable raft. They'd send up the alarm, and the boat would have to stop and rescue me. It seemed pretty foolproof. For someone who could swim.

I arranged to meet the Koozer and Nylo in a few hours, when the yacht race was due to pass us going toward Hobart.

I wrote my letter of instructions for Sister Ellery, an apology to Doc for the blatant disregard for my health I was about to take, and my will. I left everything to my nephews and my best friend Debbie and asked the Sister and Doc to witness it retroactively. I still had an hour to kill. Or, depending on how the jump went, to live.

I called home. It was Christmas morning there. Frank answered, barely audible over the laughter and ripping wrapping paper. I figured Uncle Leon was sneaking looks at PBS, Aunt Helen was bent over, shoving around olives, and Mom wasn't quite finished polishing the champagne glasses. I could hear them squeaking when she picked up the phone.

"Are you eating anything?"

"When I'm not nauseous, yes."

"Oh God. You're seasick. Why didn't you call me?"

"I'm fine, Ma. I just called to say I love you and I'm sorry I'm not there. Hug everybody, okay?"

She paused, then told me to give her love to Sister Ellery. She also said that Roger Claymore had called to wish me a Merry Christmas. He'd try again on New Year's Day.

I could have used Roger at this moment. I'd always been braver around him.

Restless, I paced on my balcony until I heard rousing cheers. The yacht racers were early. Many of the gorgeous boats were neck and neck, while a few straggled behind. I assumed one of them was Cal. It was time to get suited up, though I still hoped Gant might get here before I made my descent into international waters.

I put my hair in a bun. I didn't want it floating into my mouth. Then I put a fluorescent green scrunchie around it, for extra visibility in the water. I saw why the wetsuit had been left behind—it had a huge bloodstain and a tiny tear. My hot pink duct tape didn't match, but with any luck it would keep the water out long enough for me to be rescued.

I hooked the life jackets over my wetsuit and put the dry bag with my phones in the pocket of the one on the inside. This widened me about five feet, and with the duct tape, I resembled one of Brazil's brutalized seal toys. I hid my Balenciaga in the closet with a note and left everything else on the bedside table.

I'd arranged to meet the Koozer on Deck Four at four o'clock sharp, while the sun was still high. It was too bad the yacht racers had passed, but I could feel the engines slowing, right on time. At least with the quarantine, I wouldn't have to worry as much about being spotted in my unflattering attire. The hallway seemed empty, so I sprinted for the stairwell, wetsuit squeaking all the way. The Koozer and Nylo were waiting for me in their face masks.

"You sure? This is batshit crazy," Nylo said.

It was. And I wasn't sure. But then I thought of Harriet and Sister Ellery and all the senior citizens I would send on bucket list holidays. I wanted Pierce Butler out of commission. Besides, I had a million-dollar medical, emergency evacuation, and corpse repatriation policy, so there would be no costs for my family or Redondo Travel. And I only had to float half a mile to be in Scott's jurisdiction. If he could drop me, he could pick me up. It worked for astronauts. I wished I'd been able to kiss Doc goodbye, but right now he was a norovirus incubator, so maybe it was just as well.

I made the mistake of looking down. The white slope of the ship was Alps-like and slippery. The distant water smashed against it about every half second. To steady my stomach, I looked at Nylo instead. He explained they'd positioned a small raft on the side of the ship that I could either hold onto in the water, or get into once I was down. They'd lower it after I fell, instead of before, so it wouldn't float away without me. I felt better.

"Nylo, you're getting a vacation too," I said. "But no more drinking on the job."

"Maybe. Maybe not."

I'd just grabbed the rope when we heard it. The chopper. Scott or Gant, it didn't matter. The cavalry had arrived. I was so relieved I actually cheered. Nylo rolled his eyes.

The cabin stewards had just run down the deck to get a better look at the helicopter, when I smelled Esteé Lauder Pleasures and felt a sharp shove.

Chapter Fifty-two

Before the jab even registered, my feet were higher than my head and all of me was flipping over the railing. I reached out and just managed to grab the bottom rung with my right hand.

Someone in khaki pants rammed their heel into it.

Before I lost my grip, I strained with my other hand for the rope Nylo had tied to the raft. Maybe I could rappel down and hold onto that until I could call for help. Thank God for second grade gymnastics.

I didn't have to look down to know, despite my previous plan, I absolutely did not want to go into that water. I had to get to the raft. I kept my eyes on the rope and headed down, hand over hand—just like Sister Alicia taught us—for twenty feet, until the ship hit a wave, jolted, and I lost my grip.

I knew I should turn my fall into a dive—I'd be less likely to break my legs. But my reptile, non-swimming brain sent me the other way—Wile E. Coyote style. I spun my arms, and hit smack on top of the two life jackets—just as I reached for the inflation tab.

I probably injured a rib or two, but the jackets softened the landing enough to keep me from breaking my back. The fall still knocked the wind out of me, though. My face stung in the salt water. A wave sent me tumbling under.

I was glad I'd written a will.

I needed air. I might not know how to swim, but I knew I couldn't open my mouth until my head was out of the water.

I looked up. All I could see was my cousin Jimmy, pressing my head down in the bathtub and in the swimming pool. This was all the times I woke up as a little girl gasping for air—times a billion. It felt like one time too many.

I was freezing, my ribs hurt, my lungs were going to explode. And I was sinking. I wheeled my arms again, ramming my mouth shut so I didn't yelp from the pain. It was pointless. Finally, I stopped trying. At least if I drowned, the shark bites would be post-mortem.

Besides, everyone had gone to greet the helicopter. No one even knew I'd gone overboard. Except the killer.

Whoever heaved me over had killed Harriet and Elliot Ness. That really pissed me off. If I drowned, they'd never pay for what they'd done.

I had to find the surface. I tried to remember how Nick Nolte and Jacqueline Bissett did it in *The Deep*. Then I remembered the second life jacket. I jerked the tab. As it filled, it sent me in the right direction. I fluttered my feet to push upward. It took longer without flippers. Two more seconds and I was going to pass out.

Then, I was up, gulping air, before I got bashed by one wave, then another. At least thanks to the life jackets, I was bobbing— toward and away from the hull. I scanned the deck and glimpsed Lisa "Lele" Callahan, that boarding school bitch, leaning over the railing.

She waved and disappeared.

Where was the Koozer? Where was Gant? I tried yelling, but I couldn't even hear myself over the ship's engines.

I swore, gagging down a disgusting wash of salty sea. The Koozer had told me the ship's "treated" waste spilled right into the ocean and I couldn't spit it out fast enough. It was the first time I wished I could yell through my nose. I screamed one more time—trying to keep my mouth above water—knowing no one would hear me, maybe ever. I started feeling crazy cold. Was I dying of hypothermia? No, the duct tape had detached and tiny daggers of frigid water were shooting through the tear in my wetsuit.

I missed Frank, who'd risked his job to help, and Eddie, who still owed me bail money, and even Jimmy, that pathetic delinquent. At least when he waterboarded me, he eventually let me breathe. However suffocating they'd been, they'd always had my back. Unlike my brousins, the Bass Strait was not accountable to my Uncle Ray.

The ship was still moving at a steady pace. Away from me.

I couldn't see anyone else on board. I flailed my arms and legs.

At that moment, it felt like my whole life had been nothing but flailing—marrying Barry, running away to Africa, the Keto diet, learning Farsi, trying one cockamamie scheme after another just to show my family I was grown up. All I'd done was make it easier for some ruthless cruise hostess to shove me over a railing.

Why was I still trying so hard? Maybe I should stop. Lots of people did and they didn't wind up in the sewage treatment vortex of the Southern Hemisphere. They just kept their heads down, did what they were told, and plodded on, with a mortgage, an SUV, and eventually, cancer. If I'd done that, at least I wouldn't have to explain my various international crimes to my mother, or see her lovesick over some slick, pot-bellied widower from Queens who smelled like socks.

God, my mom. It had taken her twenty-eight years to get over my dad. I was all she had left of him. I couldn't put her through that again. Besides, if I was listed as a suicide—however "assisted" it had been by Lisa Callahan—I'd be excommunicated and my name would never be mentioned again in the Redondo family, just like cousin what's-his-name. I was not going to let that happen.

My ribs made it hard to move. Could I get the dry bag out? I imagined Jimmy was daring me to do it and gulped down the pain as I reached for it. Once I had hold of it, I flapped my legs back and forth and yelled in agony again as I tried to unzip the bag over my head.

To keep the phone above water, I had to dial with my nose. It took six tries before I hit Cal's number. My legs were turning to rubber. Even kickboxing couldn't prepare a girl for this. The waves got higher. I wasn't going to be able to keep the phone dry. Then, from six inches above my head, I heard a voice.

"Cal here!"

I shouted up toward the phone. "Cal? It's Cyd Redondo. Are you still losing?"

"What, love?"

"I got pushed off the ship. I'm floating about fifty yards from the *Tasmanian Dream*. Any chance you'd be willing to turn around and pick me up?"

"Turn around? I haven't gotten there yet. Hang on!"

A vicious wave knocked me farther from the ship and for a few minutes, I couldn't see anything. My legs were about to give out. I tried to blow the life jacket back up, but only filled it with water.

Then, there it was, the world's slowest moving yacht. Finally, I could read its name: *Le Tortue*. Like zucchini, tortoise sounded better in French.

Cal pulled me, drenched and shaking, onto the boat and, like the gentleman he was, gave me towels, brandy, and dry clothes. He managed to get through on his radio to the ship's bridge and convinced them to hoist me back onto the ship.

It took a while, as I couldn't really take pressure on my ribs, so they had to send down a chair-like hoist for me. Yesterday it would have scared me senseless, but Dr. Paglia had taught me something about odds and it was unlikely I'd fall twice in one day.

On the way up, I waved goodbye to Cal, hoping the "Sailor rescues American gone overboard" story, which I intended to plant with various international news outlets, would make up for his last place finish.

Once I disentangled myself from the hoist, I saw Gant had Butler in cuffs. The Interpol agent came forward in the same shiny Eurotrash suit and with the same limp handshake he'd had in Tanzania. I told him about Lisa.

"Yes, get her. She killed Harriet," Butler yelled. "I didn't know until today, when I saw the flowers I sent Harriet in Lele's office. She admitted it. Said if she couldn't have me, no ex-wife was going to." If I hadn't seen Lisa at the railing, I might have thought this was another one of Butler's charming lies.

I remembered the documents. They could prove her involvement. We ran to my cabin. The papers were gone. Unless she had gone overboard too, she had to be here somewhere.

The ship seemed larger and more sinister with all the passengers quarantined. I told the Koozer to take cover and Gant and I started to search. This gave me a new appreciation for the housekeepers. There were a million doorknobs to polish. From the forward deck, I saw a scuffle going on in the Bridge. We worked our way up the stairs and edged open the door.

Lisa had a gun to Captain Lindoff's head. The crew were frozen.

"I'm sorry I didn't believe you, Ms. Redondo," Captain Lindoff gasped.

"Redondo's a lunatic bimbo," Lisa said. "Out of her mind."

I had a few retorts ready, but instead I looked at Gant for guidance. I didn't want to be the reason the first female captain died at sea. I assumed he didn't either, for the PR alone.

Apparently, neither did the norovirus, as just when Lisa started to back out of the room with the Captain, Storr Bentley projectile vomited into her face, giving me and Gant a chance to grab the psychotic hostess.

She had Butler's papers down her khaki pants.

We were all quarantined together for another hour, as the Captain returned to navigate the ship into Port Melbourne. That gave me time to tell Gant the whole story. Miraculously, my BlackBerry still worked, so I emailed him Butler's confession, gave him Gary's cell phone number, and listened as he called his supervisor. It seemed he had enough evidence, as Scott met him and the prisoners at the dock. He blew me a kiss.

I hoped maybe Doc and I could manage one night in town together before I flew home, but we only got a quick, non-touching (in every sense) goodbye, as he was dressed like someone out of *Outbreak* and still had a full infirmary. He had cleared up the drug cabinet situation with Captain Lindoff, and had just gotten word that he was being promoted and sent to their more prestigious Chinese route.

He said he would write. We could both hear a voice moaning behind the door. "Sorry, it's that Hypocritical Oath thing," he said, and disappeared.

Sister Ellery was also otherwise engaged. I tried not to visualize that. Her new infatuation, plus some residual trauma from the methadone, had convinced her to come back to Bay Ridge, at least for awhile. I arranged for her to keep a credit with the cruise line and told her she could have Mrs. Barksy's apartment. I'd waited a long time to move out of my family's house. I could wait a little more.

• • ● • •

Somehow, I'd managed to get us all home on the same flight. Barry was waiting for us at JFK. "Cydhartha." He didn't have to say anything else. I knew it meant we'd finally put our disastrous marriage behind us.

Sandra, Fredo, and I said goodbye at the curb, so they could get home to Angela as if nothing had happened. Whether they could pull it off or not was not my problem. Barry had asked me to find them, and I had. As they got into the cab, I slipped Fredo the cashier's check he'd given to Butler. It was Christmas. My work was done. He gave Sister Ellery a wink behind Sandra's back. Yeah, this was going to last.

While I installed my favorite nun in Mrs. Barsky's apartment, I realized I'd forgotten to tell Gant about Elliot Ness. Had Lisa killed him too? Why? Had he photographed her going into Harriet's room? I'd never had a chance to check his flash drive. I headed down to the office.

The lights were on. Maybe Eddie was there. I unlocked the door and walked in.

It wasn't Eddie.

"Jimmy?"

"Squid."

I gave myself a minute not to start screaming, as it might alarm Sister Ellery. My brousin Jimmy, who had been involved in Uncle Ray's smuggling ring, had been banished from the family for his own safety two months earlier and was supposed to be in Fresno, laying low.

"What are you doing here?"

"Eddie said he needed somebody to run the office, seeing as how you bailed. Real sensitive, with Uncle Ray in prison and your mom going off the rails. Good work."

"Get out," I said.

"You're not the boss of me." I really was home.

"Get out!" I took off one of my heels and he headed for the door.

"Wait. Before you go, have there been any issues?"

"Nothing I couldn't handle."

That's what I was afraid of. That, the inevitable disappearance of the two hundred fifty-seven dollars I'd left in the petty cash drawer, and the sanctity of my new ergonomic chair.

I brushed it off, took the flash drive out of my purse, and pulled up the photos on my screen, hoping to find a motive for Ness' murder. I flipped through his shots. There were the Manzonis doing the Cha Cha; there was Harriet talking to Captain Lindoff; and there was Howard. There were five pictures of Howard in the cruise cabin closet. The final one had a hand over it, as though the photographer had been caught in the act.

Oh God, I thought. Hazelnut.